Burks, James (James R.),
Bird & Squirrel all tangled
up /
2019.
33305252317163
ca   07/14/22

P9-EKJ-881

James Burks

BIRD & SQUIRREL

ALL TANGLED UP

graphix

An Imprint of
SCHOLASTIC

To Steph McHugh for always facing the audience
and sharing your love of books with kids
big and small.

Copyright © 2019 by James Burks

All rights reserved. Published by Graphix, an imprint
of Scholastic Inc., *Publishers since 1920.* SCHOLASTIC,
GRAPHIX, and associated logos are trademarks and/or
registered trademarks of Scholastic Inc.

The publisher does not have any control over and does
not assume any responsibility for author or third-party
websites or their content.

No part of this publication may be reproduced,
stored in a retrieval system, or transmitted in
any form or by any means, electronic, mechanical,
photocopying, recording, or otherwise, without
written permission of the publisher. For information
regarding permission, write to Scholastic Inc.,
Attention: Permissions Department,
557 Broadway, New York, NY 10012.

This book is a work of fiction. Names, characters,
places, and incidents are either the product of
the author's imagination or are used fictitiously,
and any resemblance to actual persons, living or
dead, business establishments, events, or locales
is entirely coincidental.

Library of Congress Control Number: 2016947440

ISBN 978-1-338-25183-8 (hardcover)
ISBN 978-1-338-25175-3 (paperback)

10 9   21 22 23
Printed in China   62

First edition, February 2019

Edited by Adam Rau
Book design by Phil Falco
Creative Director: David Saylor

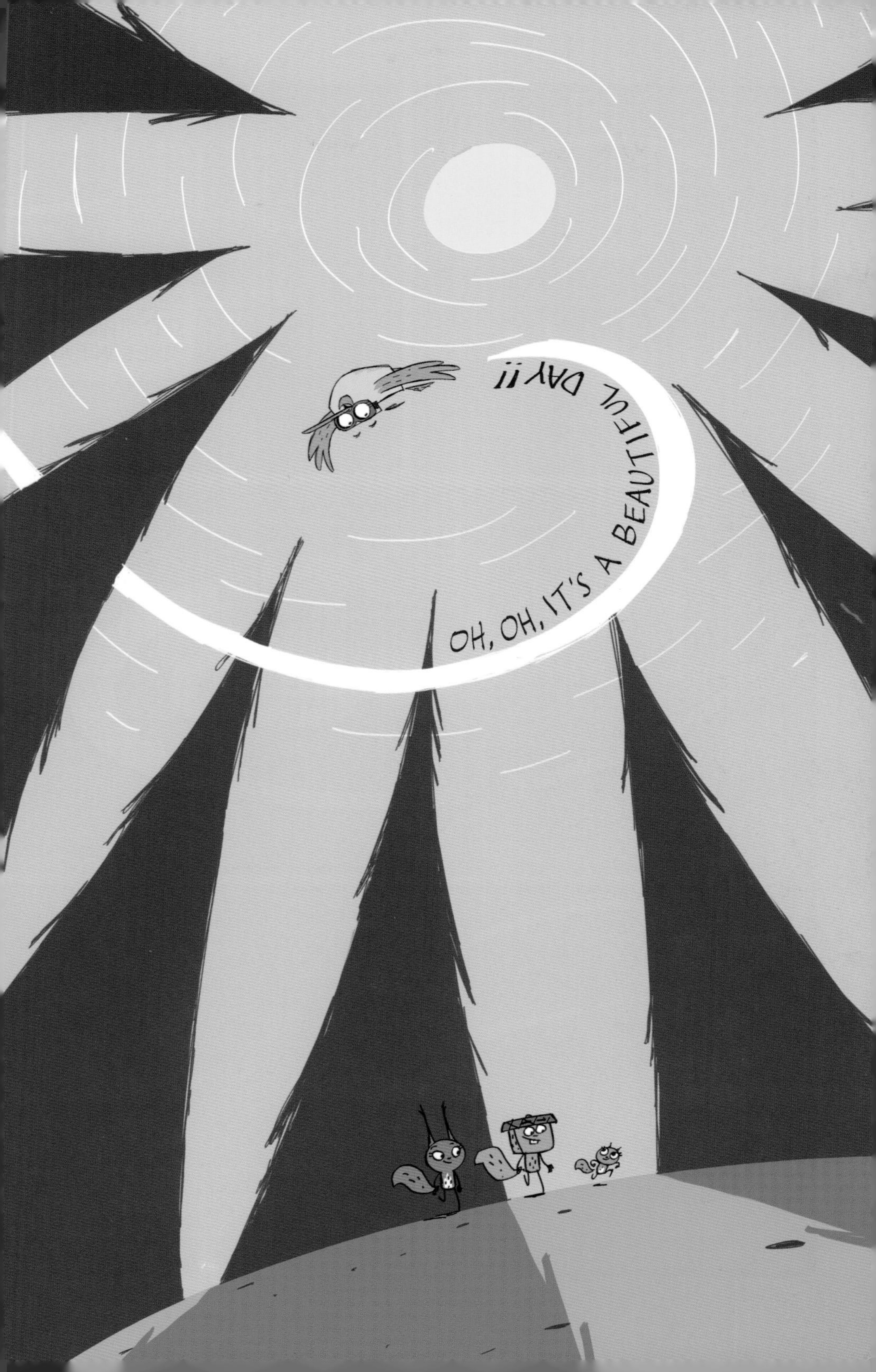
OH, OH, IT'S A BEAUTIFUL DAY!!

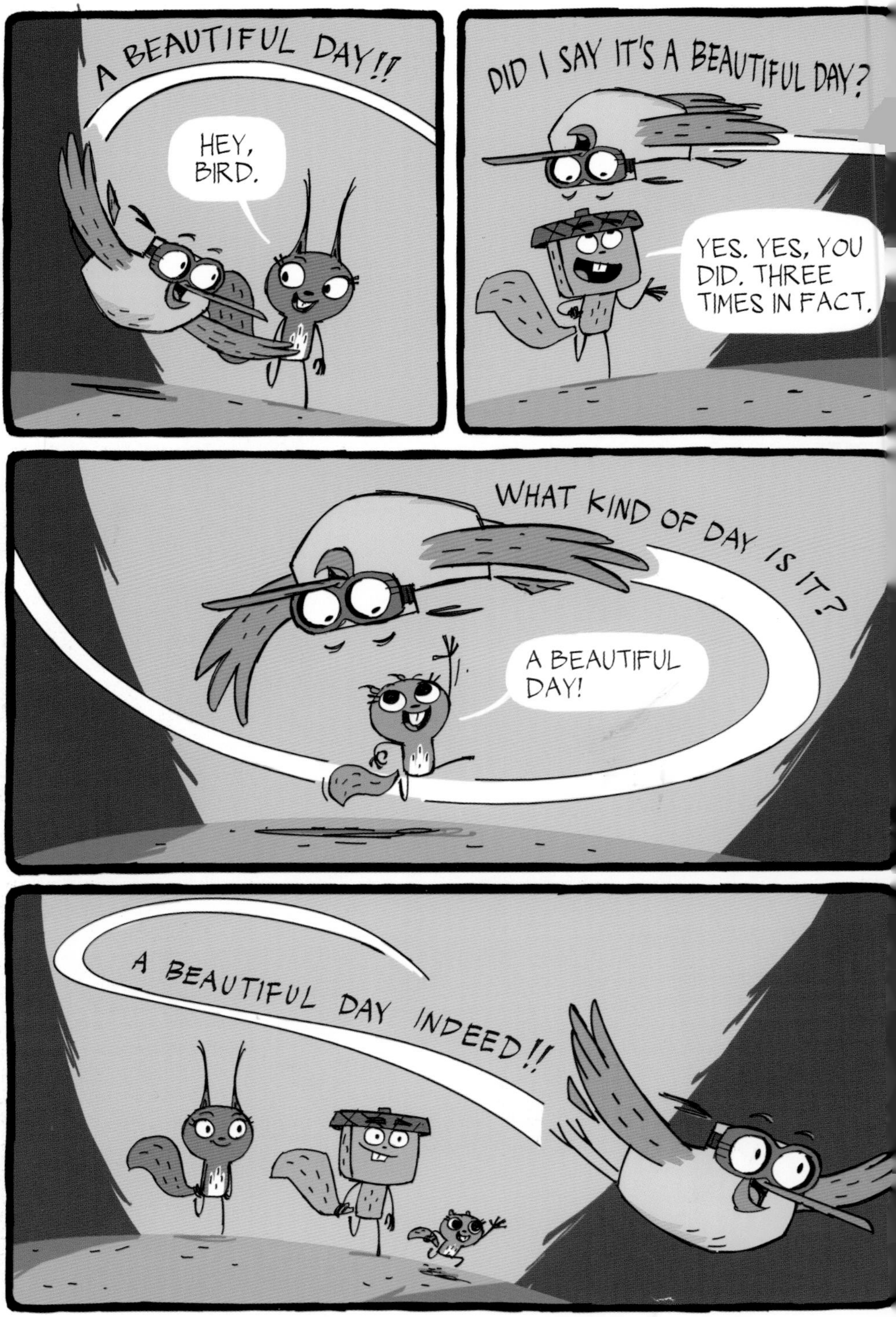
A BEAUTIFUL DAY!!
HEY, BIRD.
DID I SAY IT'S A BEAUTIFUL DAY?
YES. YES, YOU DID. THREE TIMES IN FACT.
WHAT KIND OF DAY IS IT?
A BEAUTIFUL DAY!
A BEAUTIFUL DAY INDEED!!

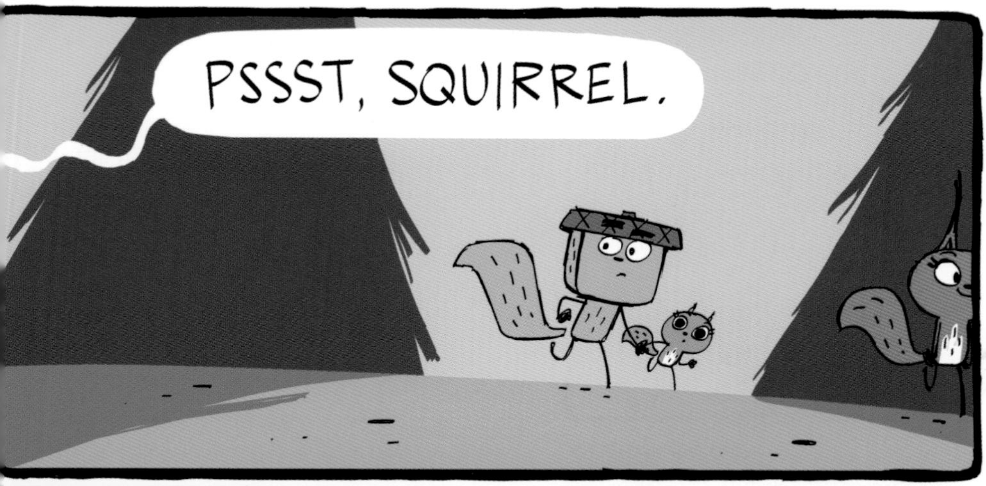
PSSST, SQUIRREL.

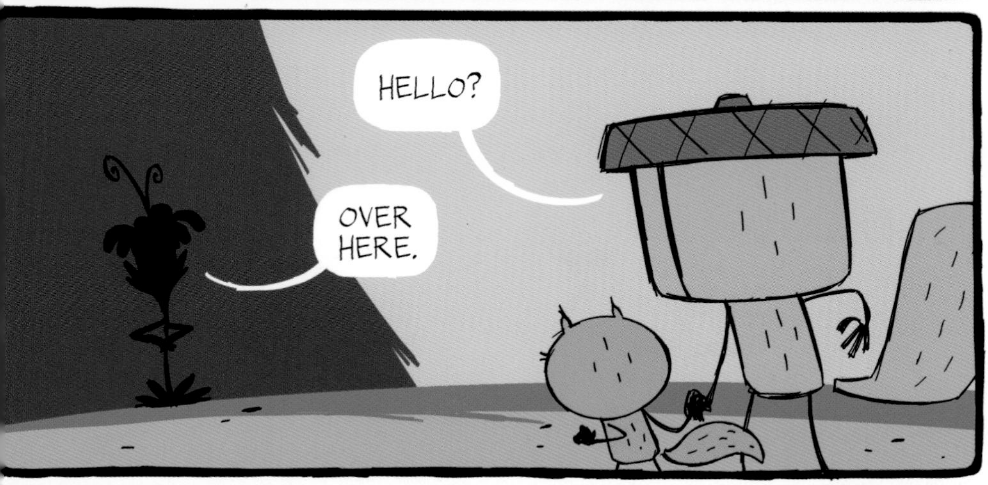
HELLO?
OVER HERE.

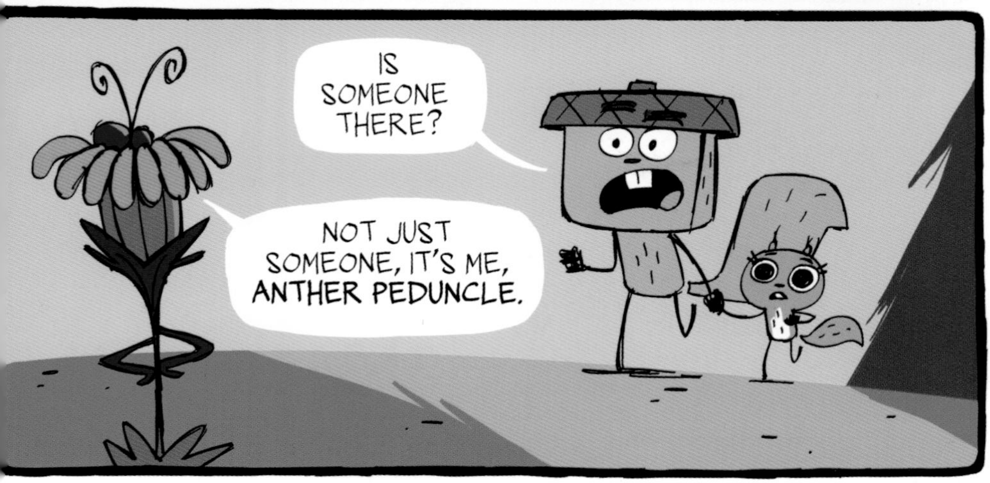
IS SOMEONE THERE?
NOT JUST SOMEONE, IT'S ME, ANTHER PEDUNCLE.

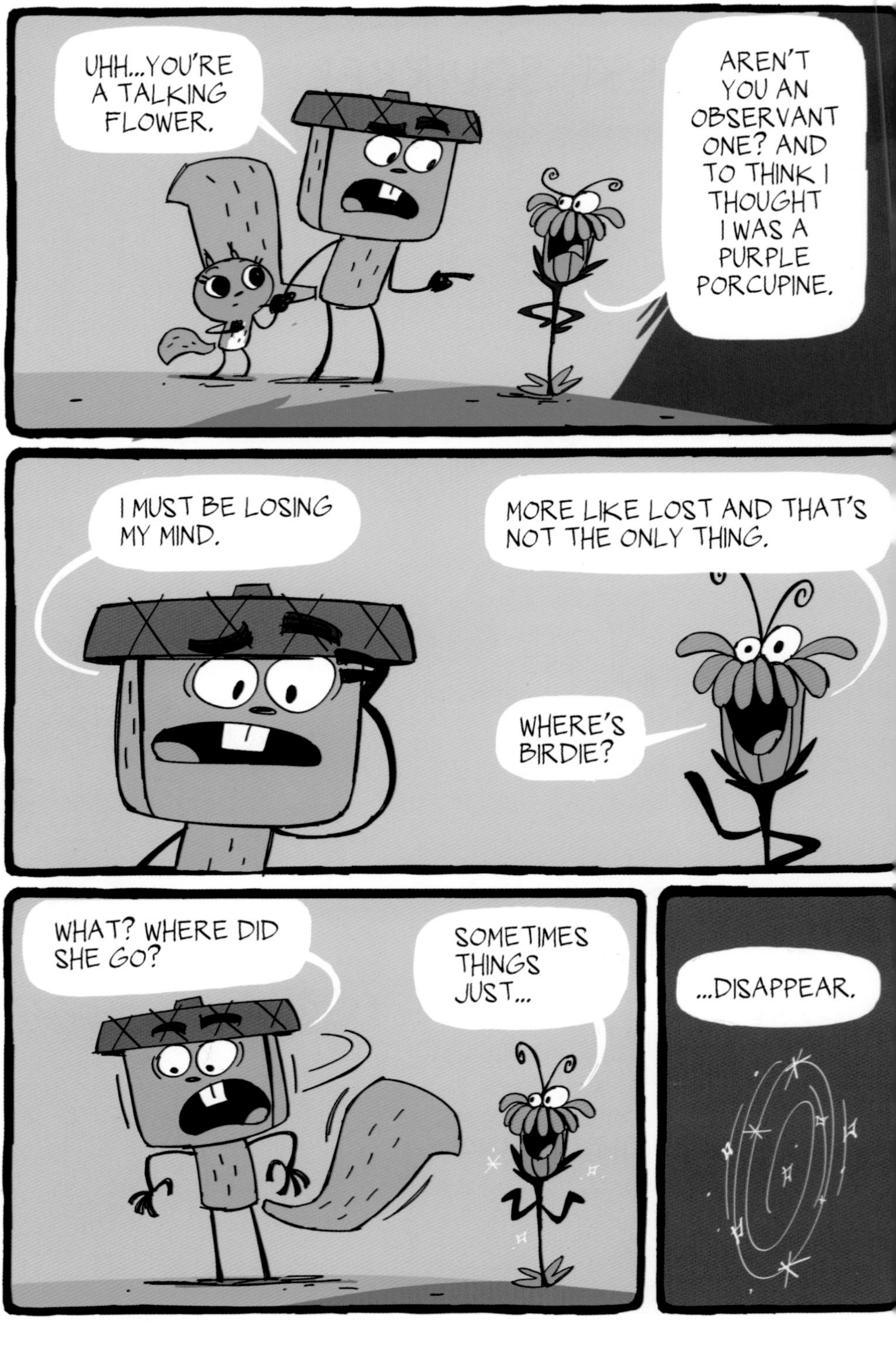
UHH...YOU'RE A TALKING FLOWER.
AREN'T YOU AN OBSERVANT ONE? AND TO THINK I THOUGHT I WAS A PURPLE PORCUPINE.
I MUST BE LOSING MY MIND.
MORE LIKE LOST AND THAT'S NOT THE ONLY THING.
WHERE'S BIRDIE?
WHAT? WHERE DID SHE GO?
SOMETIMES THINGS JUST...
...DISAPPEAR.

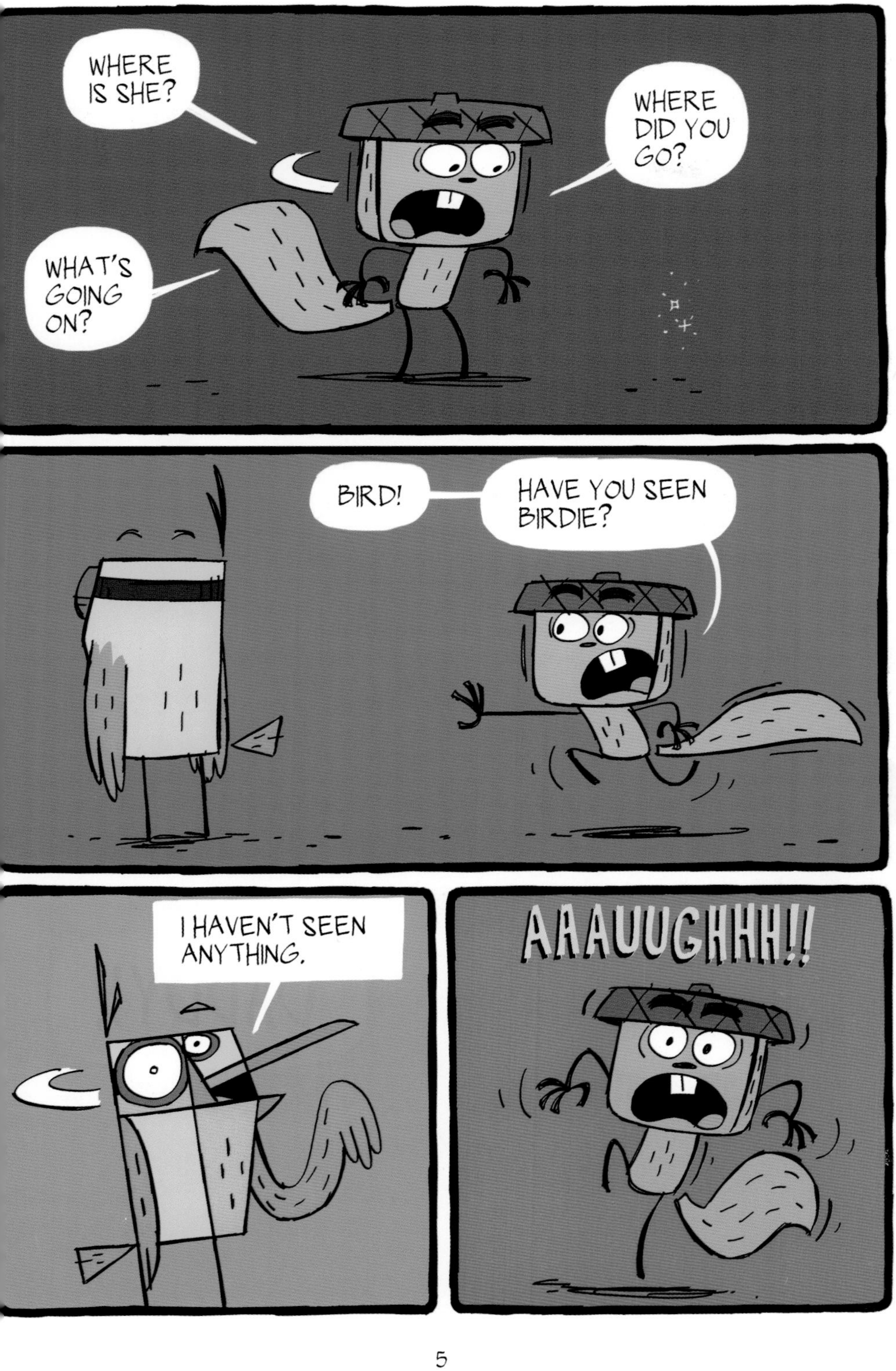
WHERE IS SHE?
WHERE DID YOU GO?
WHAT'S GOING ON?
BIRD!
HAVE YOU SEEN BIRDIE?
I HAVEN'T SEEN ANYTHING.
AAAUUGHHH!!

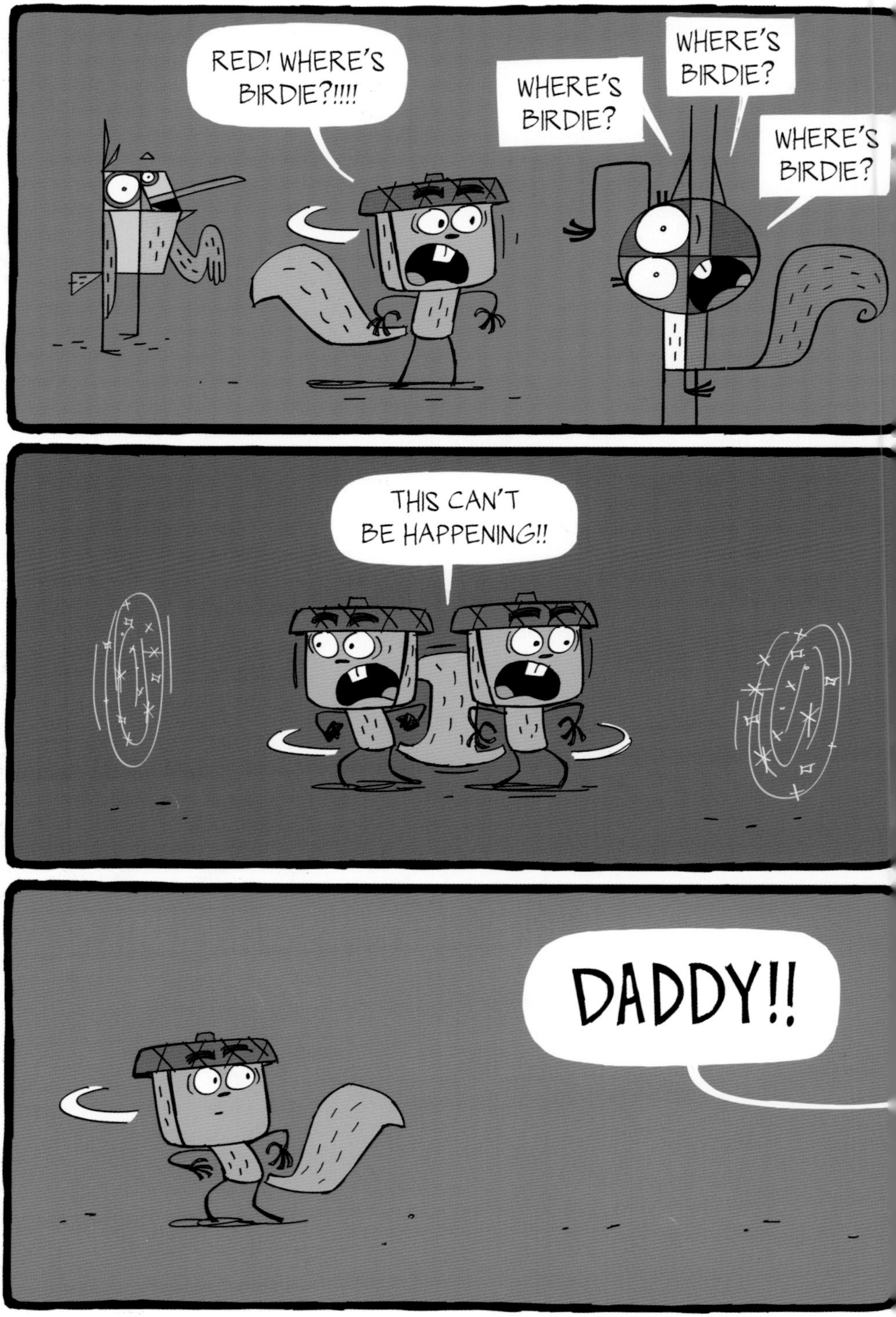
RED! WHERE'S BIRDIE?!!!!
WHERE'S BIRDIE?
WHERE'S BIRDIE?
WHERE'S BIRDIE?
THIS CAN'T BE HAPPENING!!
DADDY!!

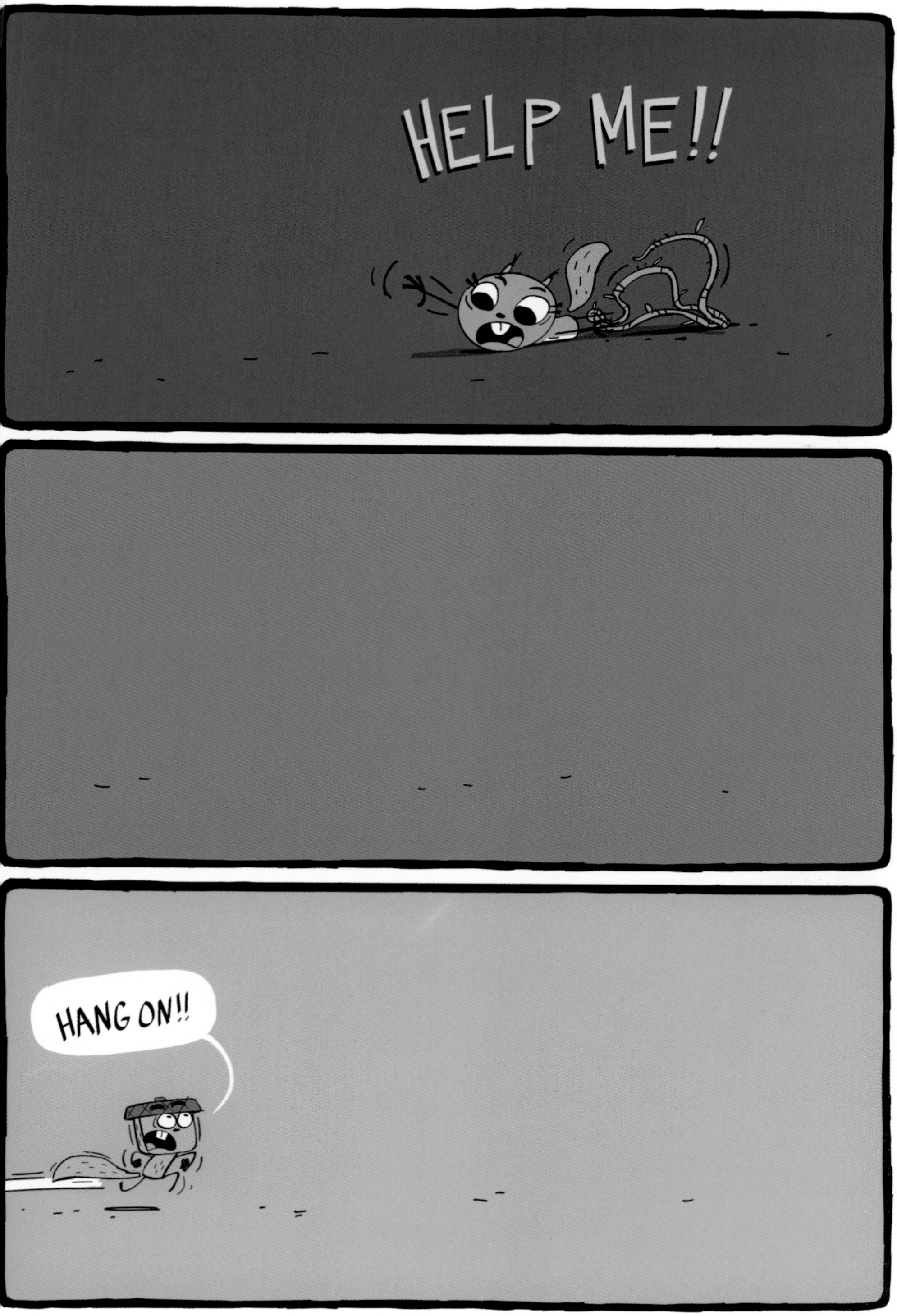
HELP ME!!
HANG ON!!

DADDY!!

I'M ALMOST THERE!

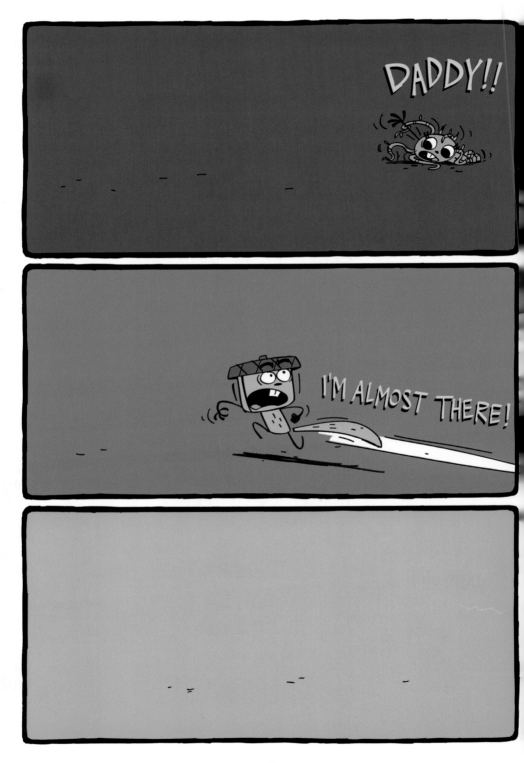

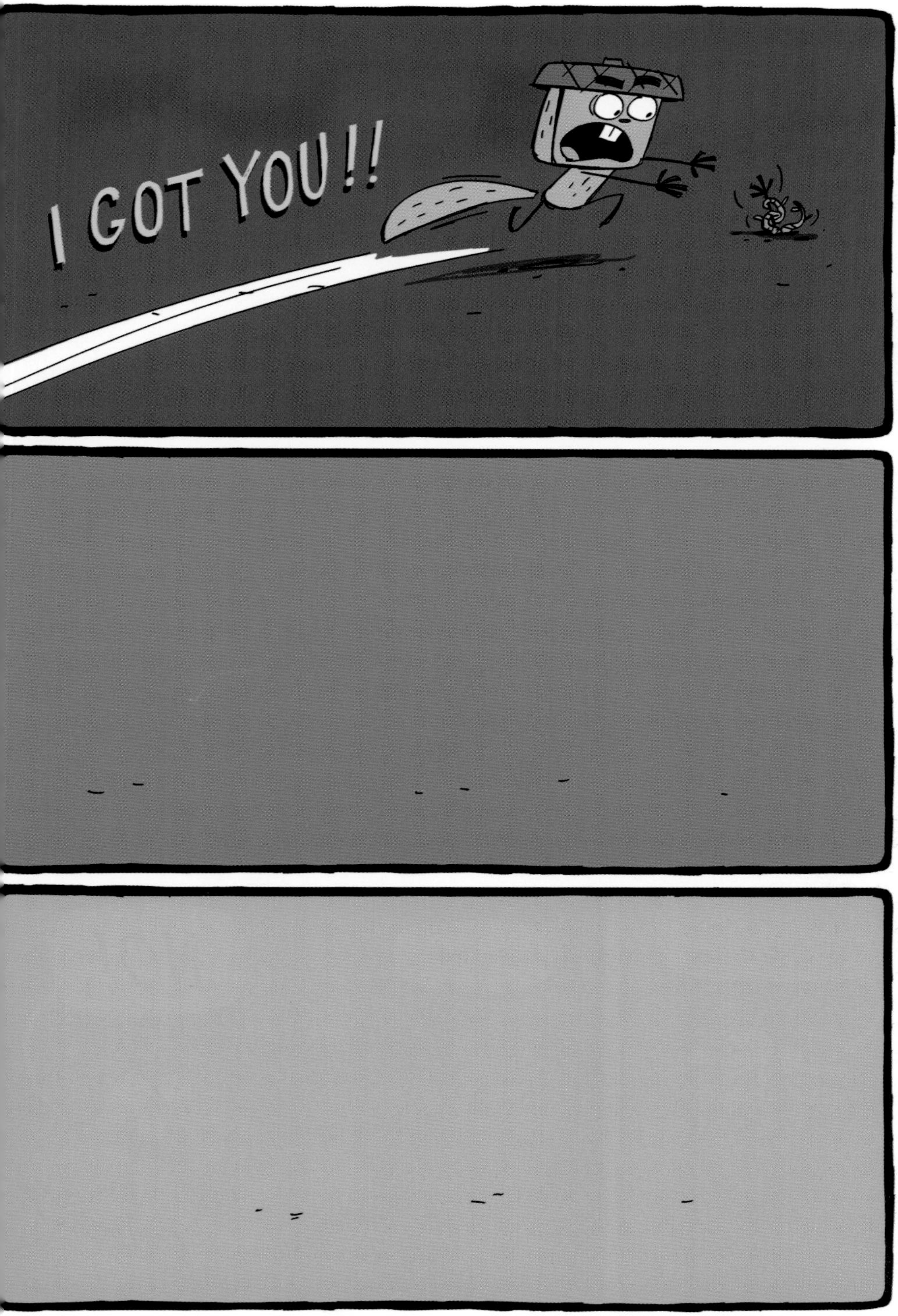
I GOT YOU!!

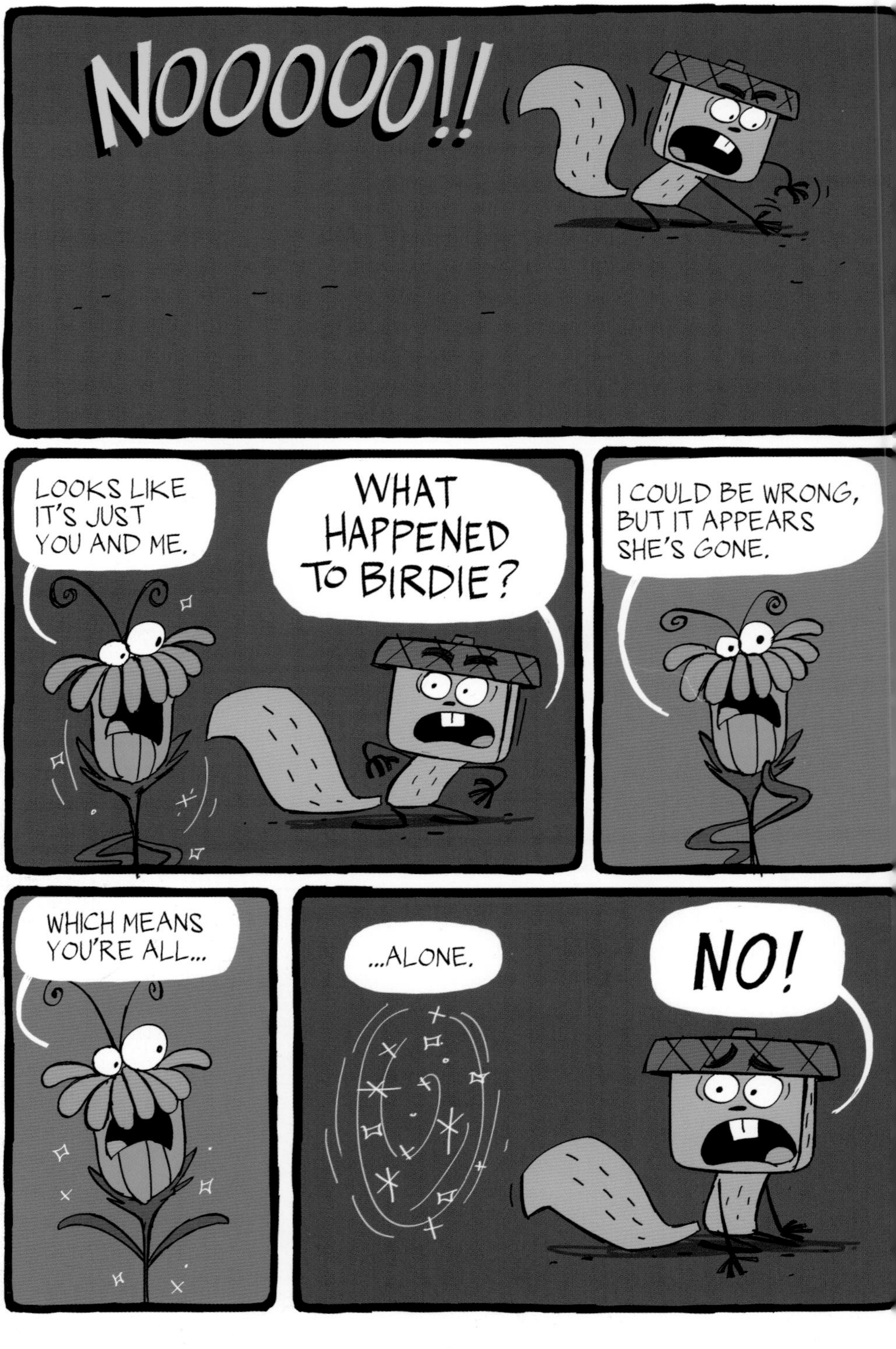
NOOOOO!!
LOOKS LIKE IT'S JUST YOU AND ME.
WHAT HAPPENED TO BIRDIE?
I COULD BE WRONG, BUT IT APPEARS SHE'S GONE.
WHICH MEANS YOU'RE ALL...
...ALONE.
NO!

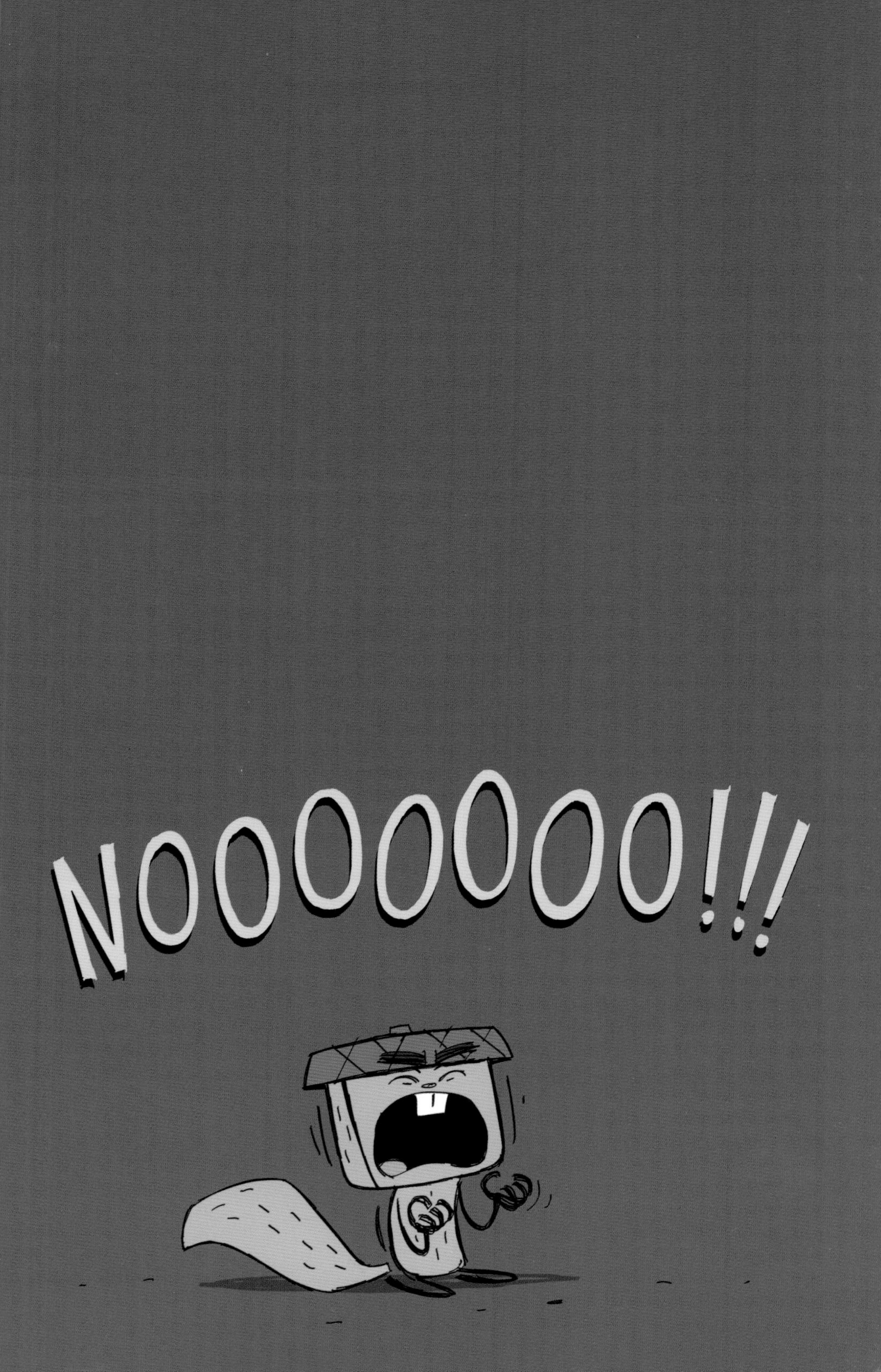
NOOOOOOO!!!

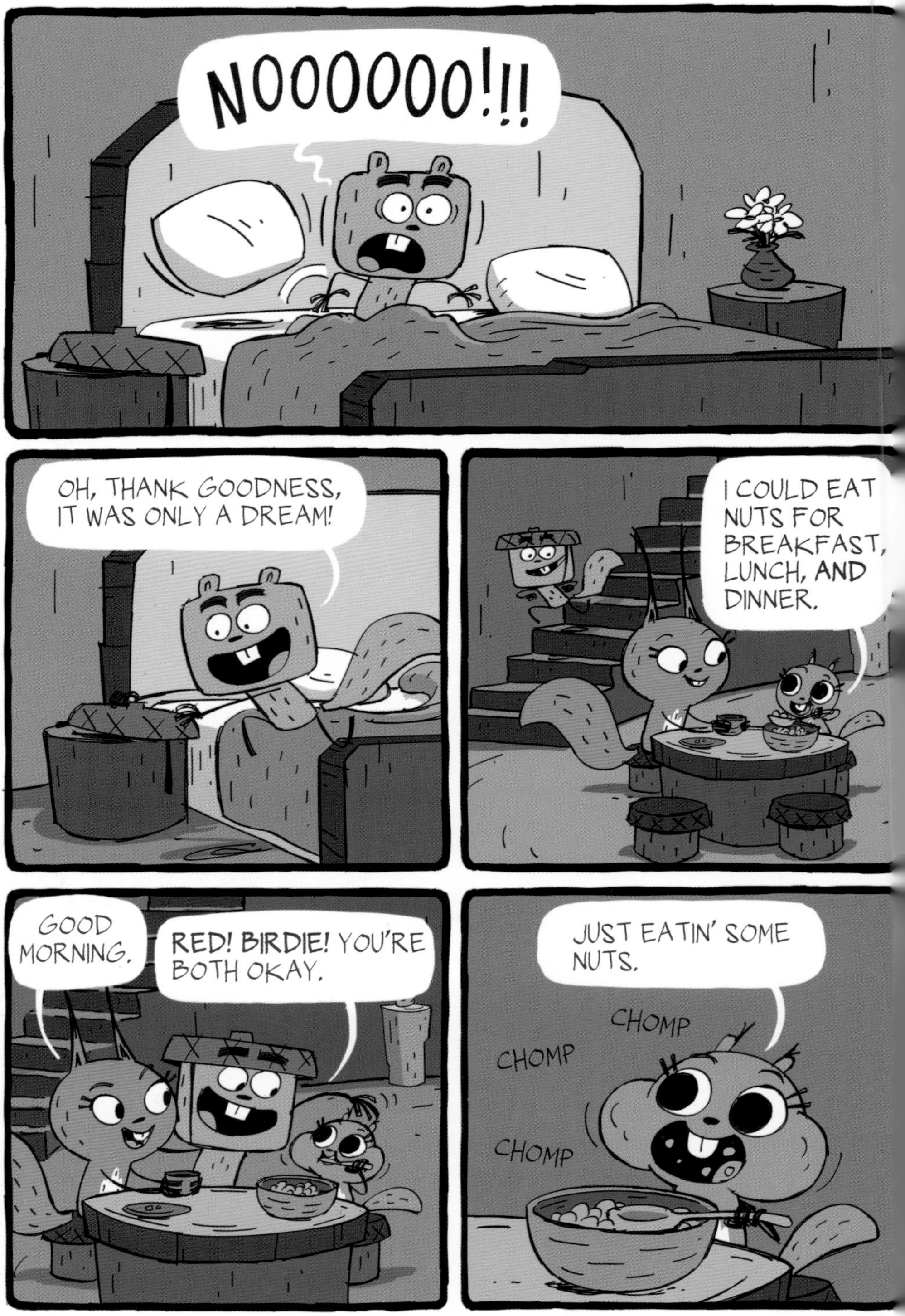
NOOOOOO!!!
OH, THANK GOODNESS, IT WAS ONLY A DREAM!
I COULD EAT NUTS FOR BREAKFAST, LUNCH, AND DINNER.
GOOD MORNING.
RED! BIRDIE! YOU'RE BOTH OKAY.
JUST EATIN' SOME NUTS.
CHOMP
CHOMP
CHOMP

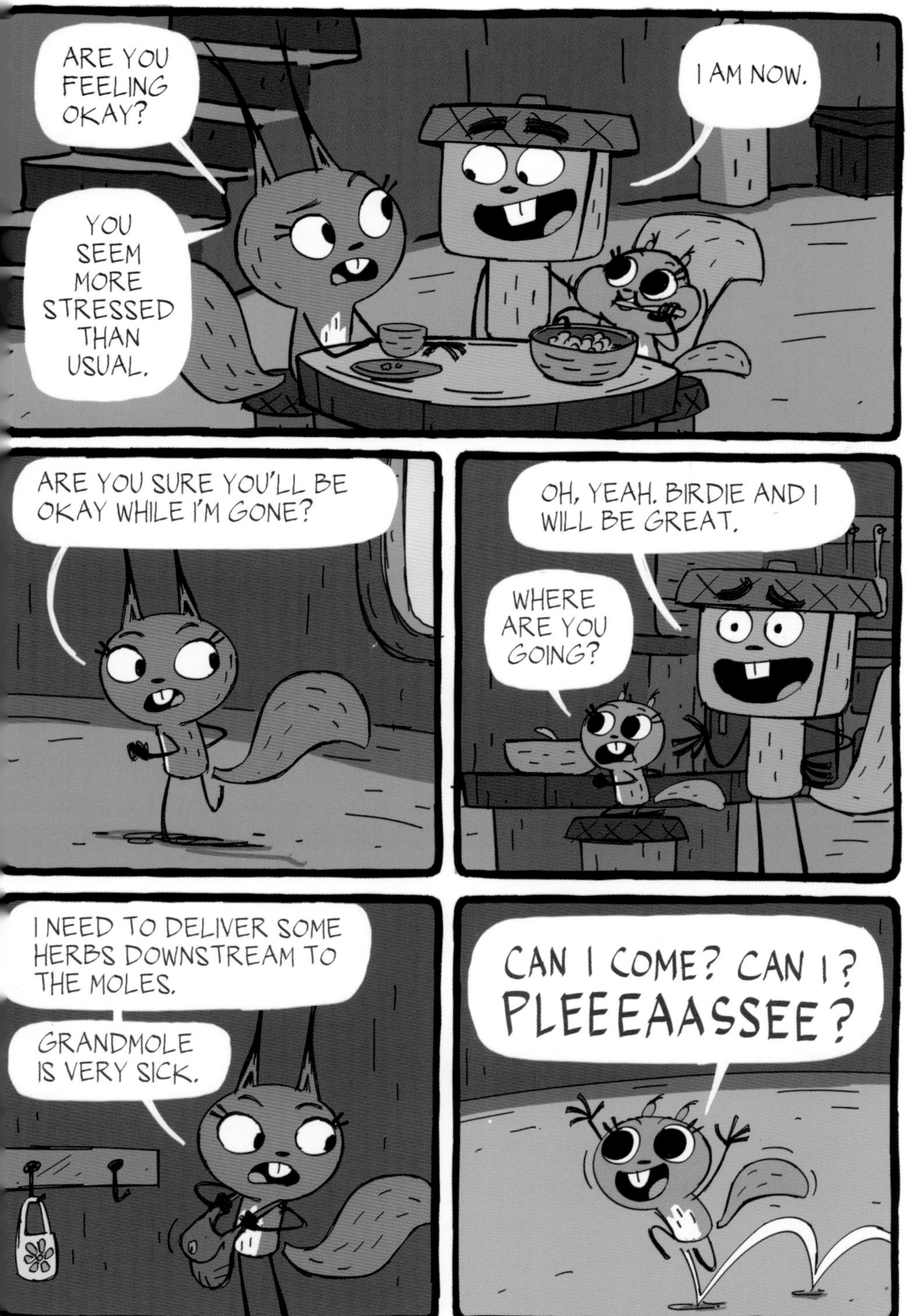
ARE YOU FEELING OKAY?
YOU SEEM MORE STRESSED THAN USUAL.
I AM NOW.
ARE YOU SURE YOU'LL BE OKAY WHILE I'M GONE?
OH, YEAH. BIRDIE AND I WILL BE GREAT.
WHERE ARE YOU GOING?
I NEED TO DELIVER SOME HERBS DOWNSTREAM TO THE MOLES.
GRANDMOLE IS VERY SICK.
CAN I COME? CAN I? PLEEEAASSEE?

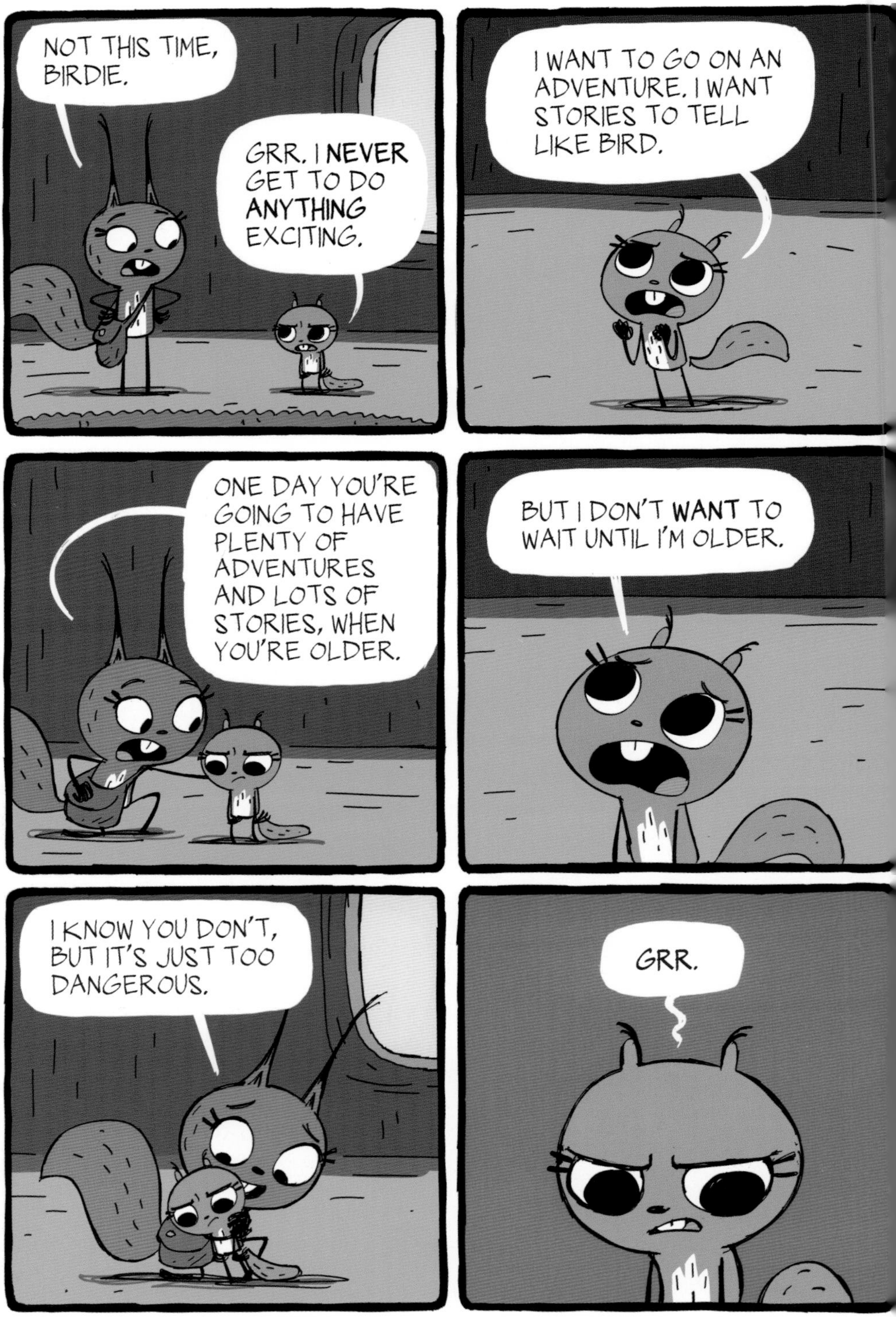
NOT THIS TIME, BIRDIE.
GRR. I **NEVER** GET TO DO **ANYTHING** EXCITING.
I WANT TO GO ON AN ADVENTURE. I WANT STORIES TO TELL LIKE BIRD.
ONE DAY YOU'RE GOING TO HAVE PLENTY OF ADVENTURES AND LOTS OF STORIES, WHEN YOU'RE OLDER.
BUT I DON'T **WANT** TO WAIT UNTIL I'M OLDER.
I KNOW YOU DON'T, BUT IT'S JUST TOO DANGEROUS.
GRR.

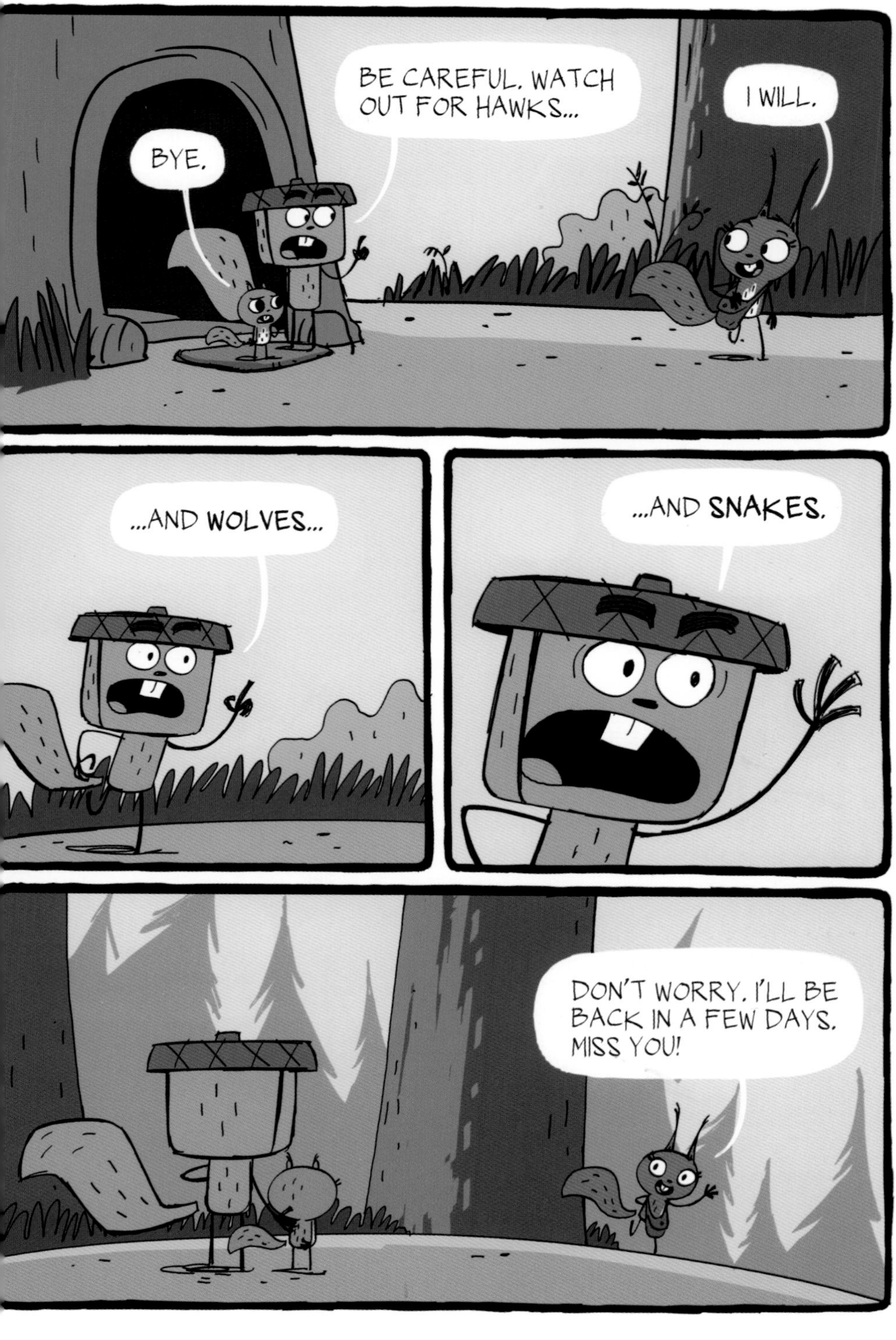
BYE.
BE CAREFUL. WATCH OUT FOR HAWKS...
I WILL.
...AND WOLVES...
...AND SNAKES.
DON'T WORRY. I'LL BE BACK IN A FEW DAYS. MISS YOU!

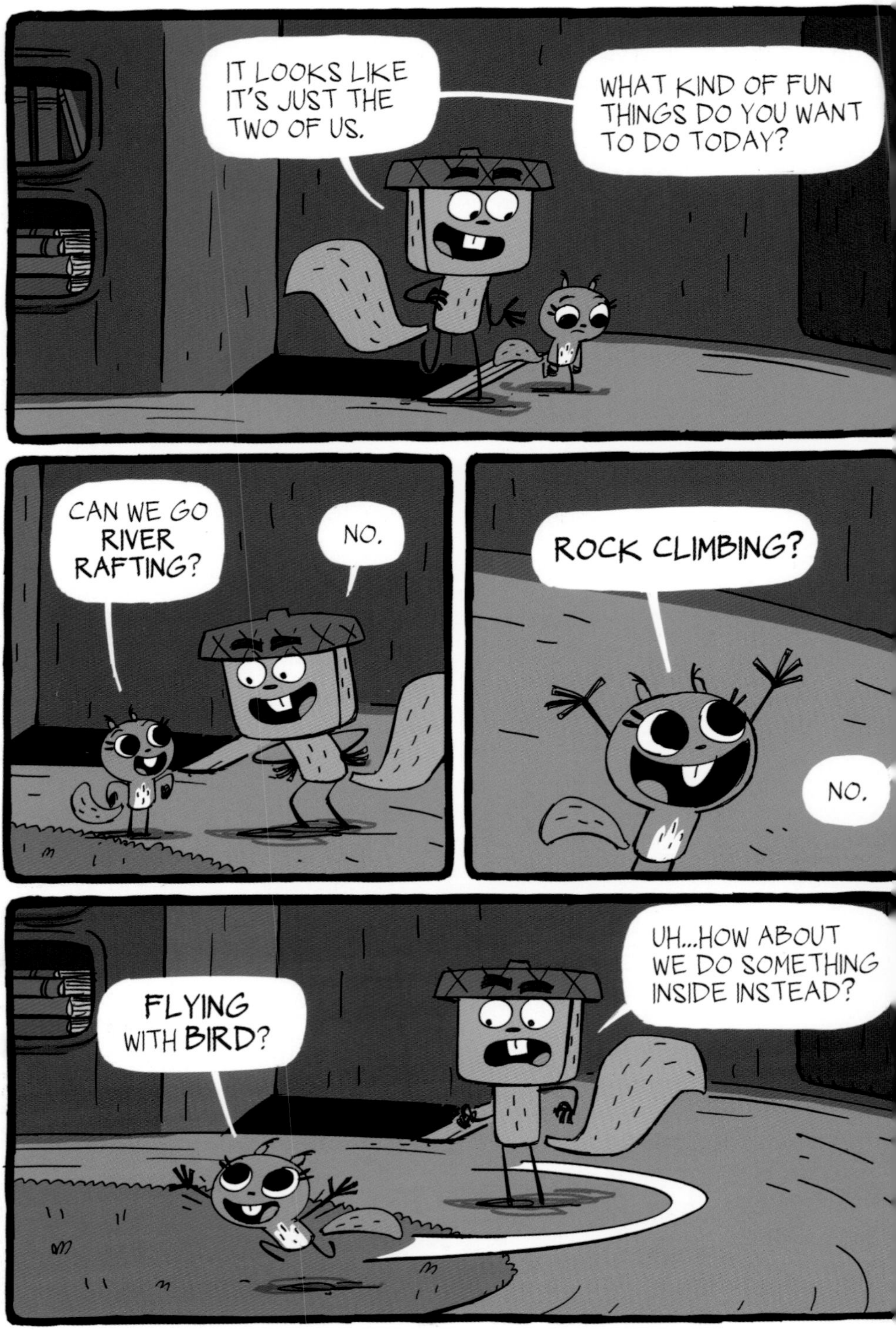
IT LOOKS LIKE IT'S JUST THE TWO OF US.
WHAT KIND OF FUN THINGS DO YOU WANT TO DO TODAY?
CAN WE GO RIVER RAFTING?
NO.
ROCK CLIMBING?
NO.
FLYING WITH BIRD?
UH...HOW ABOUT WE DO SOMETHING INSIDE INSTEAD?

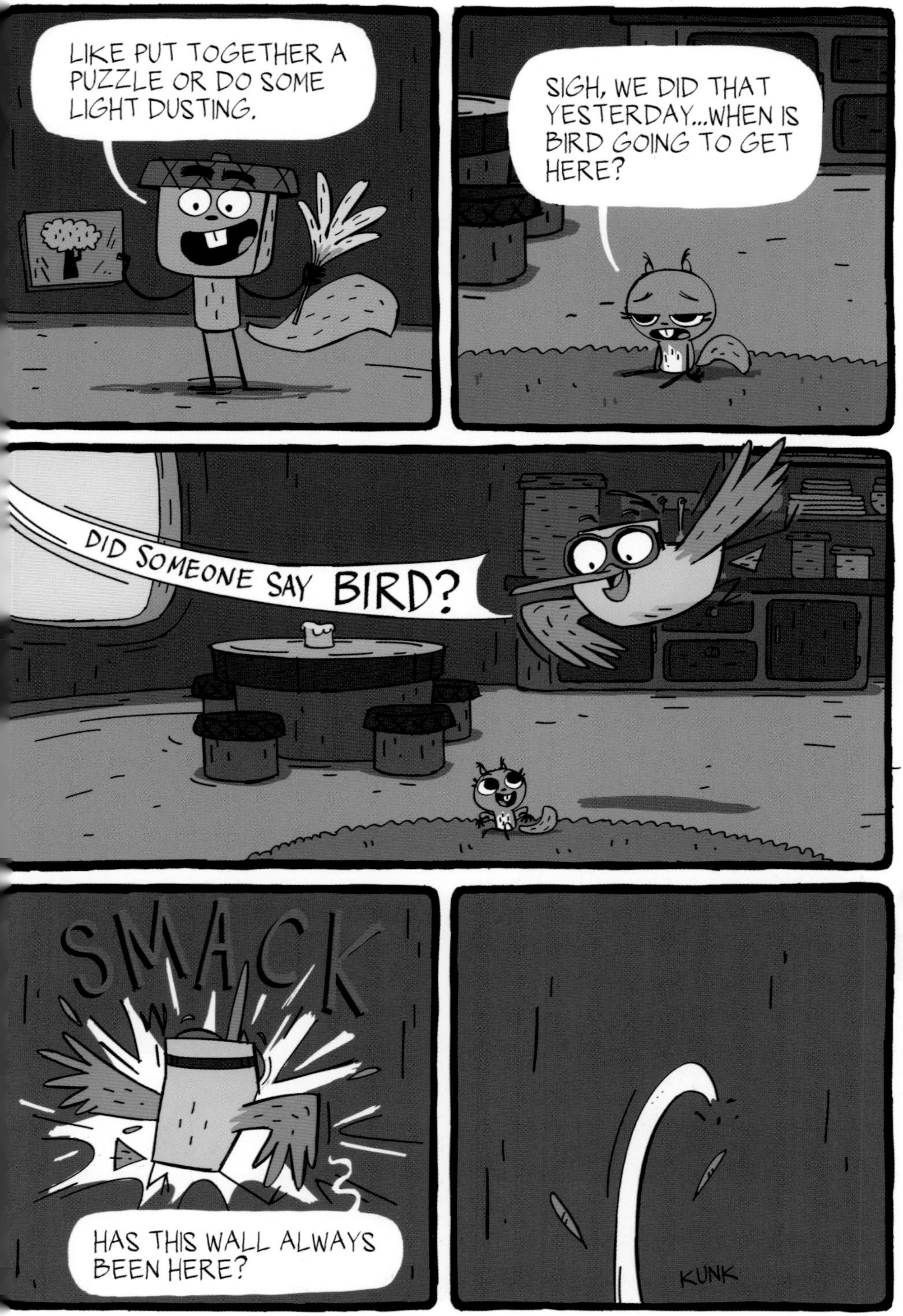
LIKE PUT TOGETHER A PUZZLE OR DO SOME LIGHT DUSTING.
SIGH, WE DID THAT YESTERDAY...WHEN IS BIRD GOING TO GET HERE?
DID SOMEONE SAY BIRD?
SMACK
HAS THIS WALL ALWAYS BEEN HERE?
KUNK

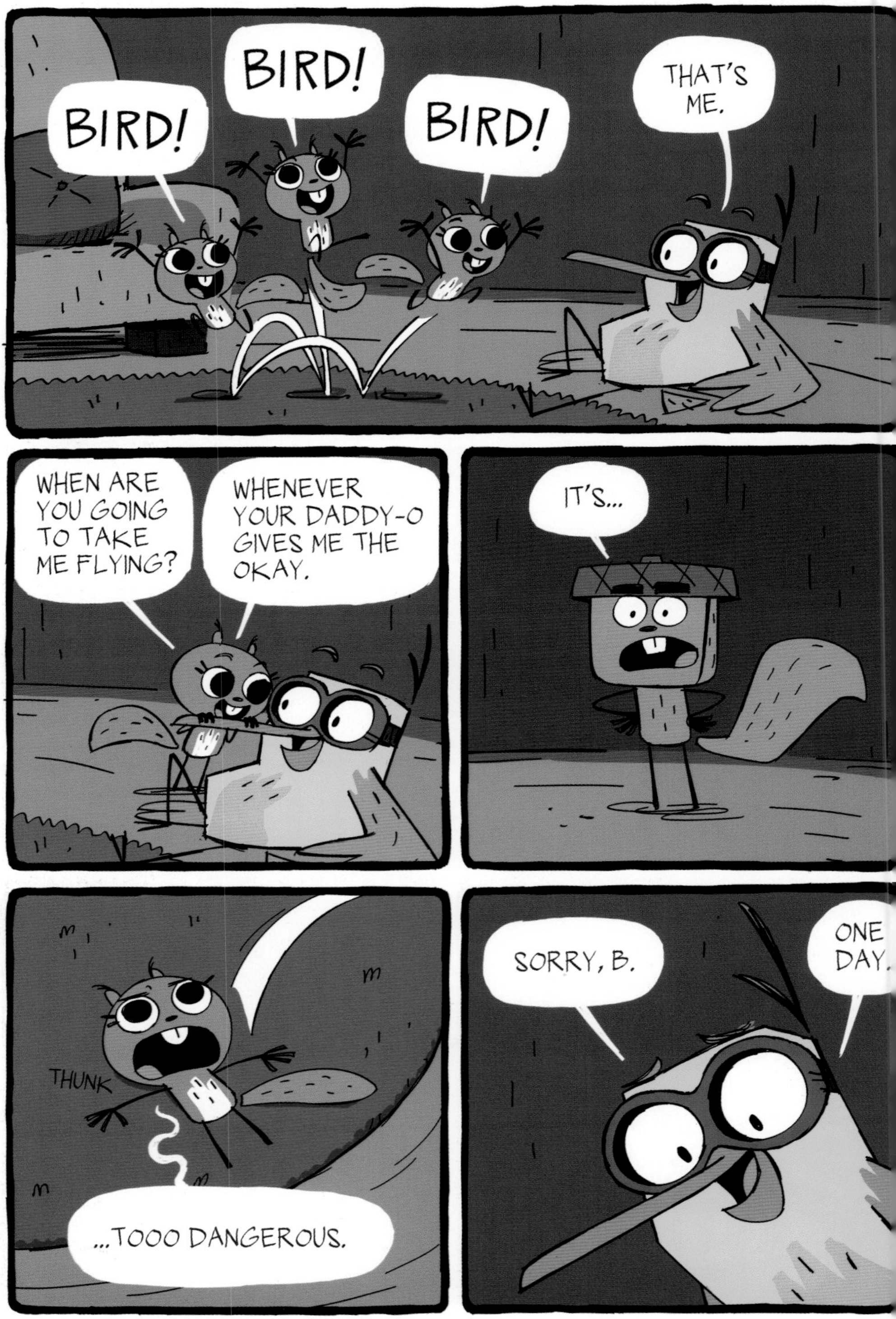
BIRD!
BIRD!
BIRD!
THAT'S ME.
WHEN ARE YOU GOING TO TAKE ME FLYING?
WHENEVER YOUR DADDY-O GIVES ME THE OKAY.
IT'S...
THUNK
...TOOO DANGEROUS.
SORRY, B.
ONE DAY.

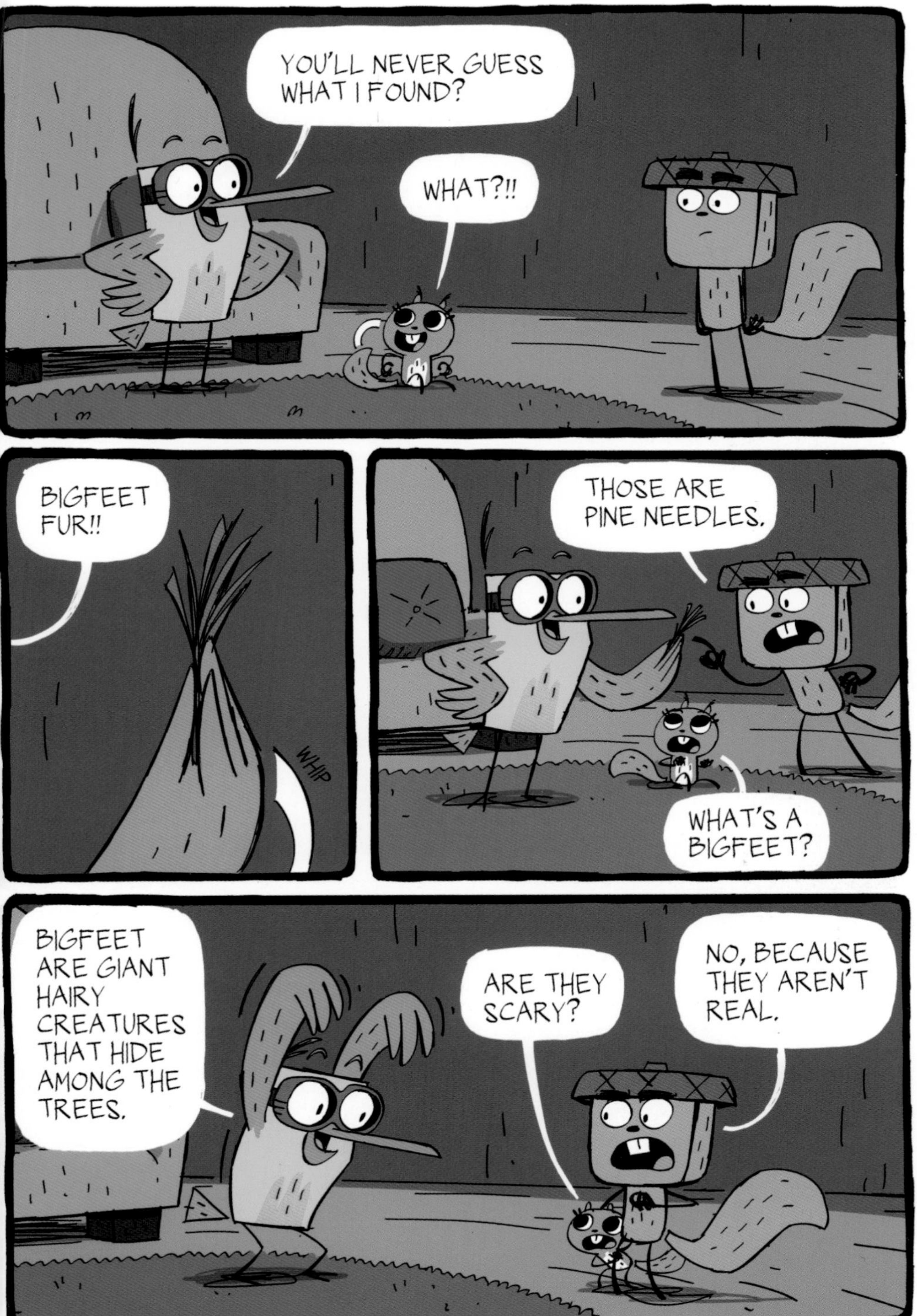
YOU'LL NEVER GUESS WHAT I FOUND?
WHAT?!!
BIGFEET FUR!!
WHIP
THOSE ARE PINE NEEDLES.
WHAT'S A BIGFEET?
BIGFEET ARE GIANT HAIRY CREATURES THAT HIDE AMONG THE TREES.
ARE THEY SCARY?
NO, BECAUSE THEY AREN'T REAL.

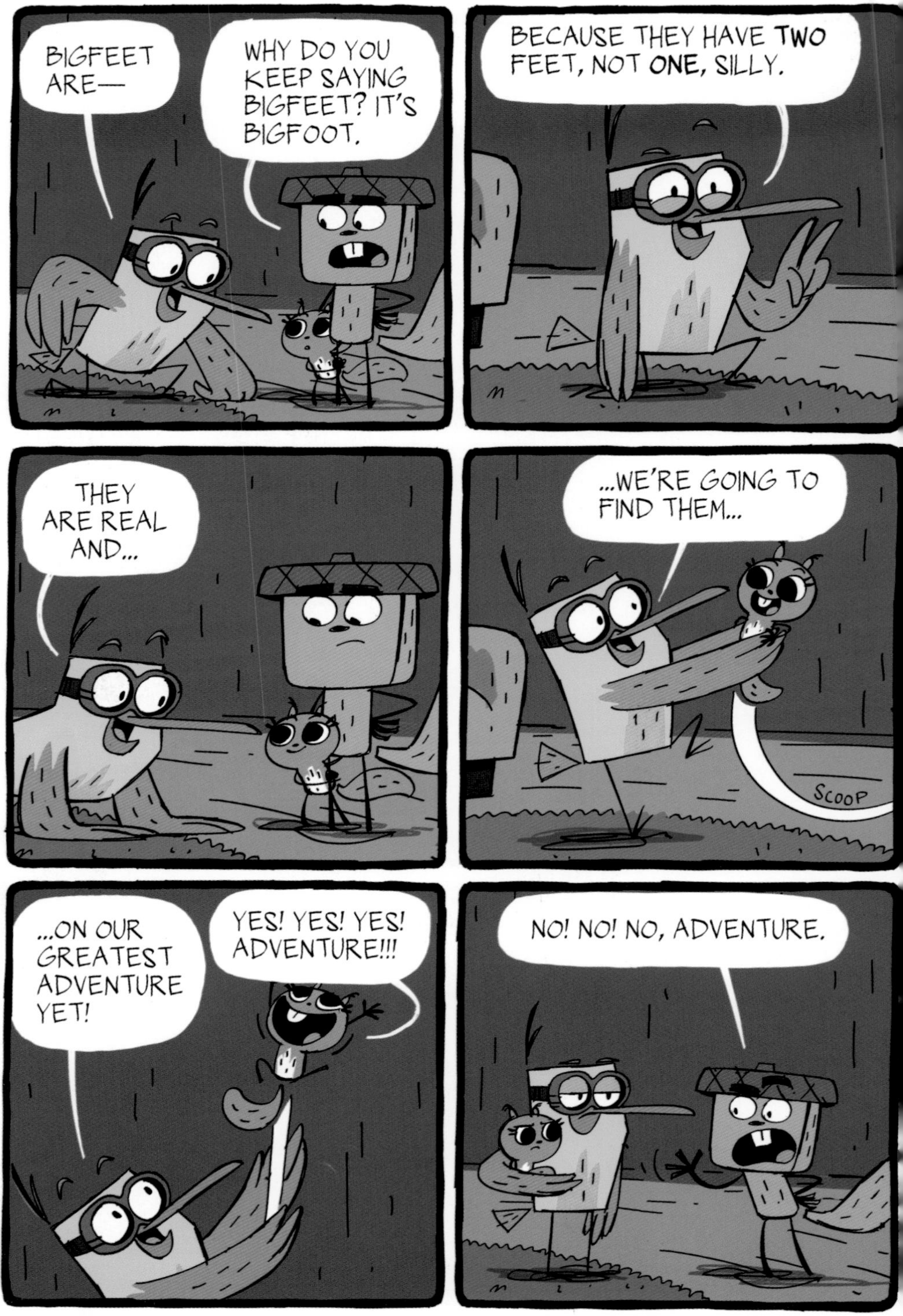
BIGFEET ARE—
WHY DO YOU KEEP SAYING BIGFEET? IT'S BIGFOOT.
BECAUSE THEY HAVE **TWO** FEET, NOT **ONE**, SILLY.
THEY ARE REAL AND...
...WE'RE GOING TO FIND THEM...
SCOOP
...ON OUR GREATEST ADVENTURE YET!
YES! YES! YES! ADVENTURE!!!
NO! NO! NO, ADVENTURE.

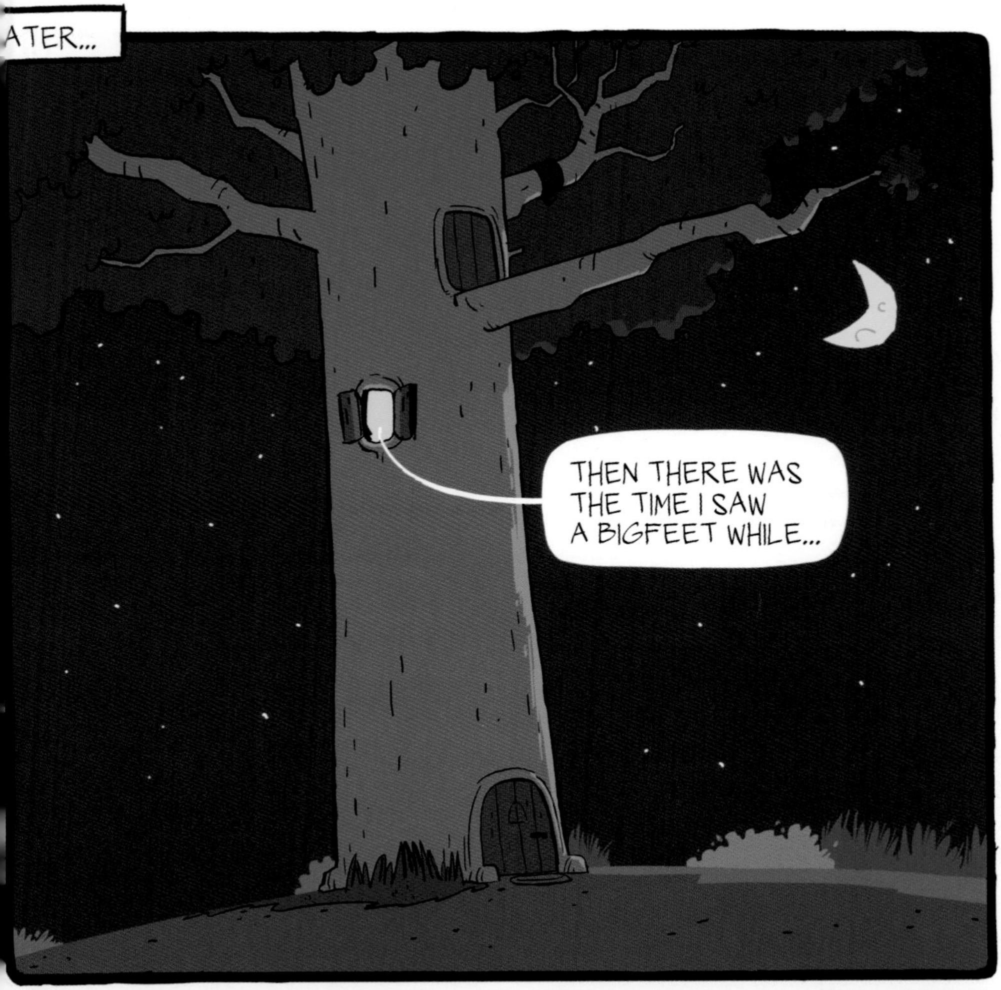
ATER...
THEN THERE WAS THE TIME I SAW A BIGFEET WHILE...

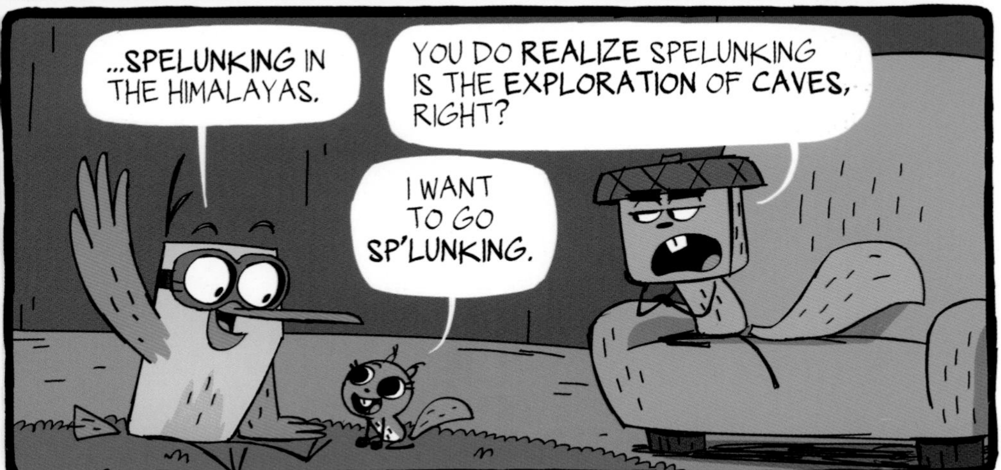
...SPELUNKING IN THE HIMALAYAS.
YOU DO REALIZE SPELUNKING IS THE EXPLORATION OF CAVES, RIGHT?
I WANT TO GO SP'LUNKING.

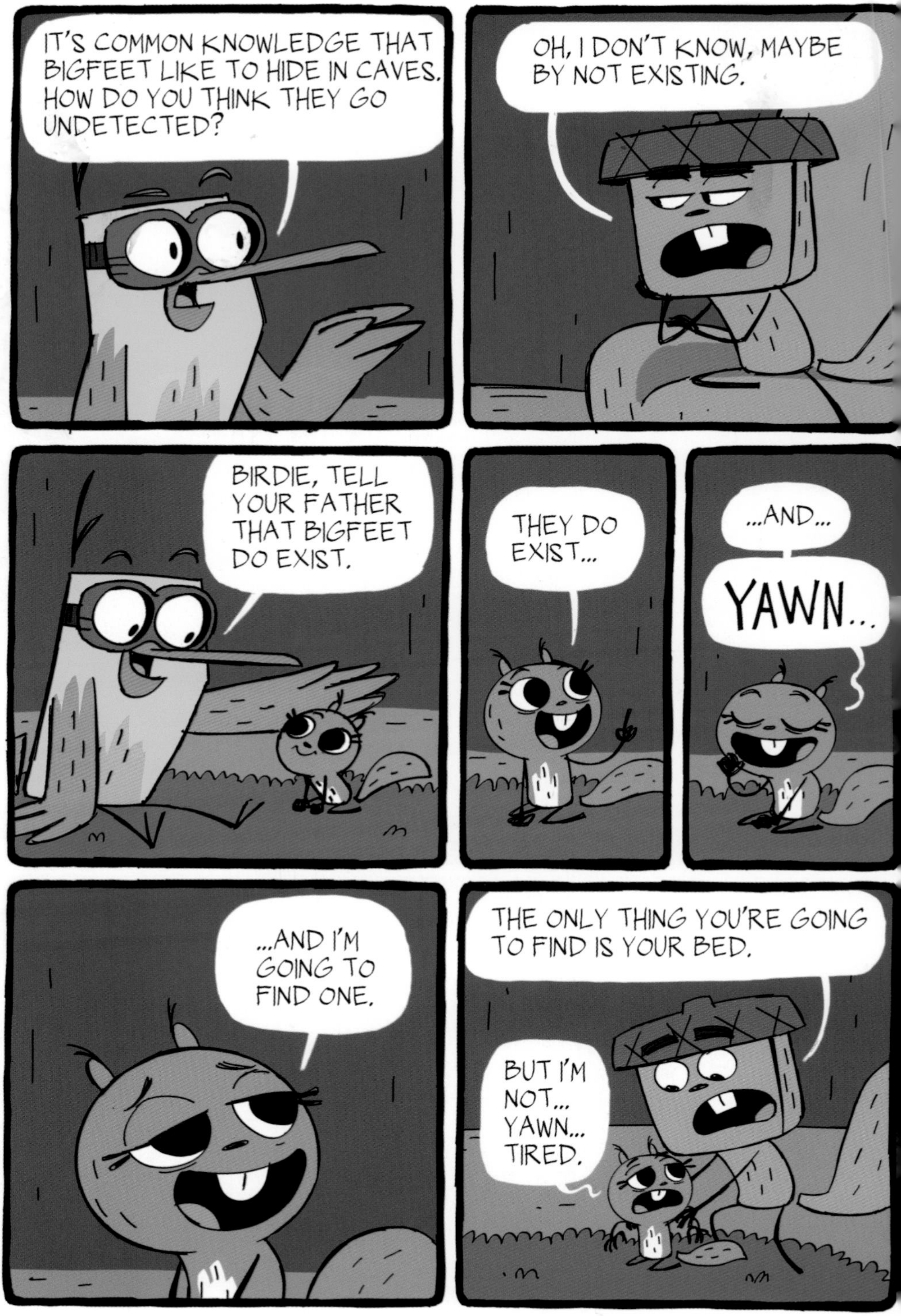
IT'S COMMON KNOWLEDGE THAT BIGFEET LIKE TO HIDE IN CAVES. HOW DO YOU THINK THEY GO UNDETECTED?
OH, I DON'T KNOW, MAYBE BY NOT EXISTING.
BIRDIE, TELL YOUR FATHER THAT BIGFEET DO EXIST.
THEY DO EXIST...
...AND...
YAWN...
...AND I'M GOING TO FIND ONE.
THE ONLY THING YOU'RE GOING TO FIND IS YOUR BED.
BUT I'M NOT... YAWN... TIRED.

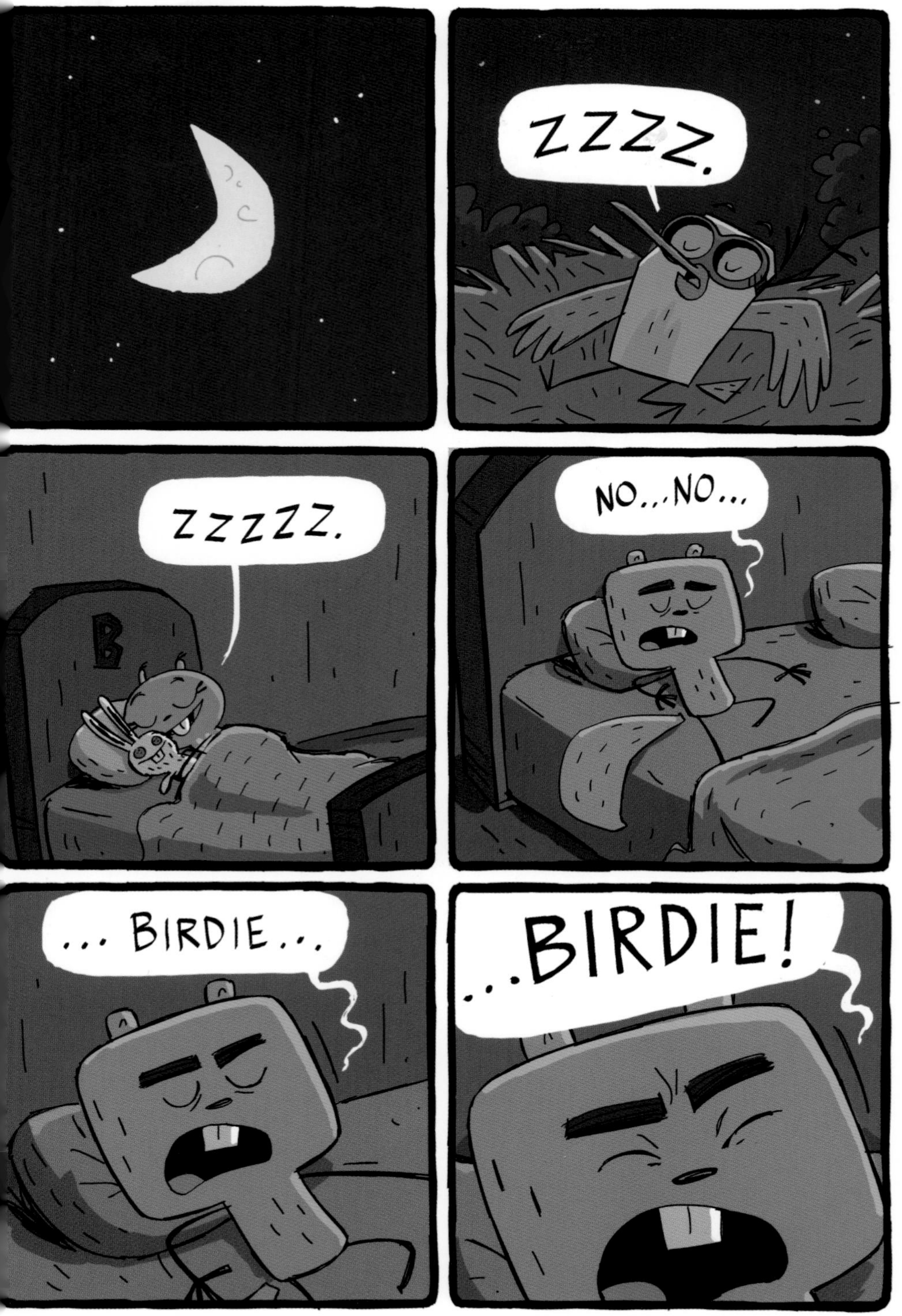
ZZZZ.
ZZZZZ.
NO...NO...
... BIRDIE...
...BIRDIE!

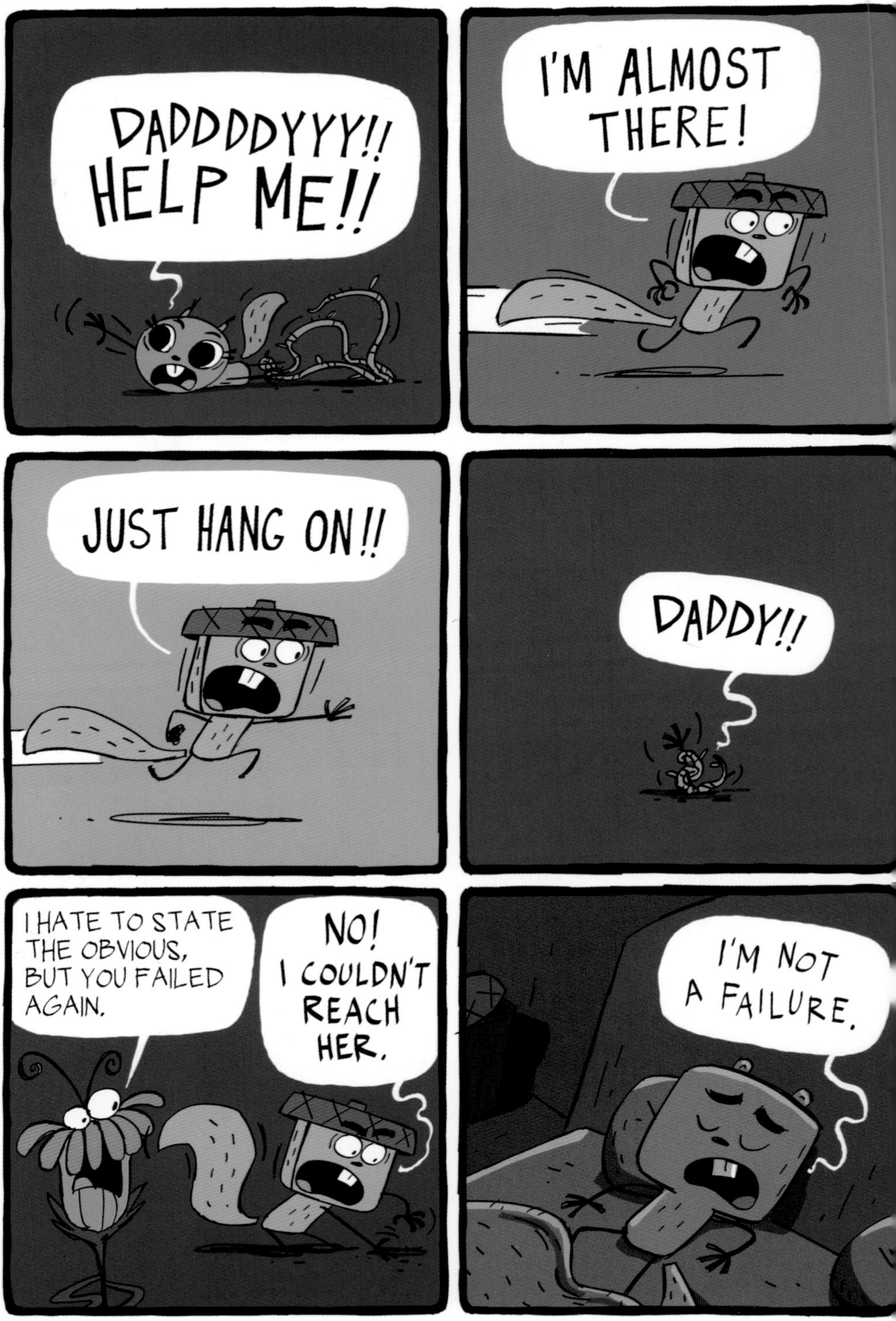
DADDDDYYY!! HELP ME!!
I'M ALMOST THERE!
JUST HANG ON!!
DADDY!!
I HATE TO STATE THE OBVIOUS, BUT YOU FAILED AGAIN.
NO! I COULDN'T REACH HER.
I'M NOT A FAILURE.

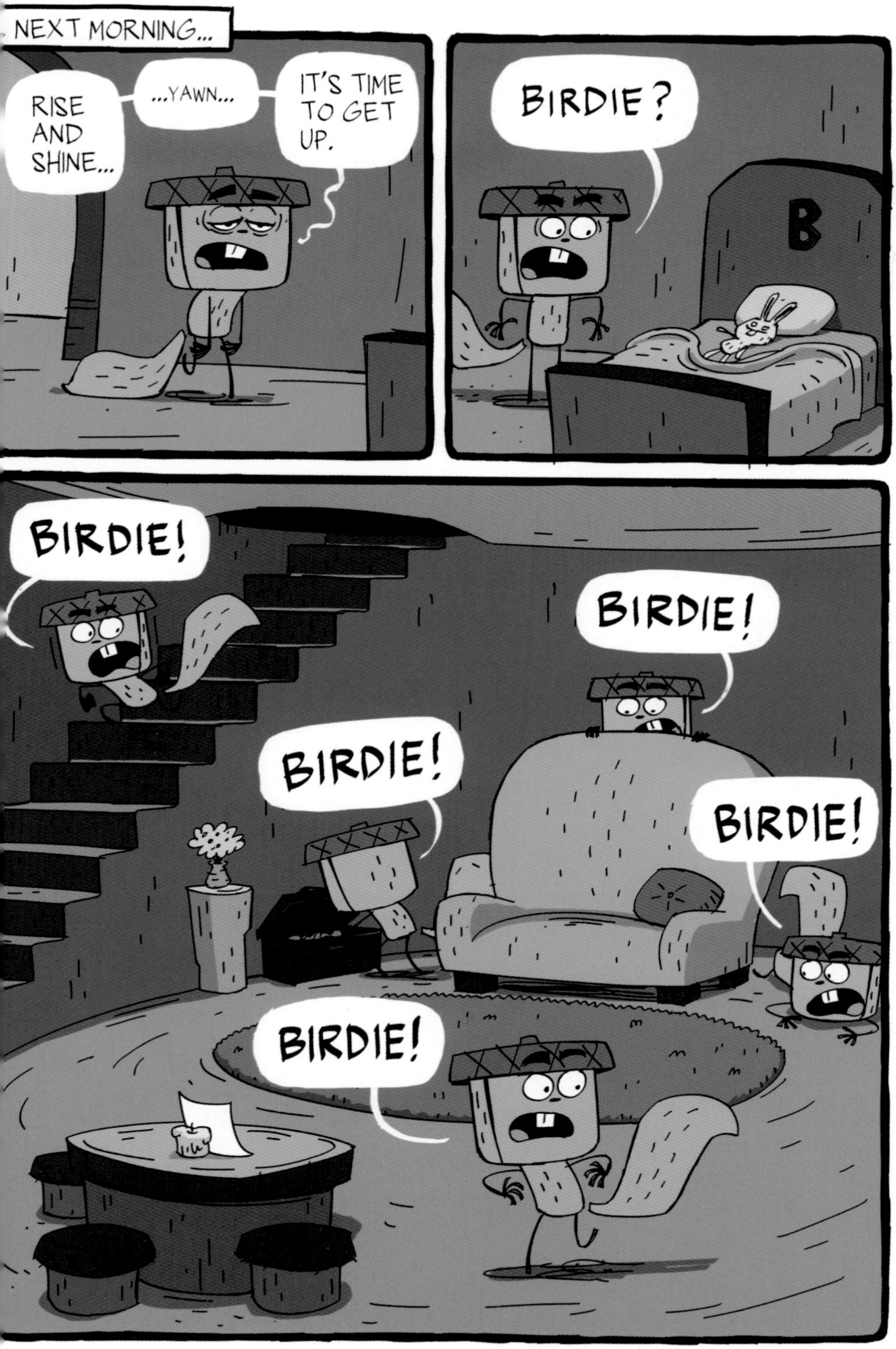
NEXT MORNING...
RISE AND SHINE...
...YAWN...
IT'S TIME TO GET UP.
BIRDIE?
B
BIRDIE!
BIRDIE!
BIRDIE!
BIRDIE!
BIRDIE!

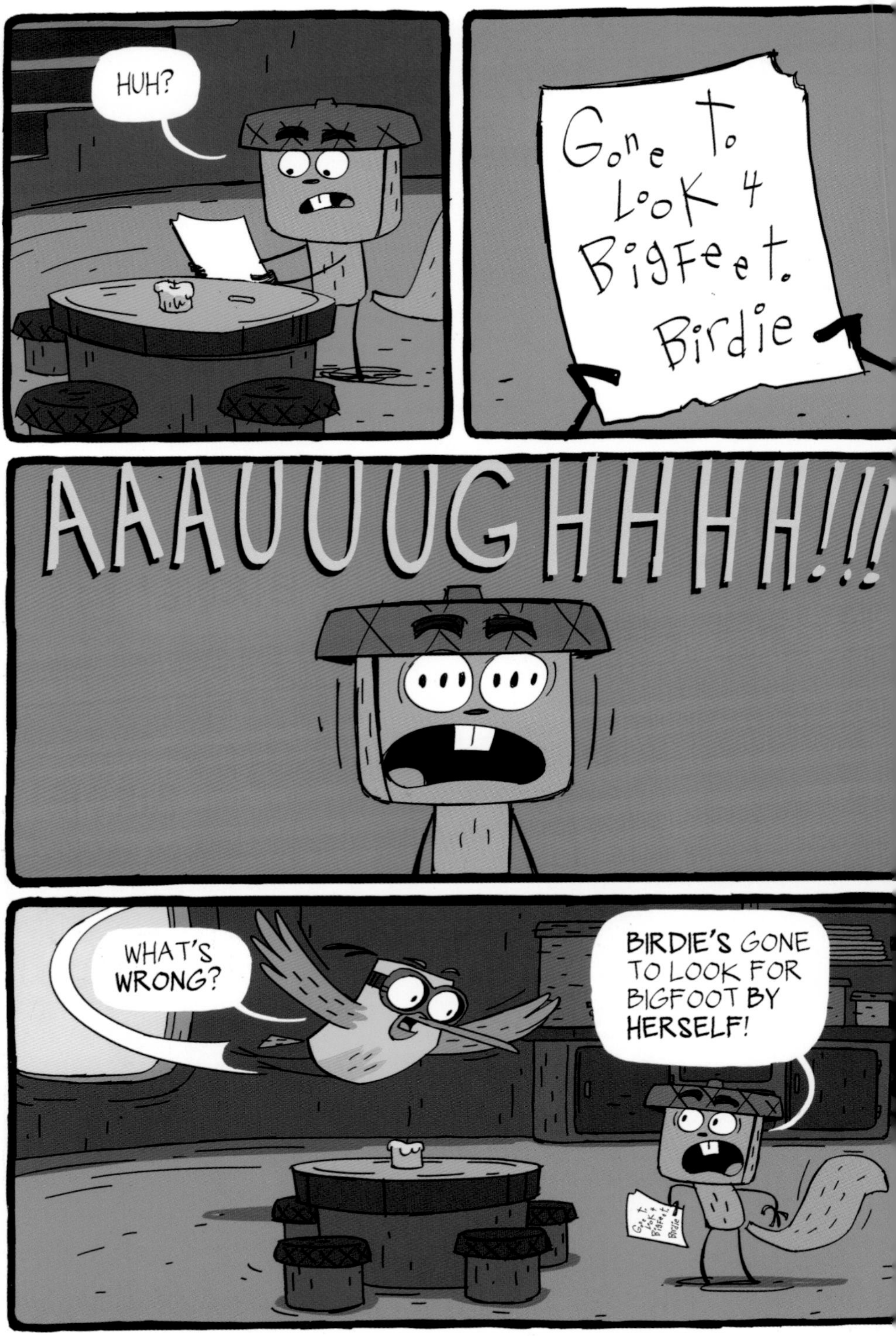
HUH?
Gone To Look 4 BigFeet. Birdie
AAAUUUGHHHH!!!
WHAT'S WRONG?
BIRDIE'S GONE TO LOOK FOR BIGFOOT BY HERSELF!

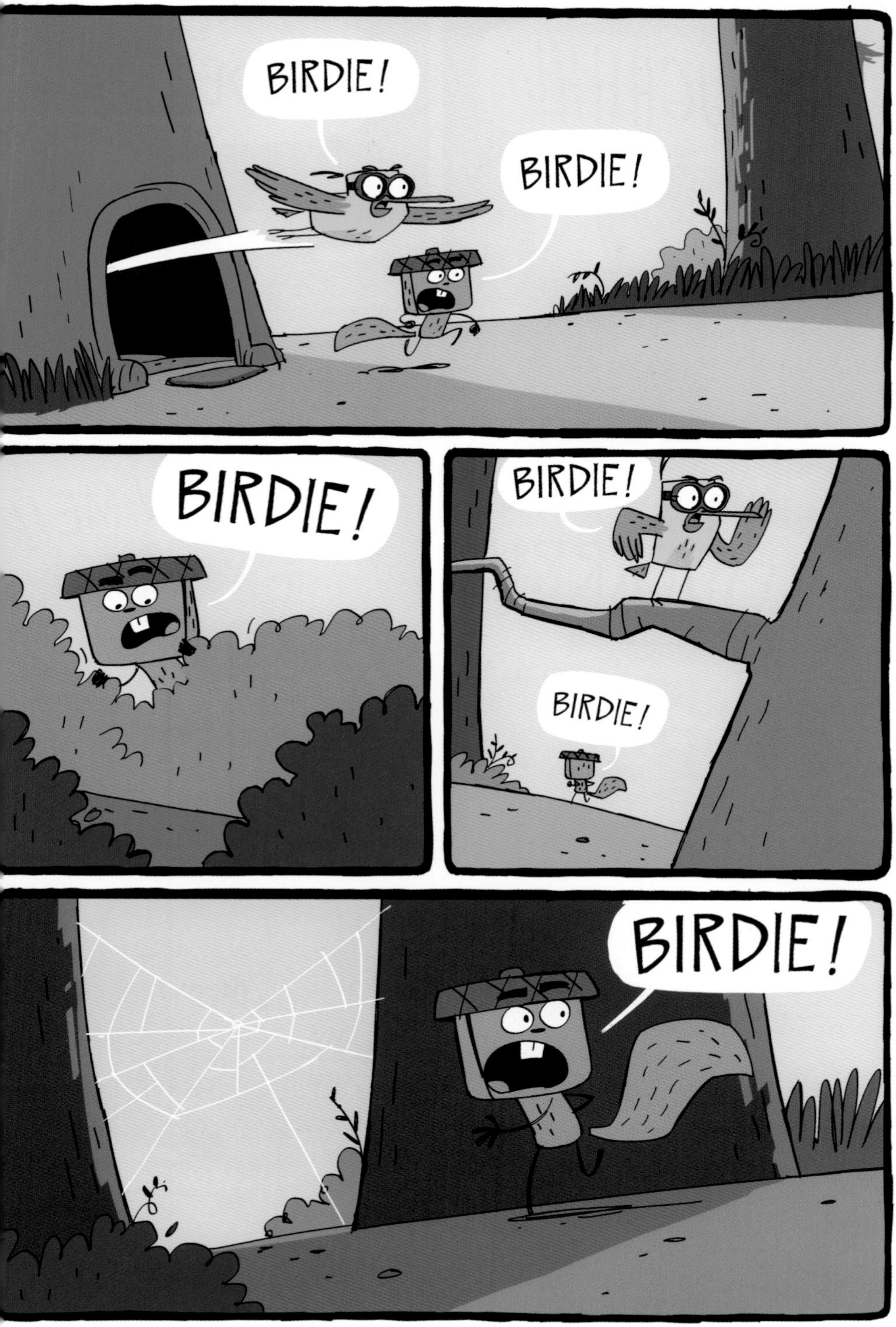
BIRDIE!
BIRDIE!
BIRDIE!
BIRDIE!
BIRDIE!
BIRDIE!

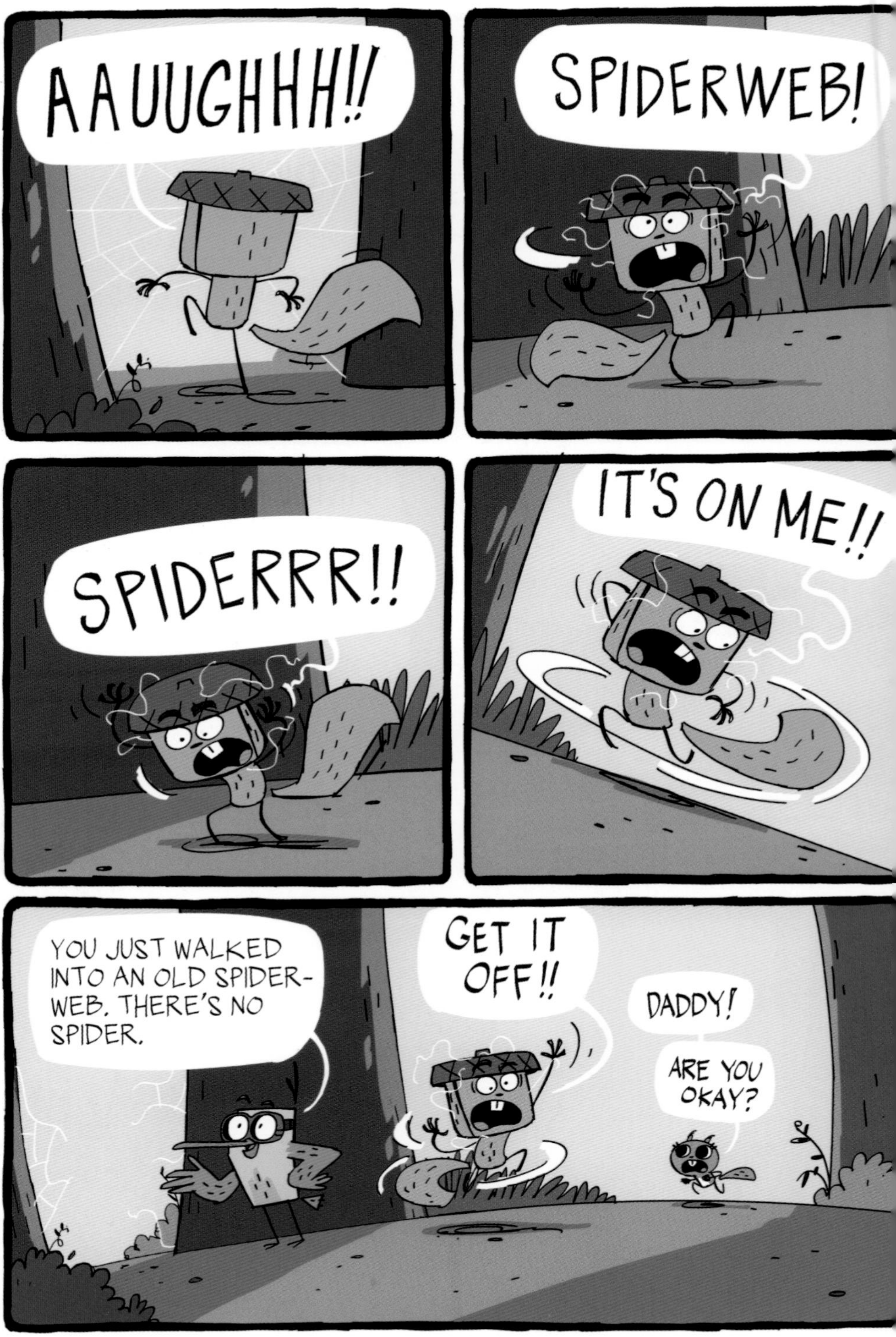
AAUUGHHH!!
SPIDERWEB!
SPIDERRR!!
IT'S ON ME!!
YOU JUST WALKED INTO AN OLD SPIDER-WEB. THERE'S NO SPIDER.
GET IT OFF!!
DADDY!
ARE YOU OKAY?

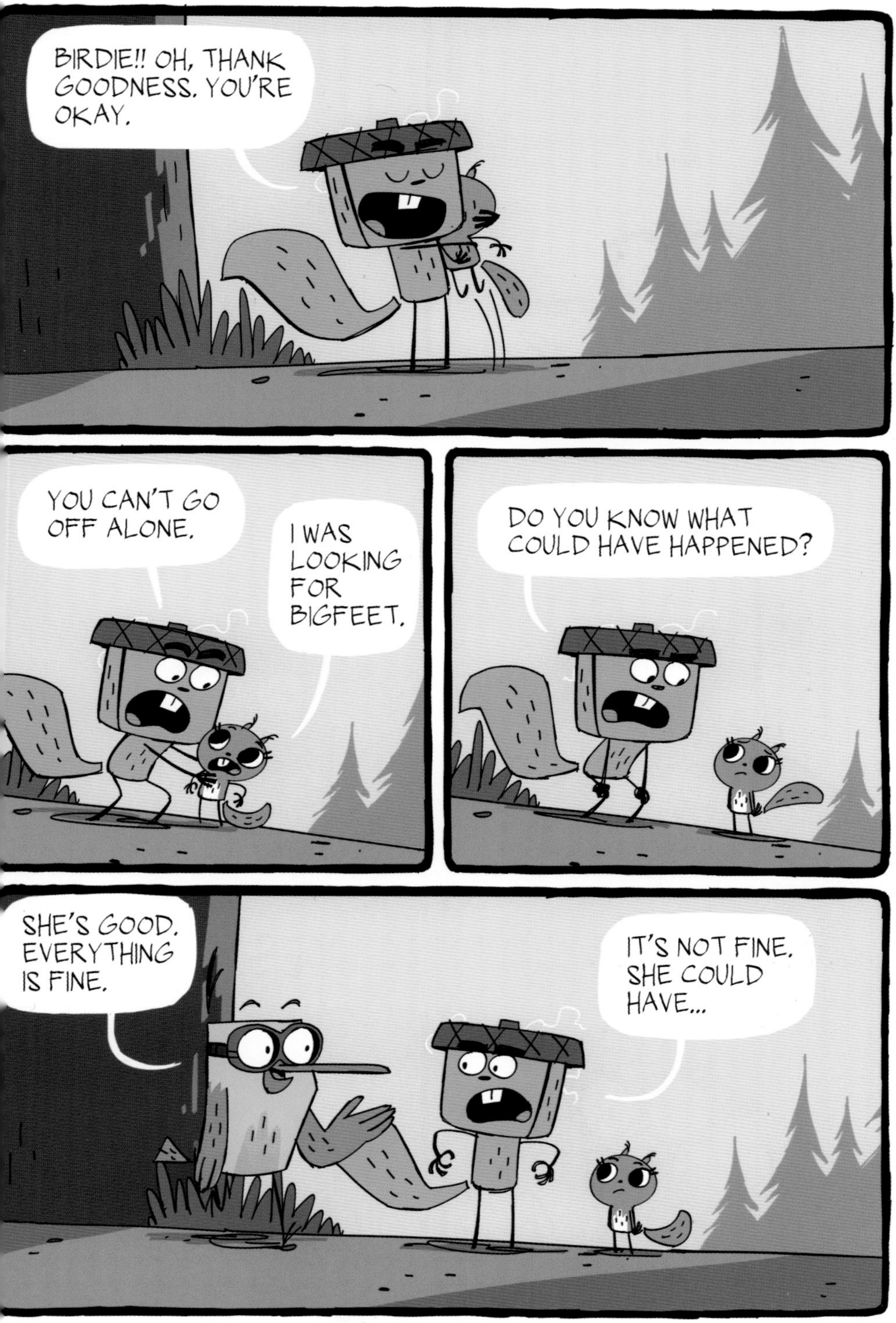
BIRDIE!! OH, THANK GOODNESS. YOU'RE OKAY.
YOU CAN'T GO OFF ALONE.
I WAS LOOKING FOR BIGFEET.
DO YOU KNOW WHAT COULD HAVE HAPPENED?
SHE'S GOOD. EVERYTHING IS FINE.
IT'S NOT FINE. SHE COULD HAVE...

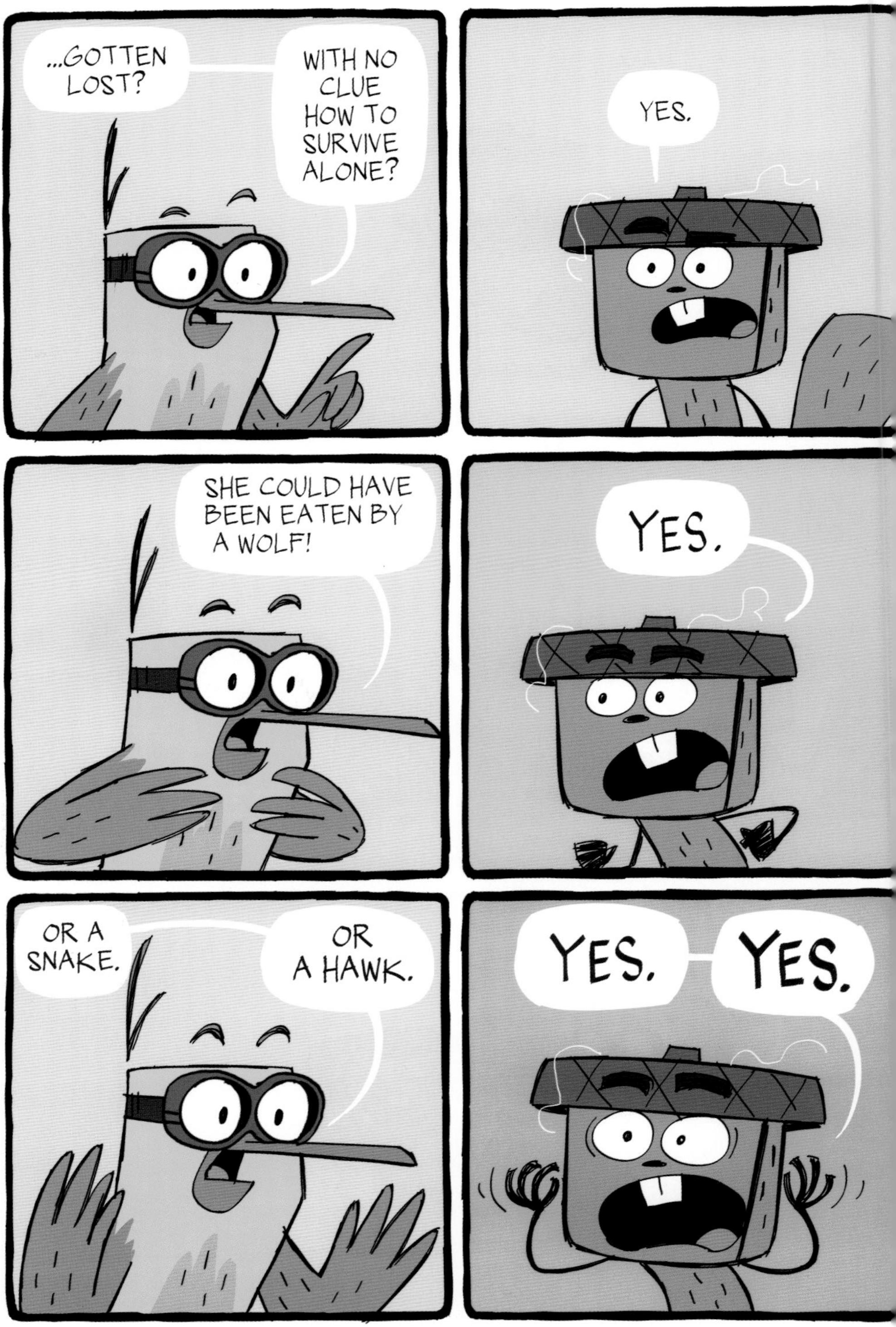
...GOTTEN LOST?
WITH NO CLUE HOW TO SURVIVE ALONE?
YES.
SHE COULD HAVE BEEN EATEN BY A WOLF!
YES.
OR A SNAKE.
OR A HAWK.
YES.
YES.

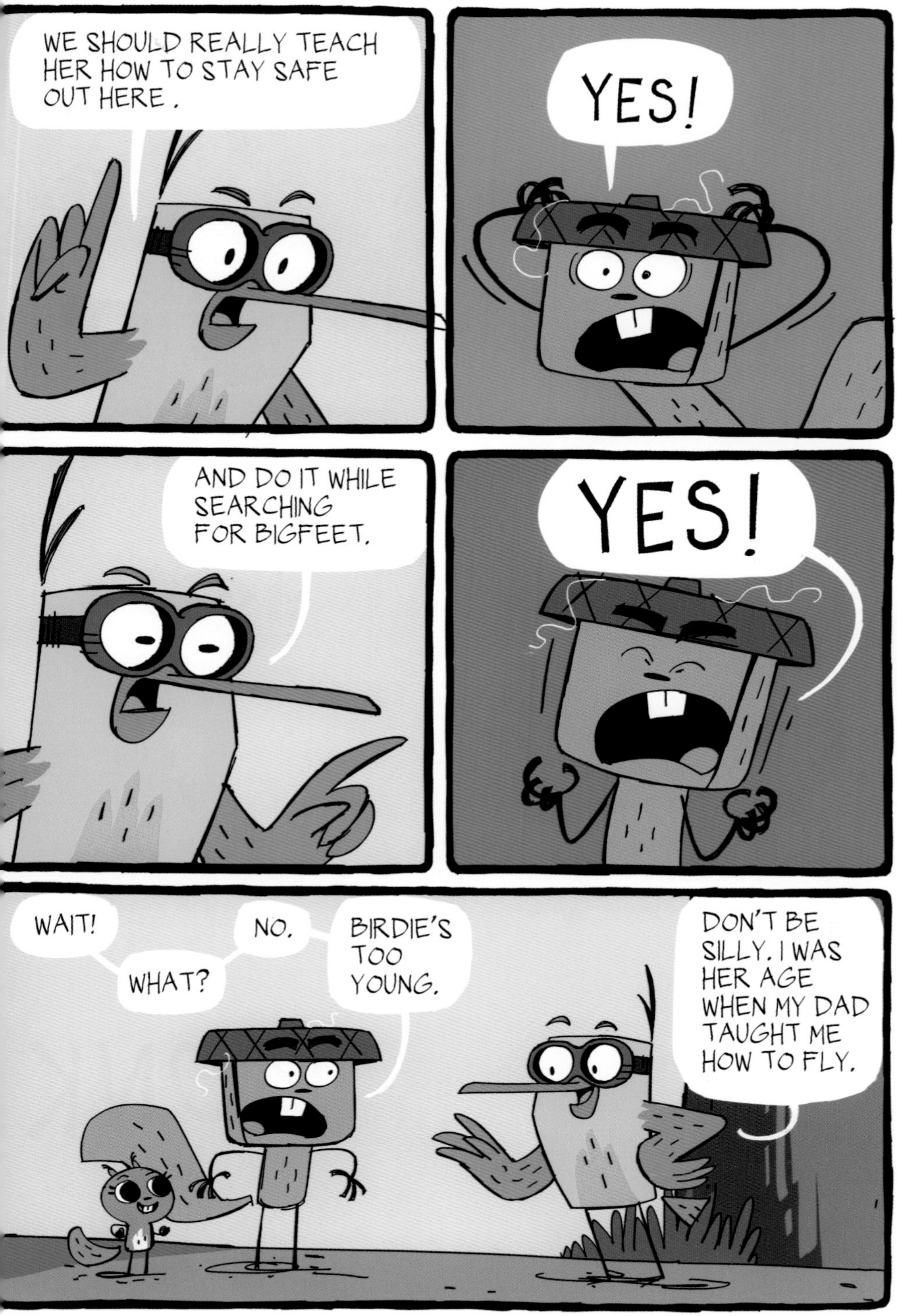
WE SHOULD REALLY TEACH HER HOW TO STAY SAFE OUT HERE.
YES!
AND DO IT WHILE SEARCHING FOR BIGFEET.
YES!
WAIT!
WHAT?
NO.
BIRDIE'S TOO YOUNG.
DON'T BE SILLY. I WAS HER AGE WHEN MY DAD TAUGHT ME HOW TO FLY.

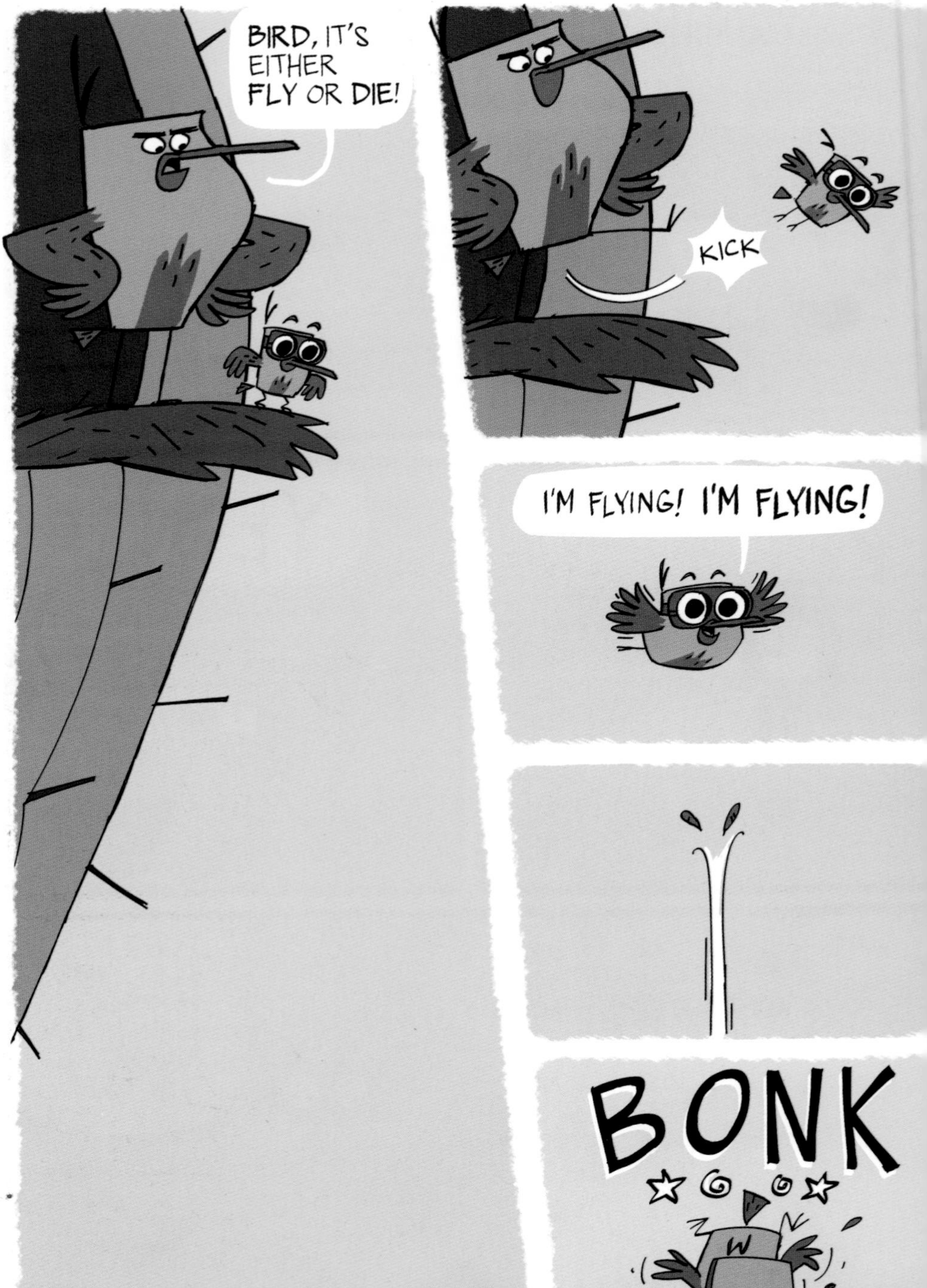
BIRD, IT'S EITHER FLY OR DIE!
KICK
I'M FLYING! I'M FLYING!
BONK

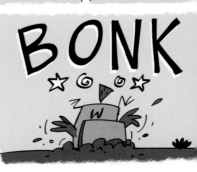

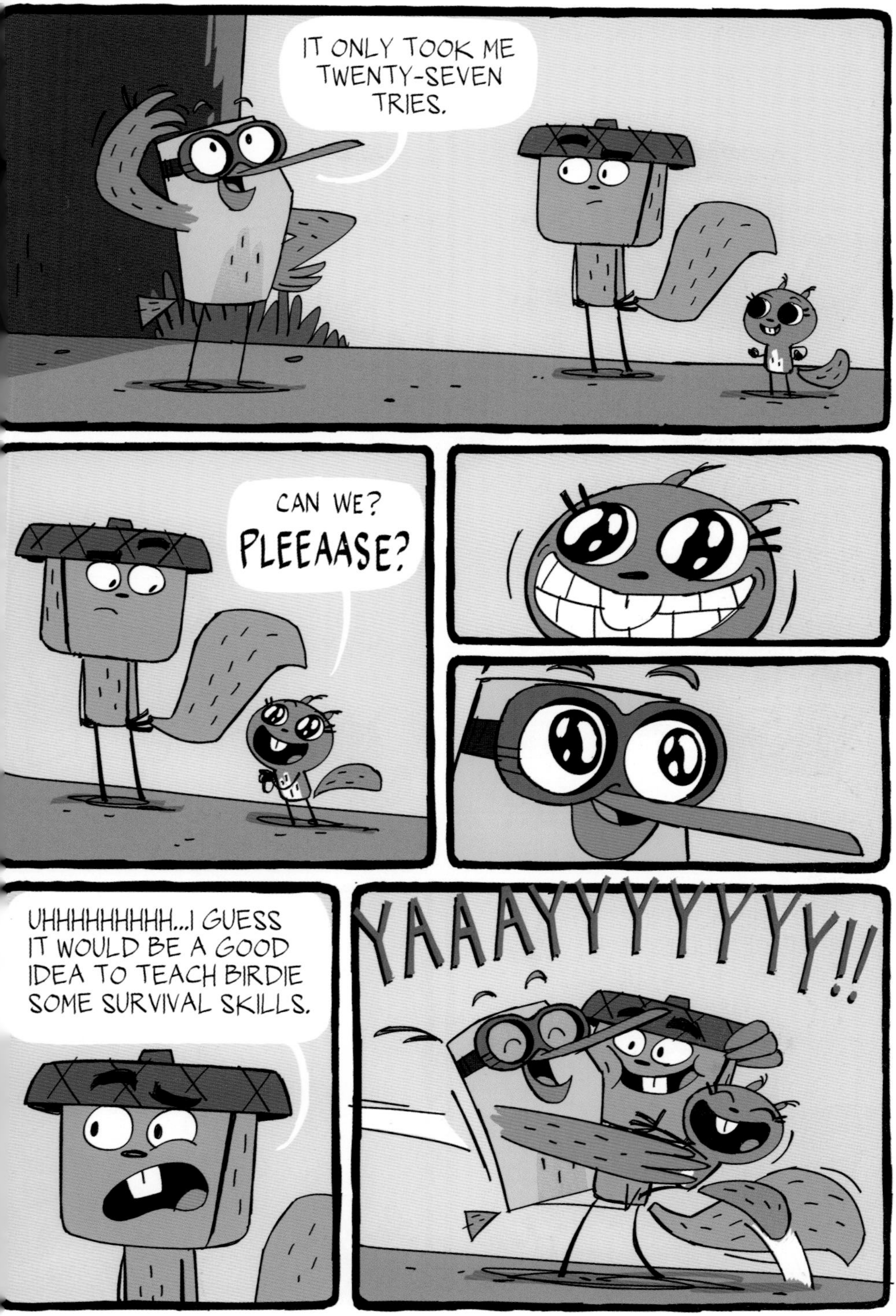
IT ONLY TOOK ME TWENTY-SEVEN TRIES.
CAN WE? PLEEAASE?
UHHHHHHHHH...I GUESS IT WOULD BE A GOOD IDEA TO TEACH BIRDIE SOME SURVIVAL SKILLS.
YAAAYYYYYYYY!!

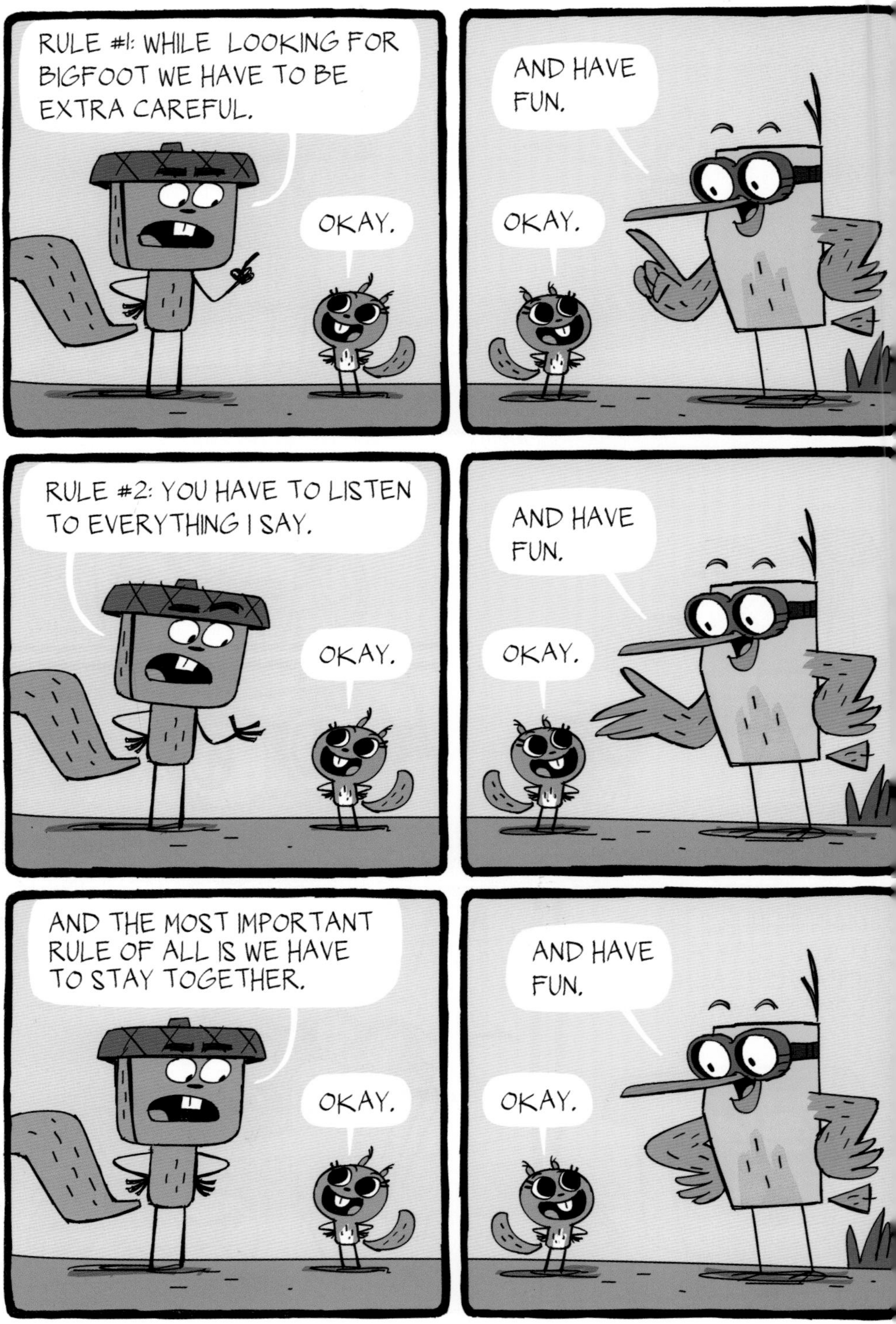
RULE #1: WHILE LOOKING FOR BIGFOOT WE HAVE TO BE EXTRA CAREFUL.
OKAY.
AND HAVE FUN.
OKAY.
RULE #2: YOU HAVE TO LISTEN TO EVERYTHING I SAY.
OKAY.
AND HAVE FUN.
OKAY.
AND THE MOST IMPORTANT RULE OF ALL IS WE HAVE TO STAY TOGETHER.
OKAY.
AND HAVE FUN.
OKAY.

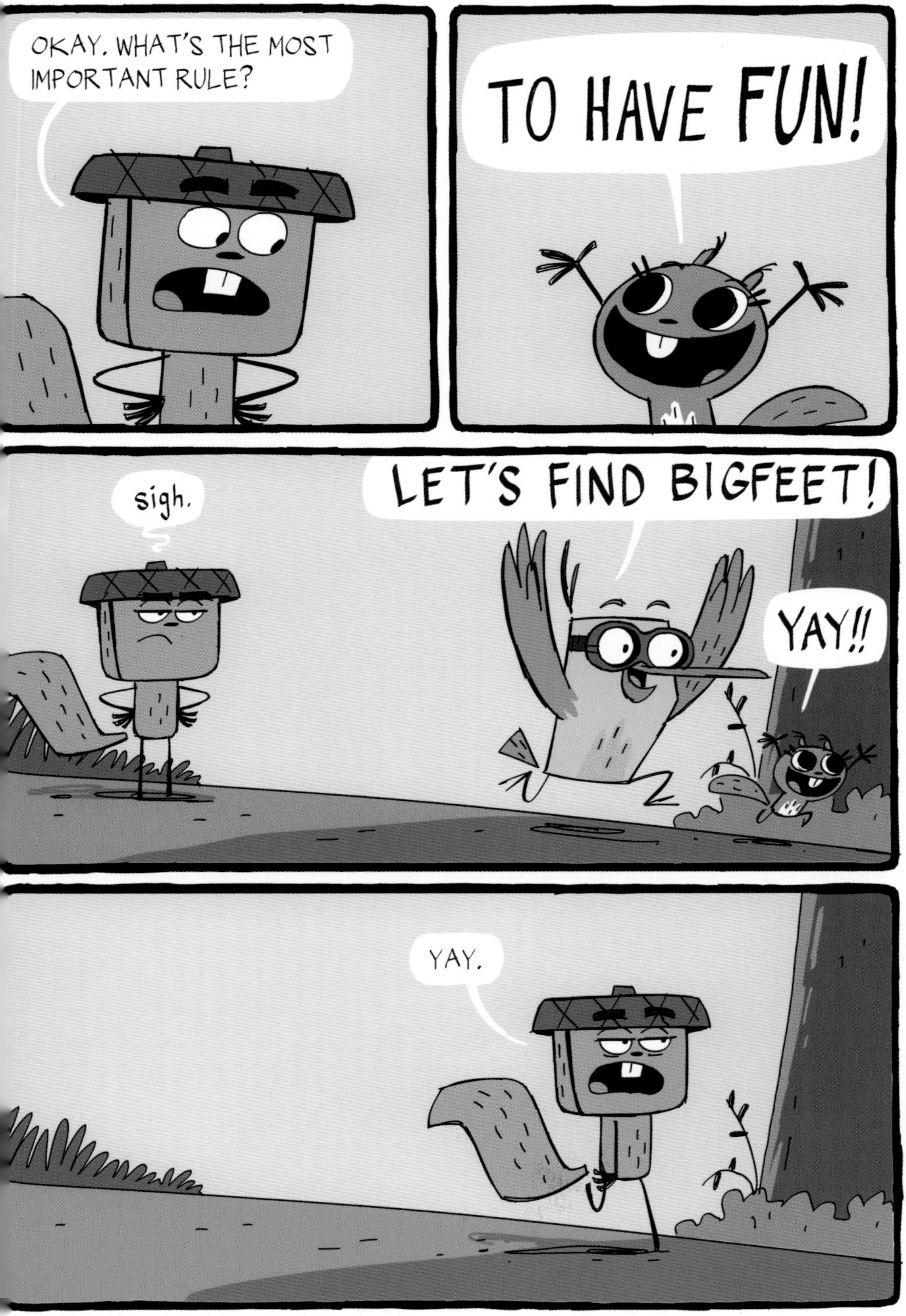
OKAY. WHAT'S THE MOST IMPORTANT RULE?
TO HAVE FUN!
sigh.
LET'S FIND BIGFEET!
YAY!!
YAY.

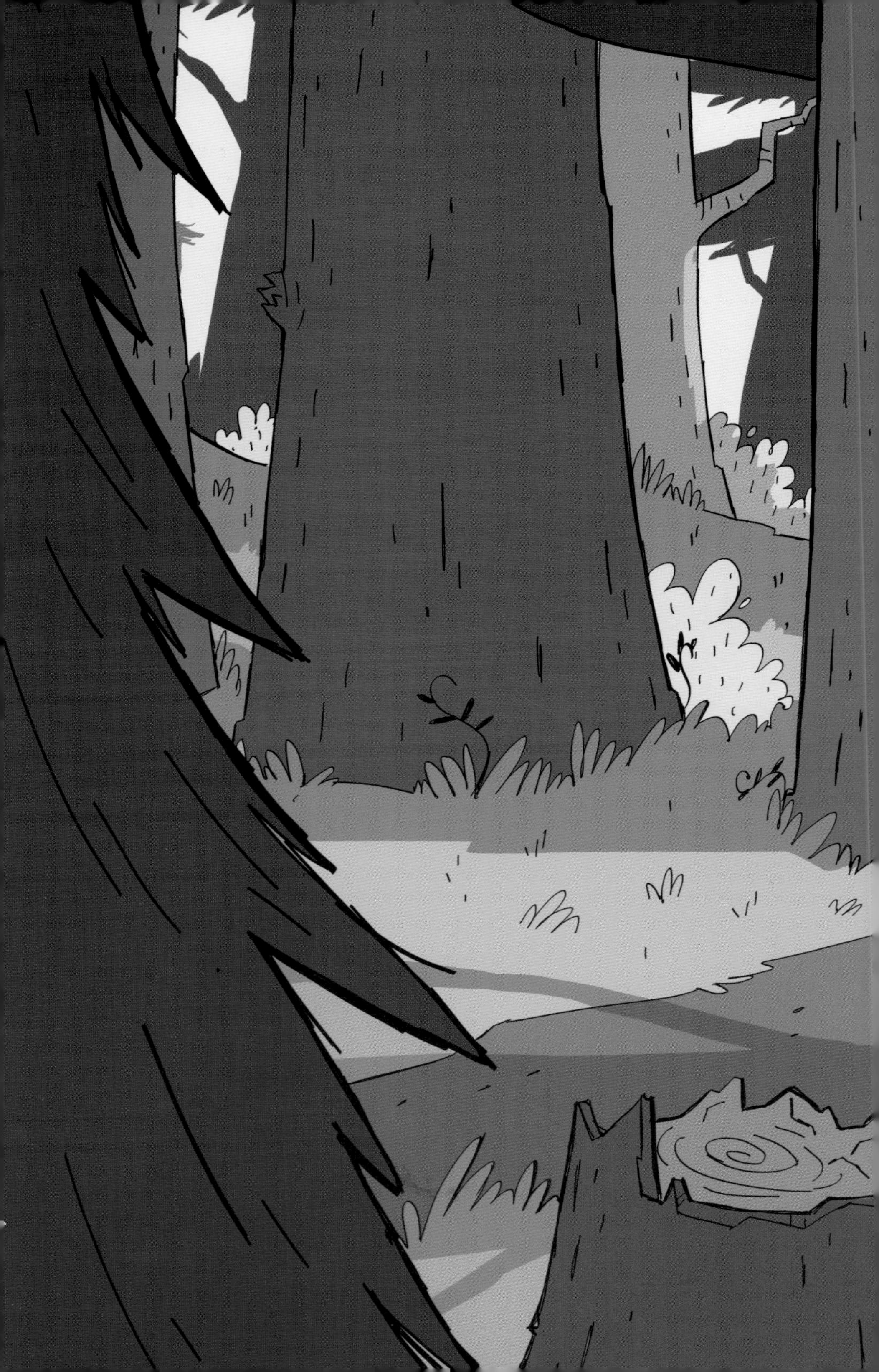

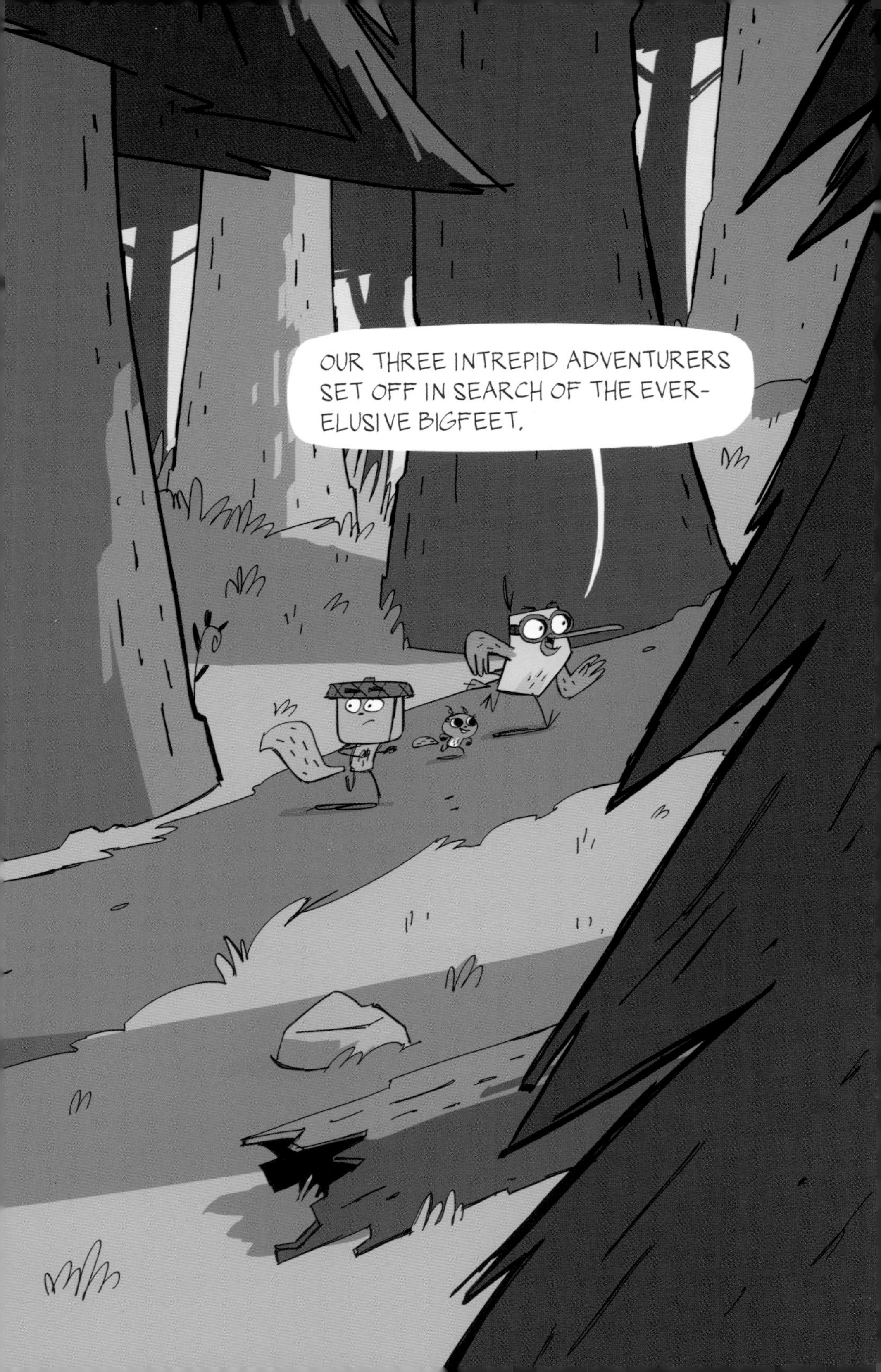
OUR THREE INTREPID ADVENTURERS SET OFF IN SEARCH OF THE EVER-ELUSIVE BIGFEET.

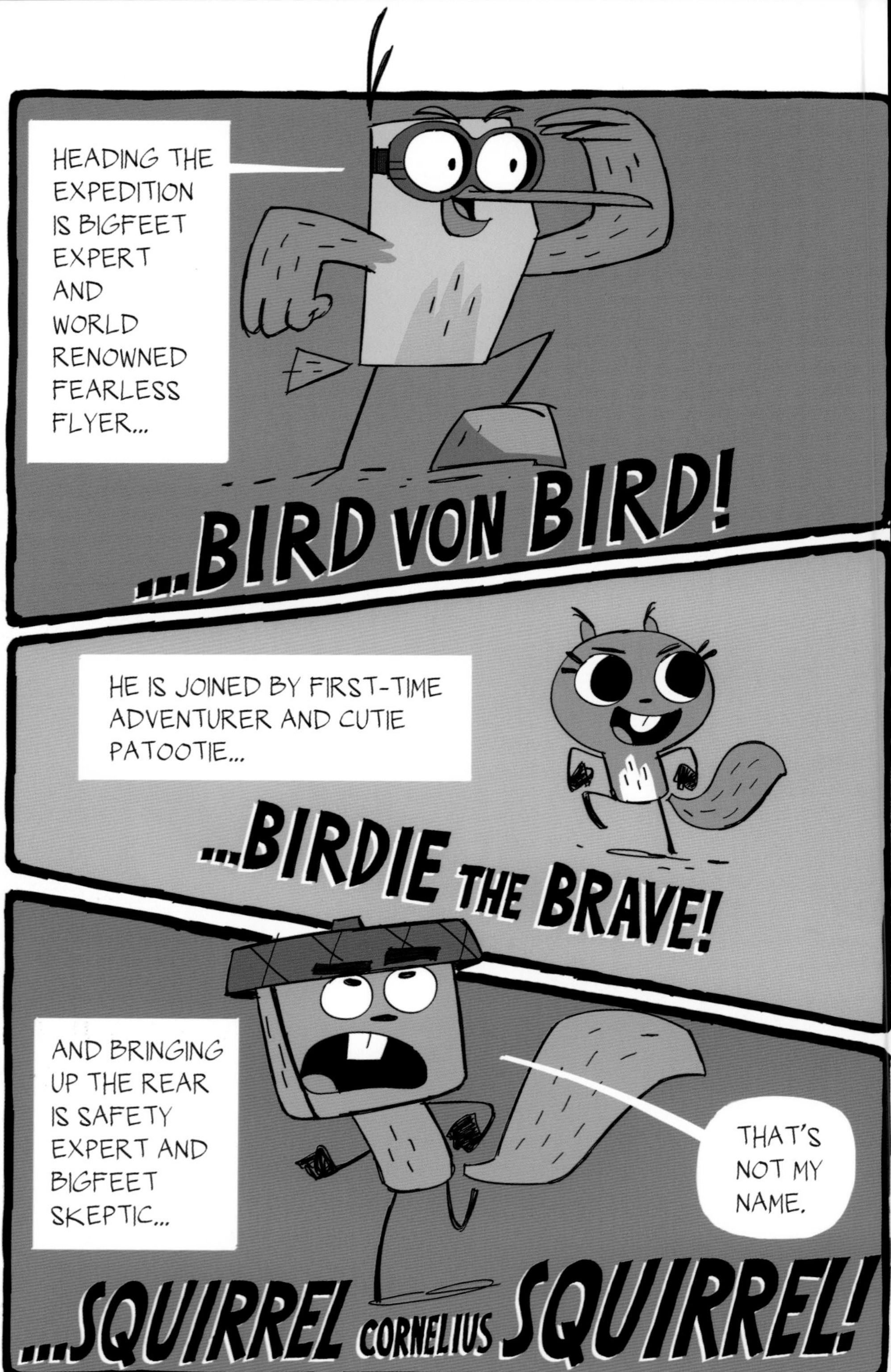
HEADING THE EXPEDITION IS BIGFEET EXPERT AND WORLD RENOWNED FEARLESS FLYER...
...BIRD VON BIRD!
HE IS JOINED BY FIRST-TIME ADVENTURER AND CUTIE PATOOTIE...
...BIRDIE THE BRAVE!
AND BRINGING UP THE REAR IS SAFETY EXPERT AND BIGFEET SKEPTIC...
THAT'S NOT MY NAME.
...SQUIRREL CORNELIUS SQUIRREL!

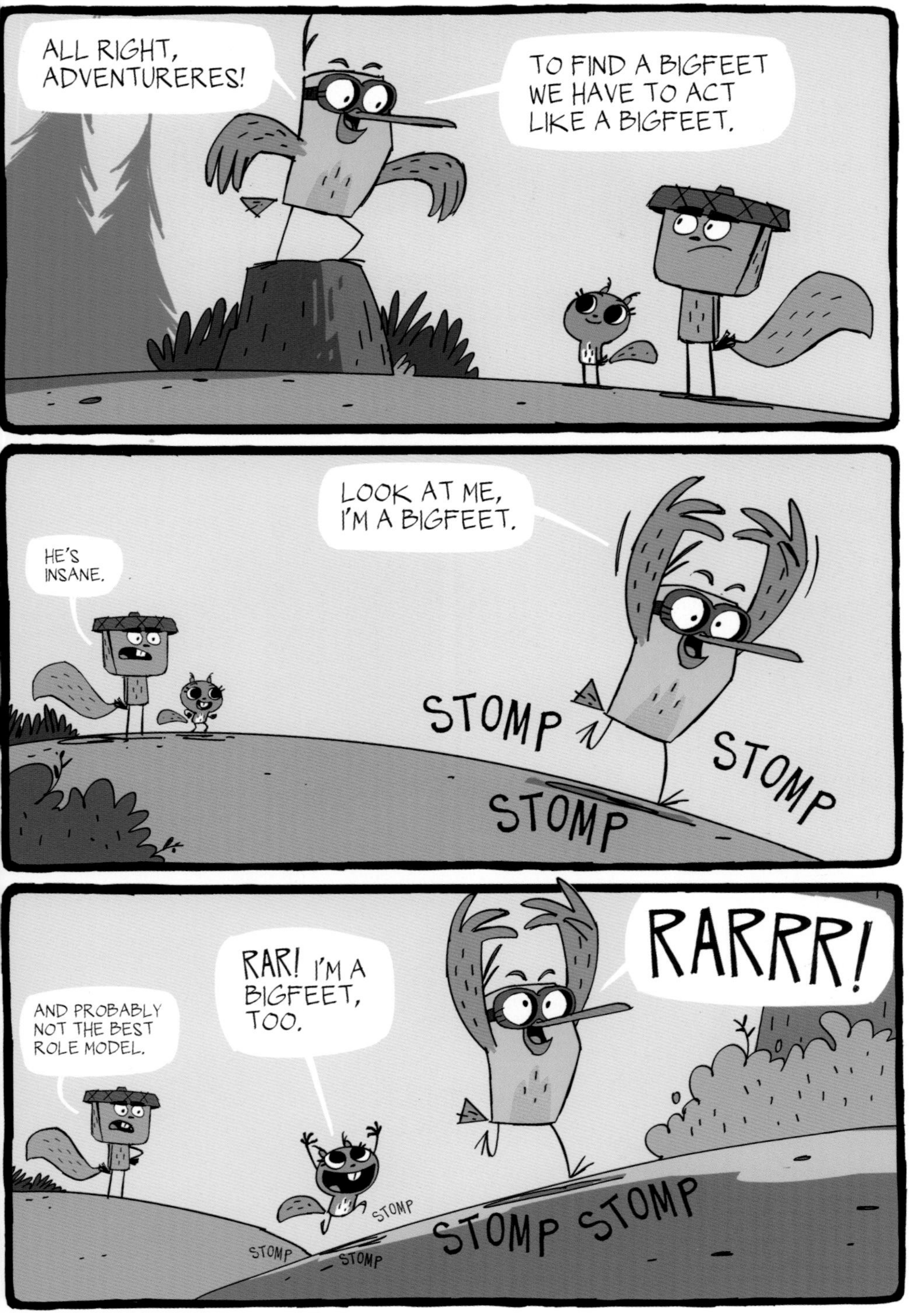
ALL RIGHT, ADVENTURERES!
TO FIND A BIGFEET WE HAVE TO ACT LIKE A BIGFEET.
HE'S INSANE.
LOOK AT ME, I'M A BIGFEET.
STOMP
STOMP
STOMP
AND PROBABLY NOT THE BEST ROLE MODEL.
RAR! I'M A BIGFEET, TOO.
RARRR!
STOMP
STOMP
STOMP
STOMP STOMP

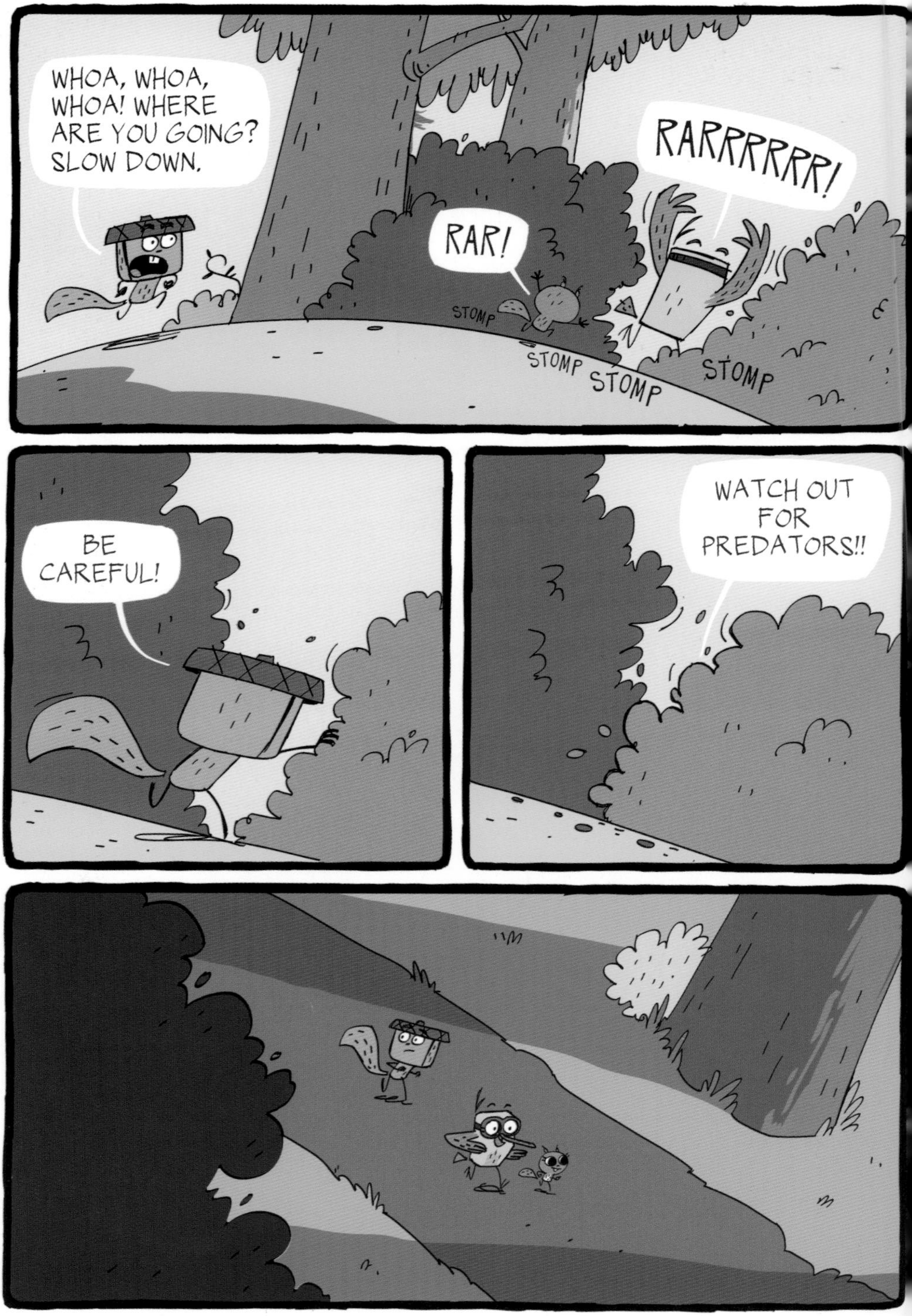
WHOA, WHOA, WHOA! WHERE ARE YOU GOING? SLOW DOWN.
RARRRRRR!
RAR!
STOMP
STOMP STOMP
STOMP
BE CAREFUL!
WATCH OUT FOR PREDATORS!!

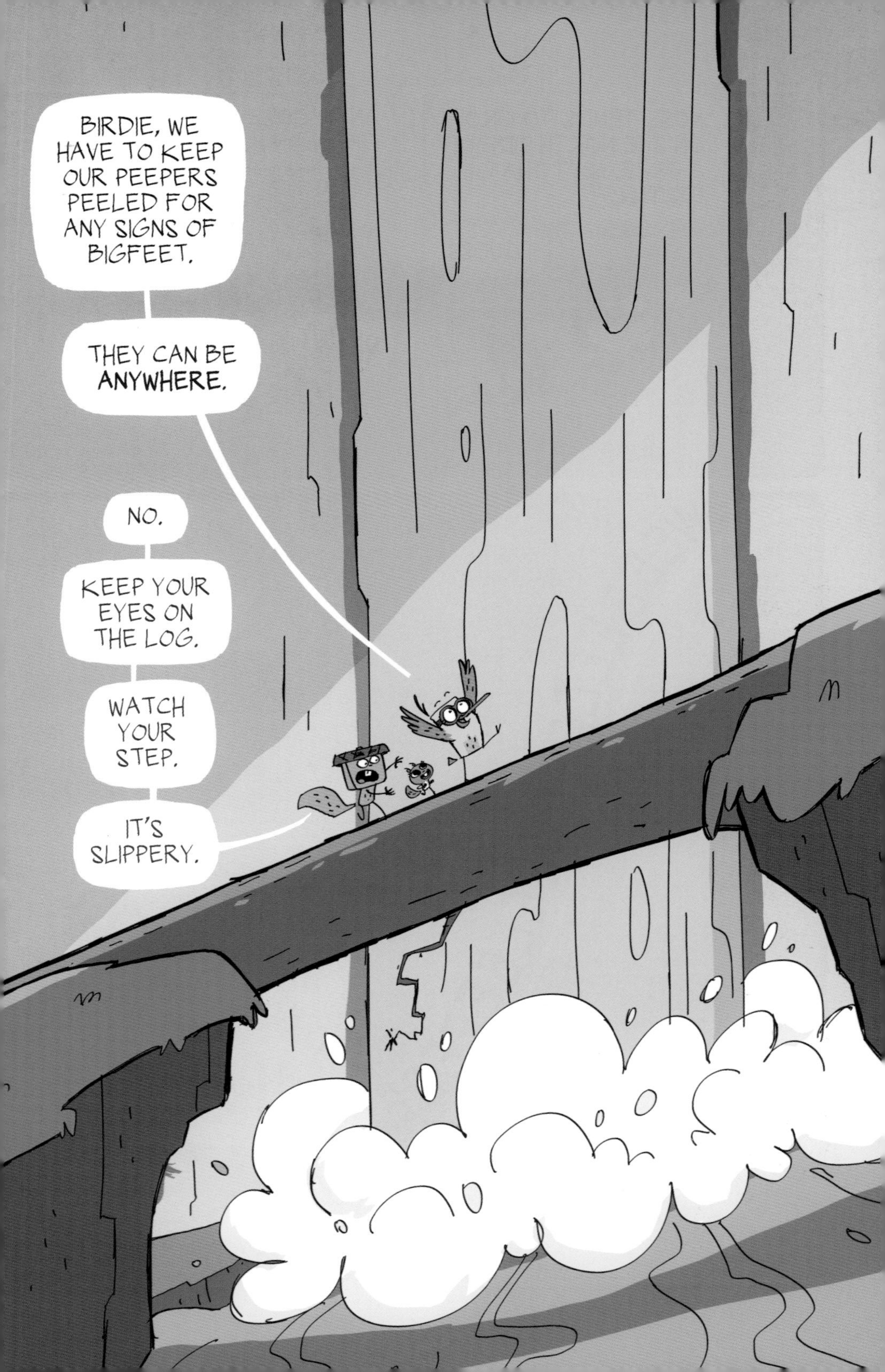
BIRDIE, WE HAVE TO KEEP OUR PEEPERS PEELED FOR ANY SIGNS OF BIGFEET.
THEY CAN BE **ANYWHERE.**
NO.
KEEP YOUR EYES ON THE LOG.
WATCH YOUR STEP.
IT'S SLIPPERY.

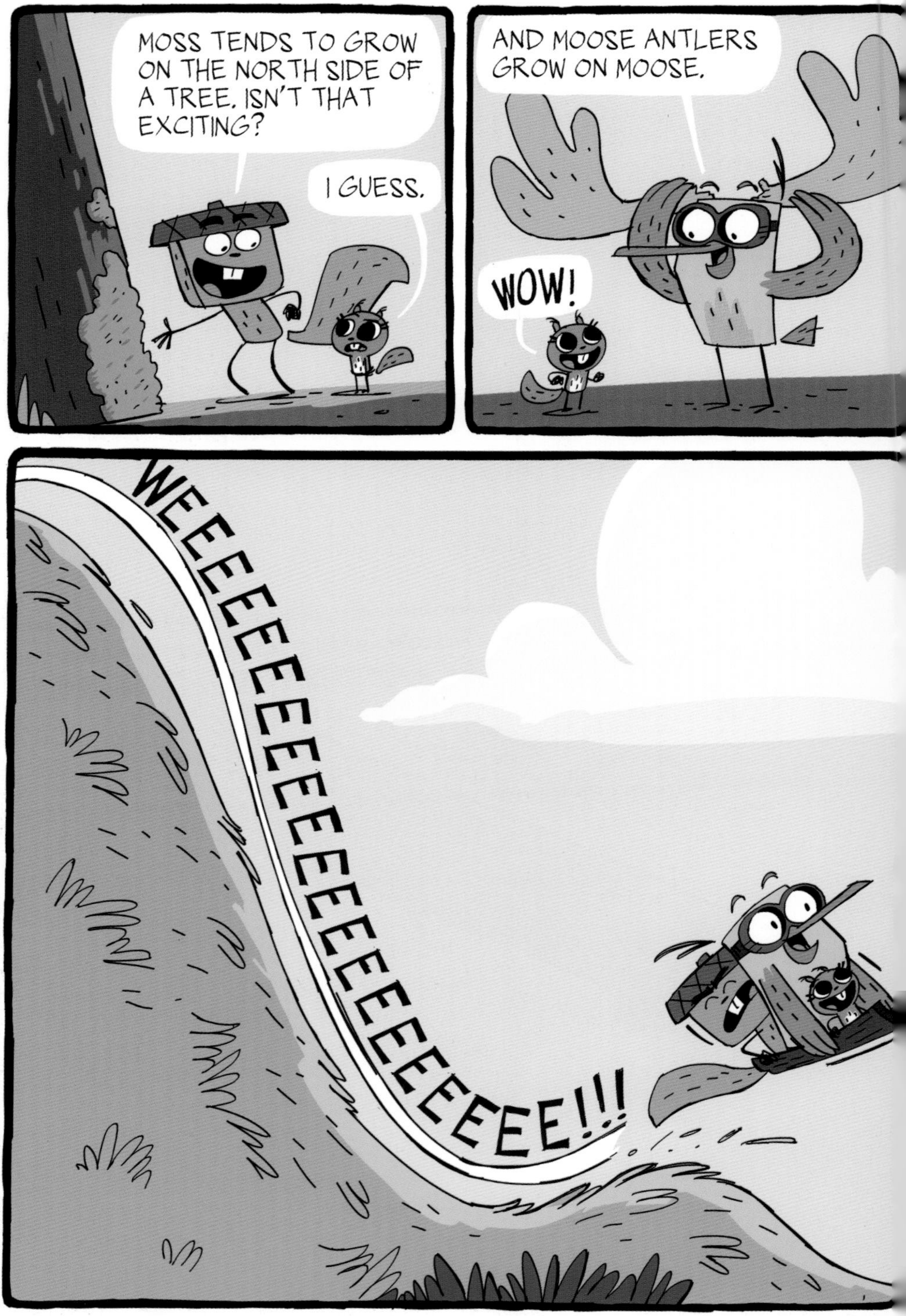
MOSS TENDS TO GROW ON THE NORTH SIDE OF A TREE. ISN'T THAT EXCITING?
I GUESS.
AND MOOSE ANTLERS GROW ON MOOSE.
WOW!
WEEEEEEEEEEEEEEEEEEEEEEE!!!

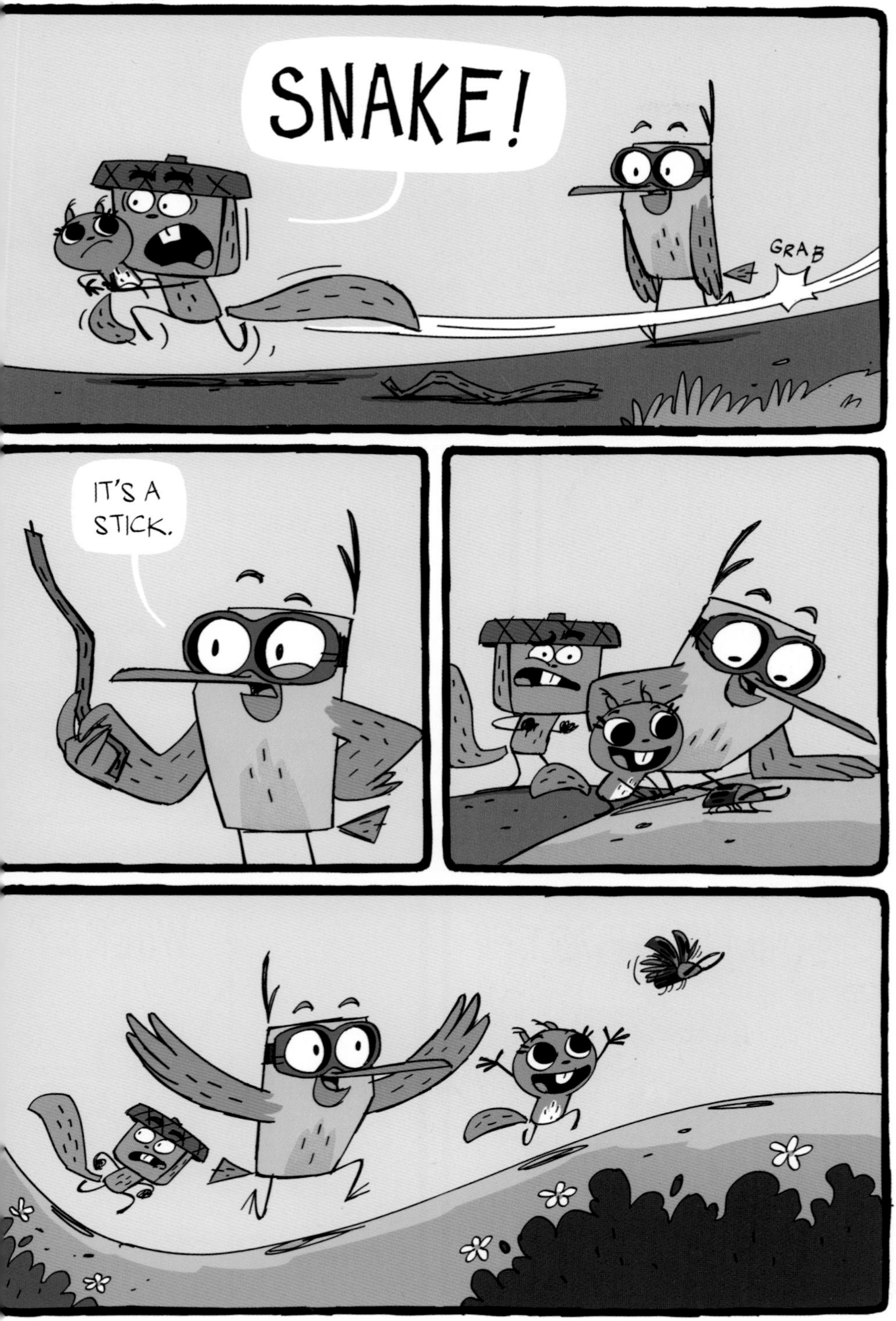
SNAKE!
GRAB
IT'S A STICK.

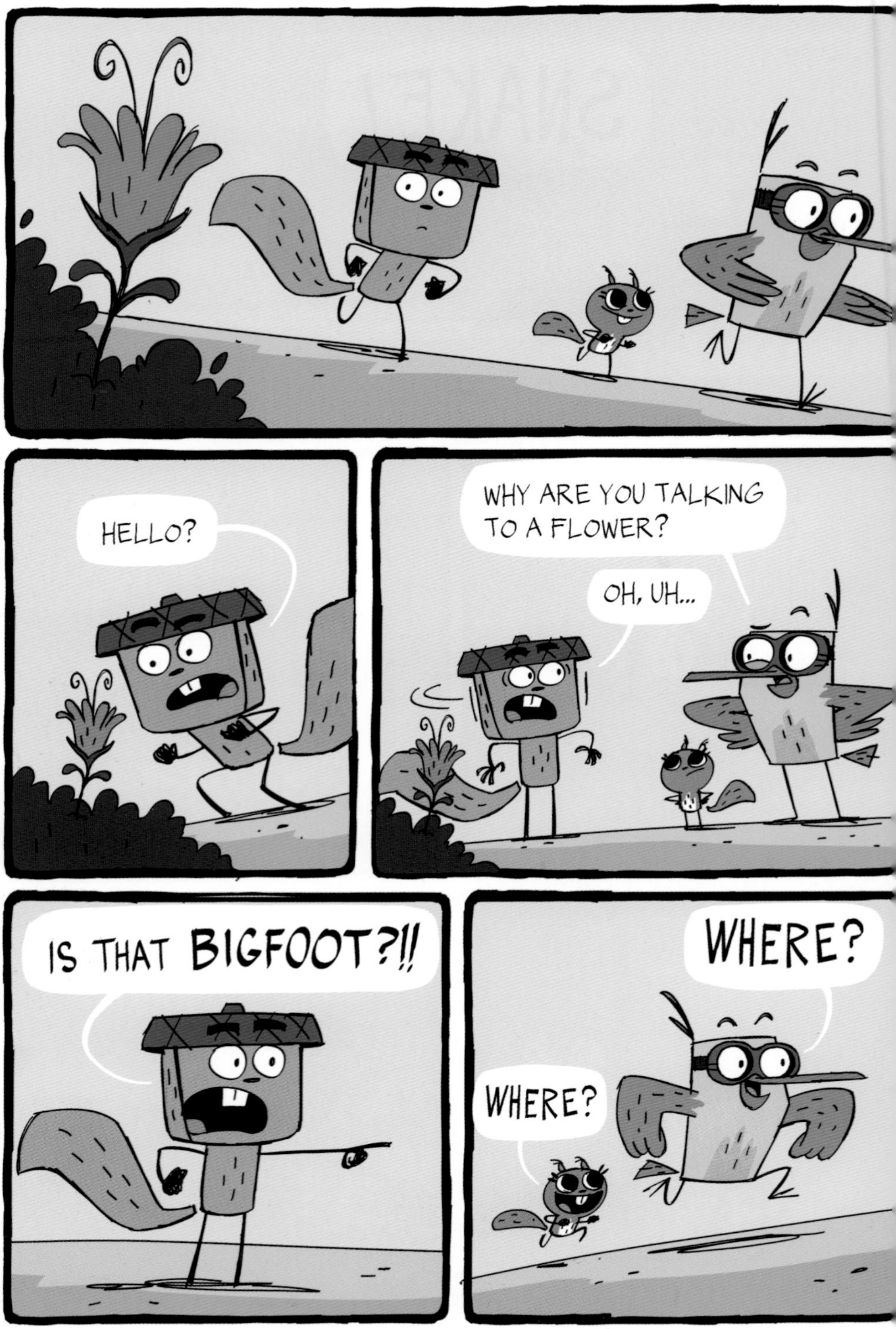
HELLO?
WHY ARE YOU TALKING TO A FLOWER?
OH, UH...
IS THAT BIGFOOT?!!
WHERE?
WHERE?

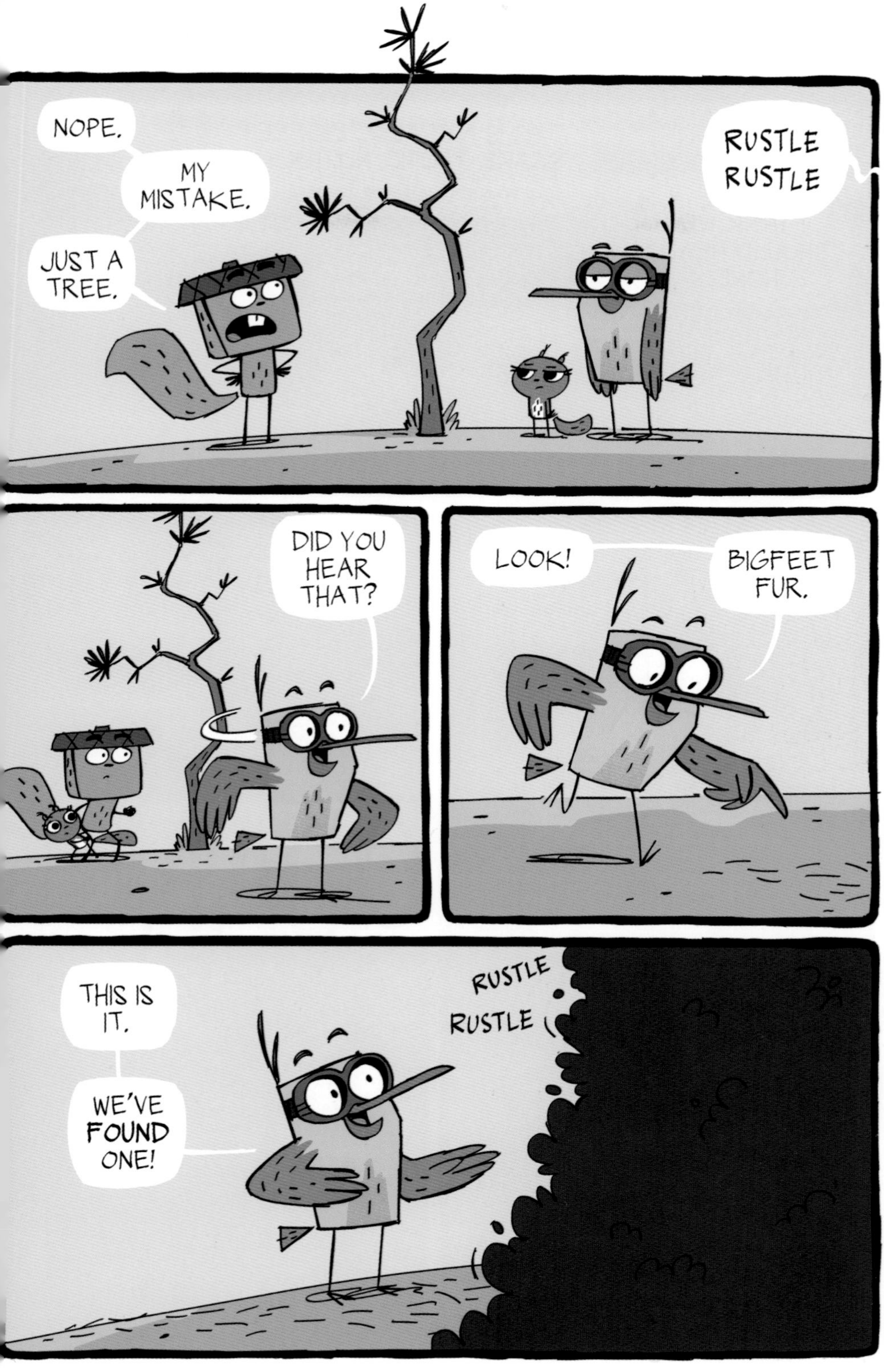

NOPE.
MY MISTAKE.
JUST A TREE.
RUSTLE RUSTLE
DID YOU HEAR THAT?
LOOK!
BIGFEET FUR.
THIS IS IT.
WE'VE **FOUND** ONE!
RUSTLE
RUSTLE

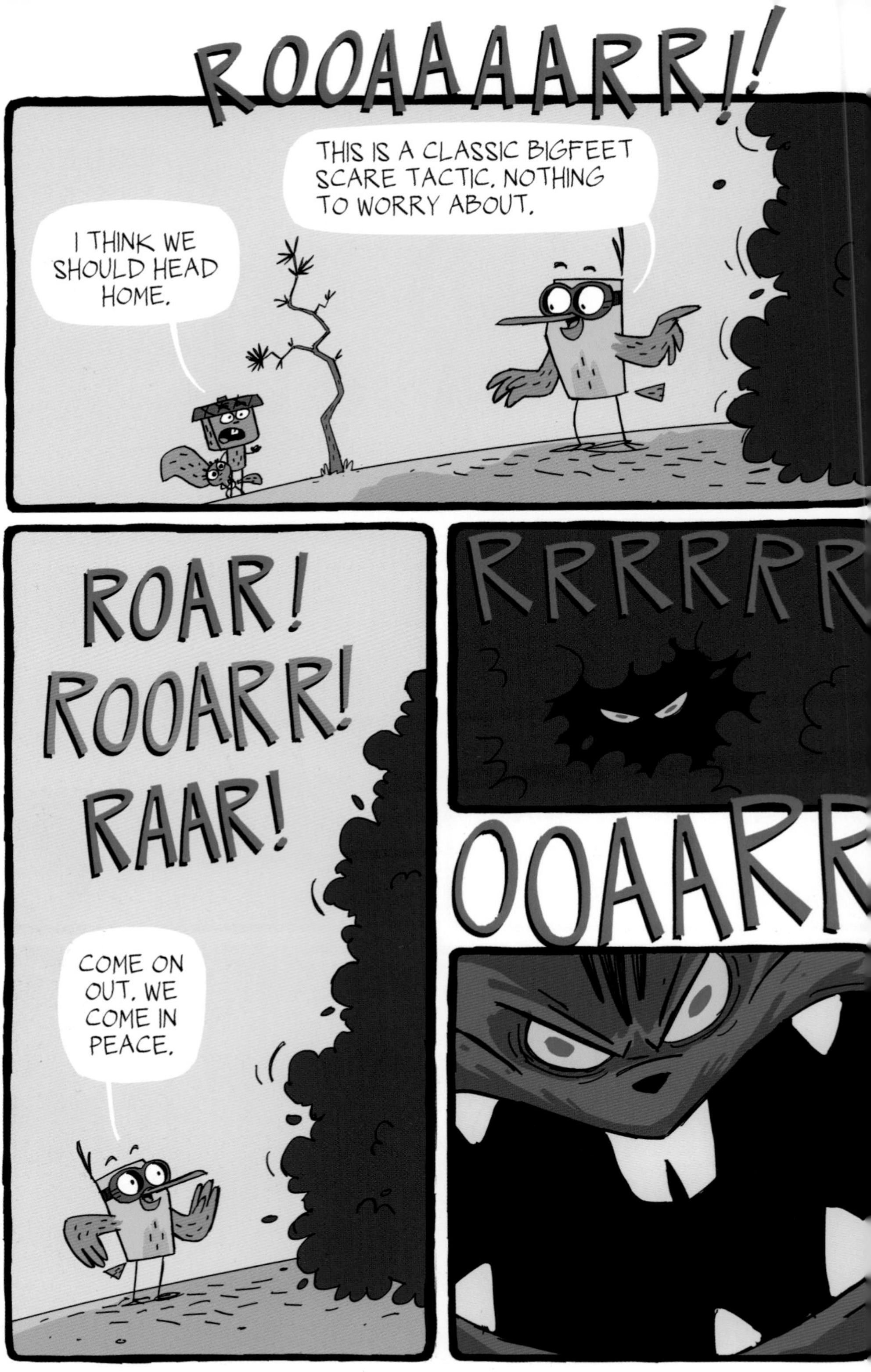
ROOAAAARR!!
I THINK WE SHOULD HEAD HOME.
THIS IS A CLASSIC BIGFEET SCARE TACTIC. NOTHING TO WORRY ABOUT.
ROAR! ROOARR! RAAR!
COME ON OUT. WE COME IN PEACE.
RRRRRR
OOARR

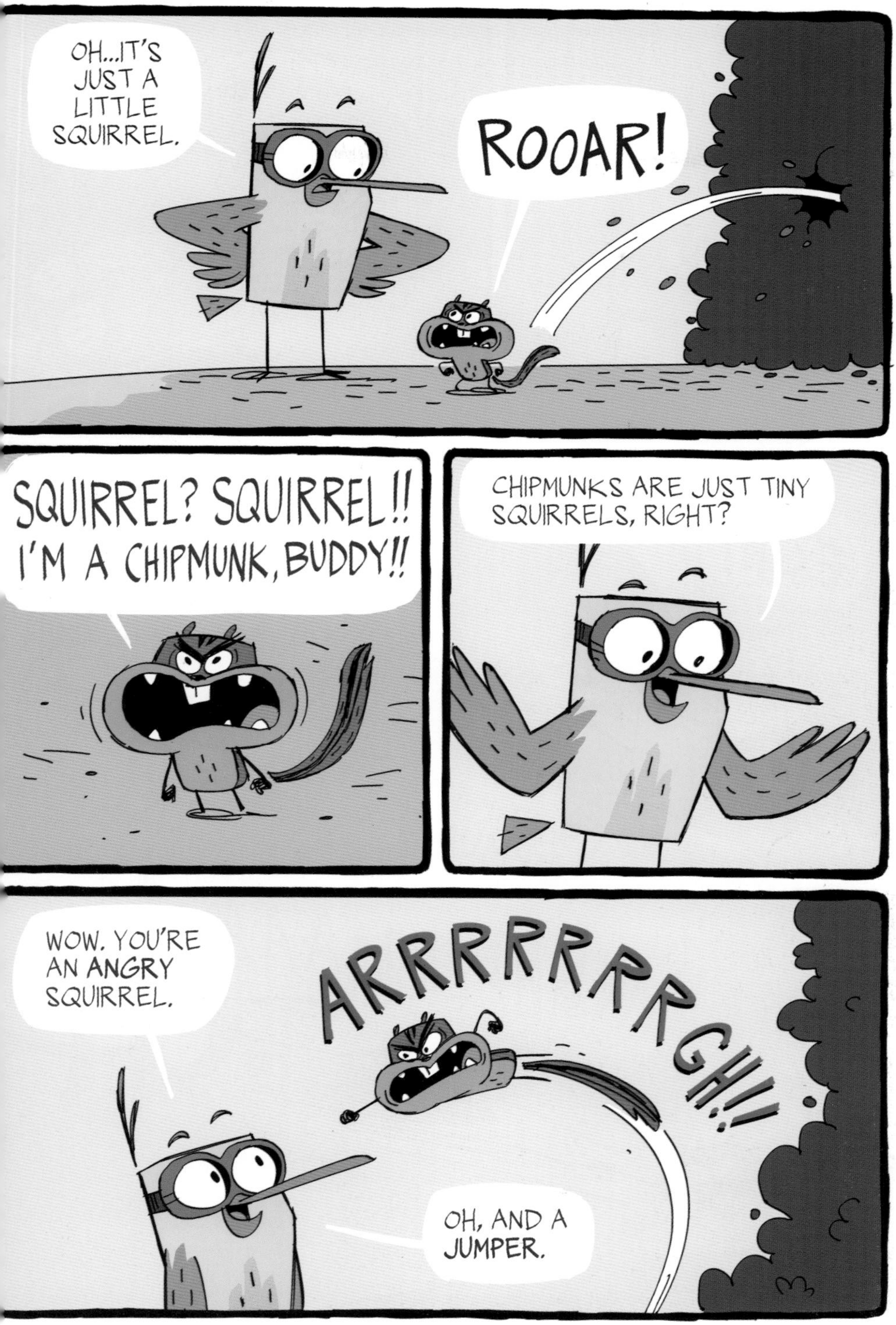
OH...IT'S JUST A LITTLE SQUIRREL.
ROOAR!
SQUIRREL? SQUIRREL!! I'M A CHIPMUNK, BUDDY!!
CHIPMUNKS ARE JUST TINY SQUIRRELS, RIGHT?
WOW. YOU'RE AN ANGRY SQUIRREL.
ARRRRRRRRGH!!
OH, AND A JUMPER.

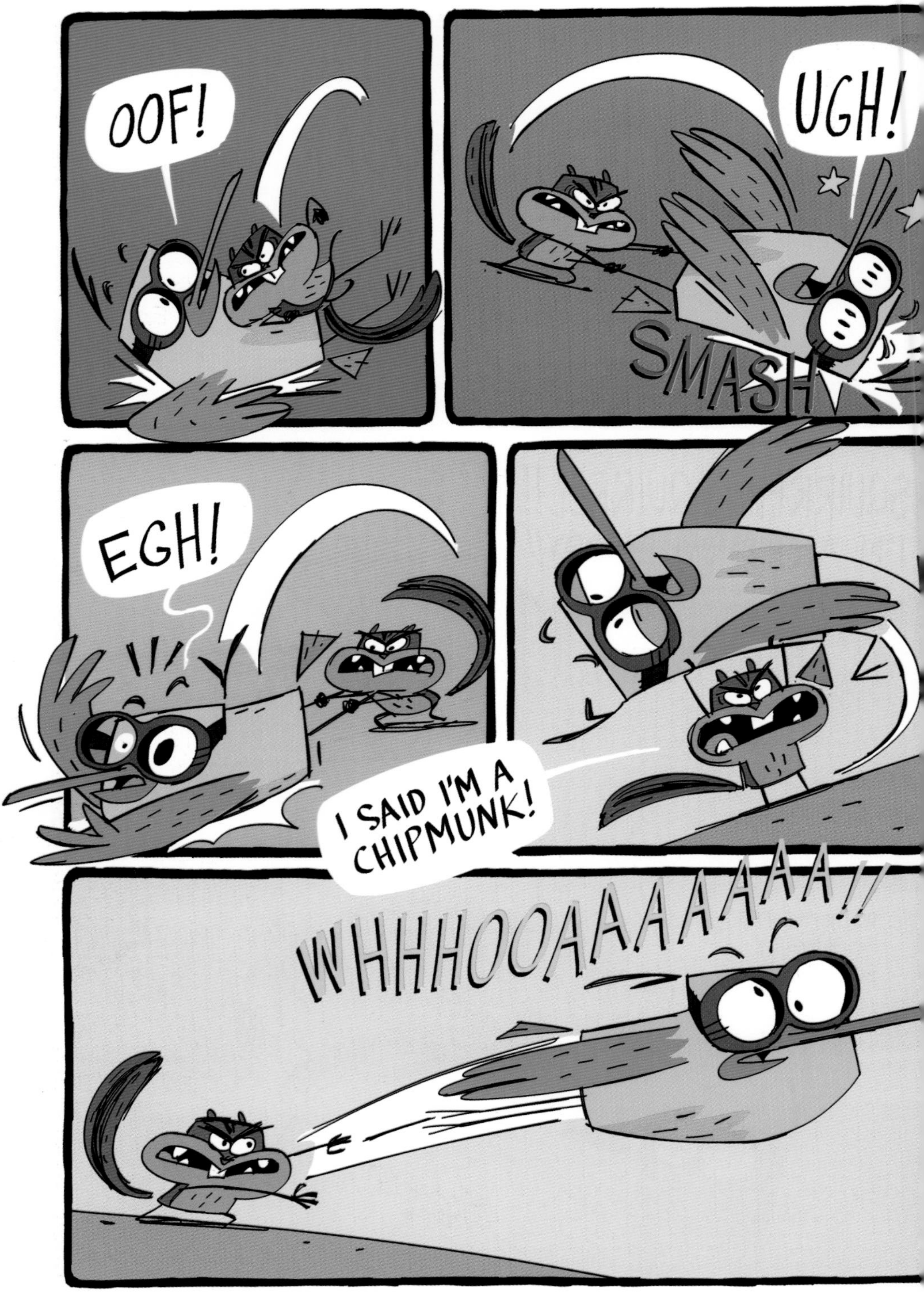
OOF!
UGH!
SMASH
EGH!
I SAID I'M A CHIPMUNK!
WHHHOOAAAAAAAA!!

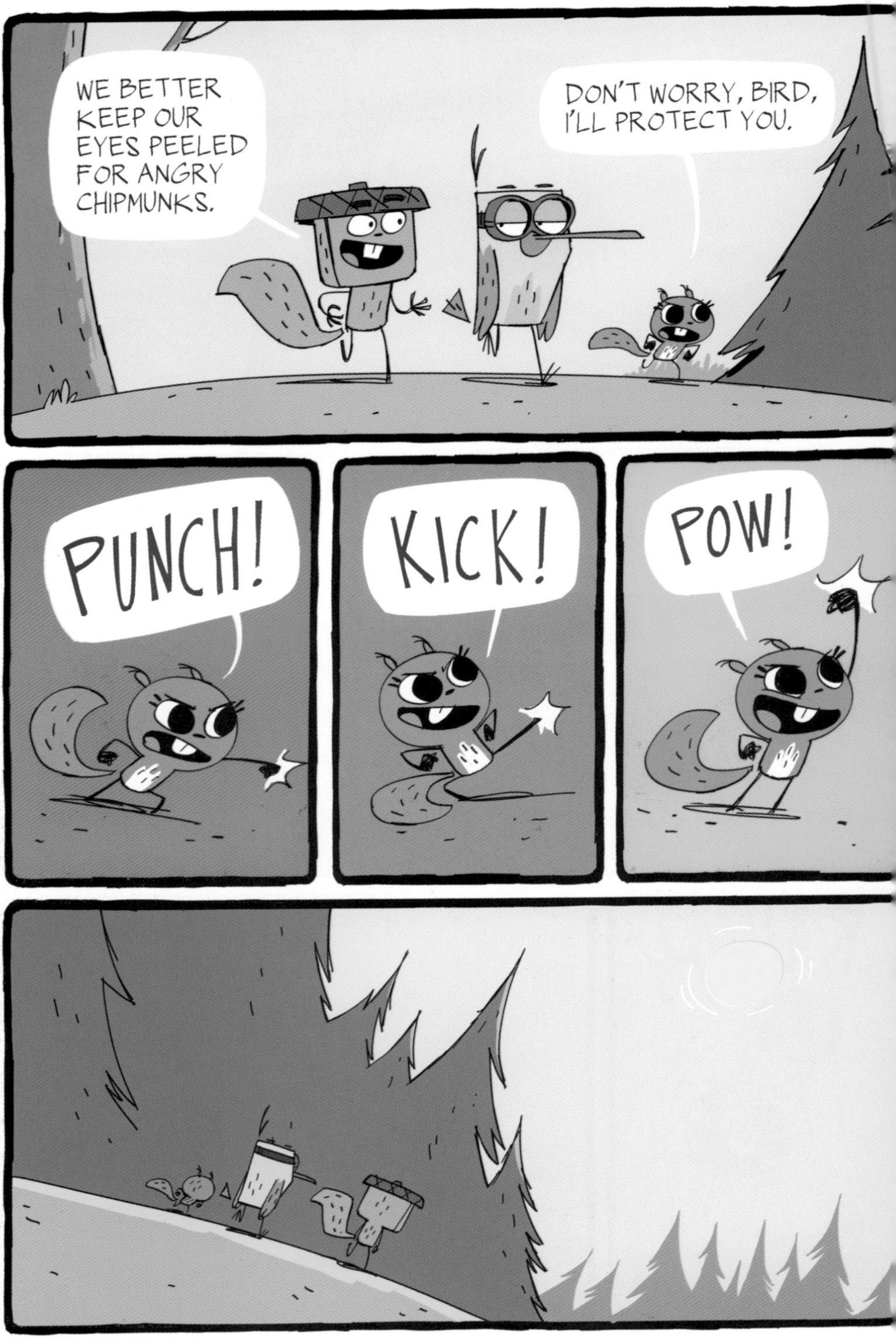
WE BETTER KEEP OUR EYES PEELED FOR ANGRY CHIPMUNKS.
DON'T WORRY, BIRD, I'LL PROTECT YOU.
PUNCH!
KICK!
POW!

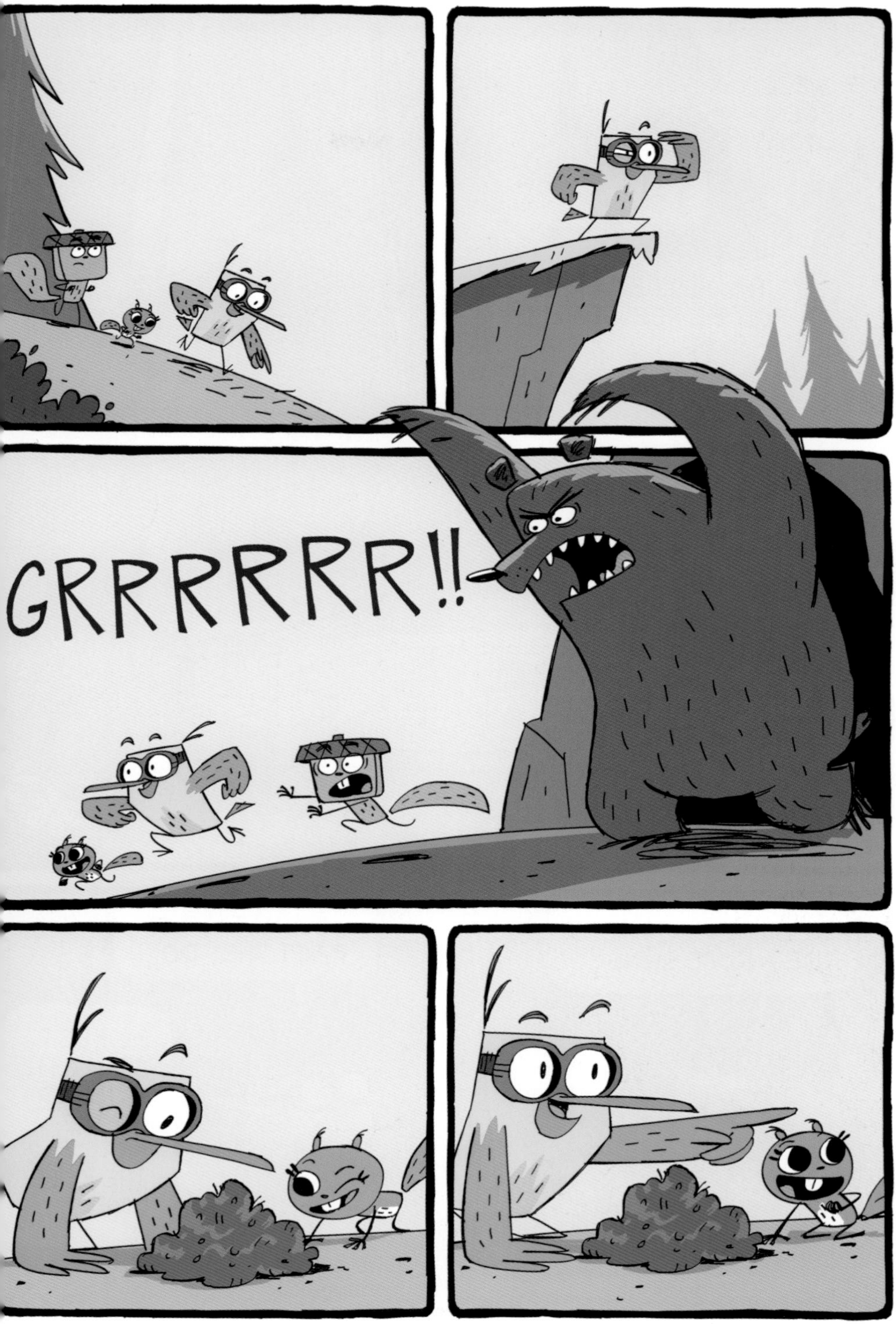
GRRRRRR!!

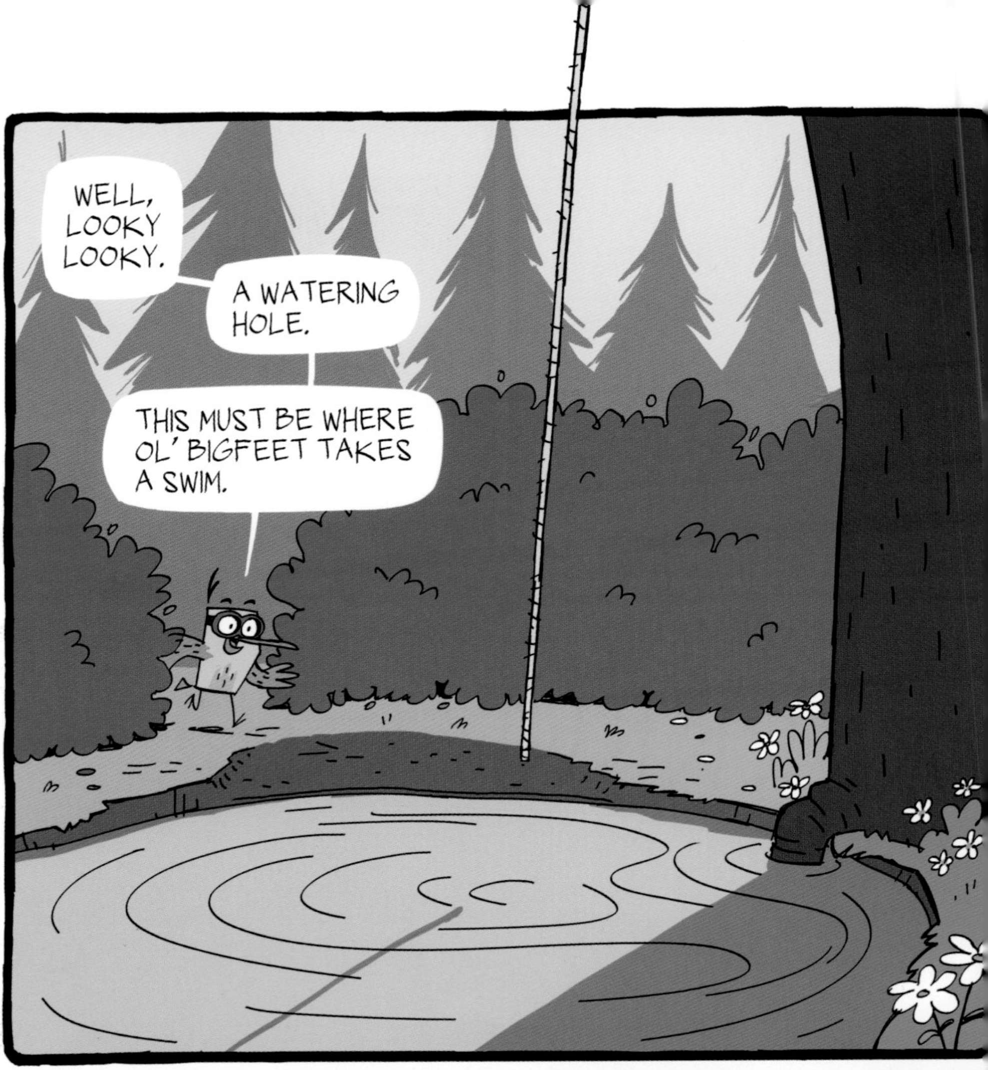
WELL, LOOKY LOOKY.
A WATERING HOLE.
THIS MUST BE WHERE OL' BIGFEET TAKES A SWIM.

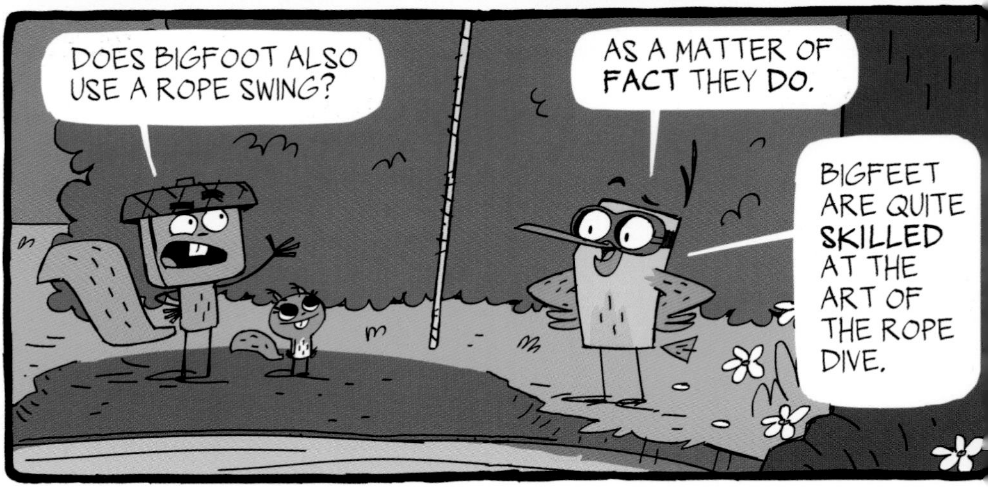
DOES BIGFOOT ALSO USE A ROPE SWING?
AS A MATTER OF **FACT** THEY **DO.**
BIGFEET ARE QUITE **SKILLED** AT THE ART OF THE ROPE DIVE.

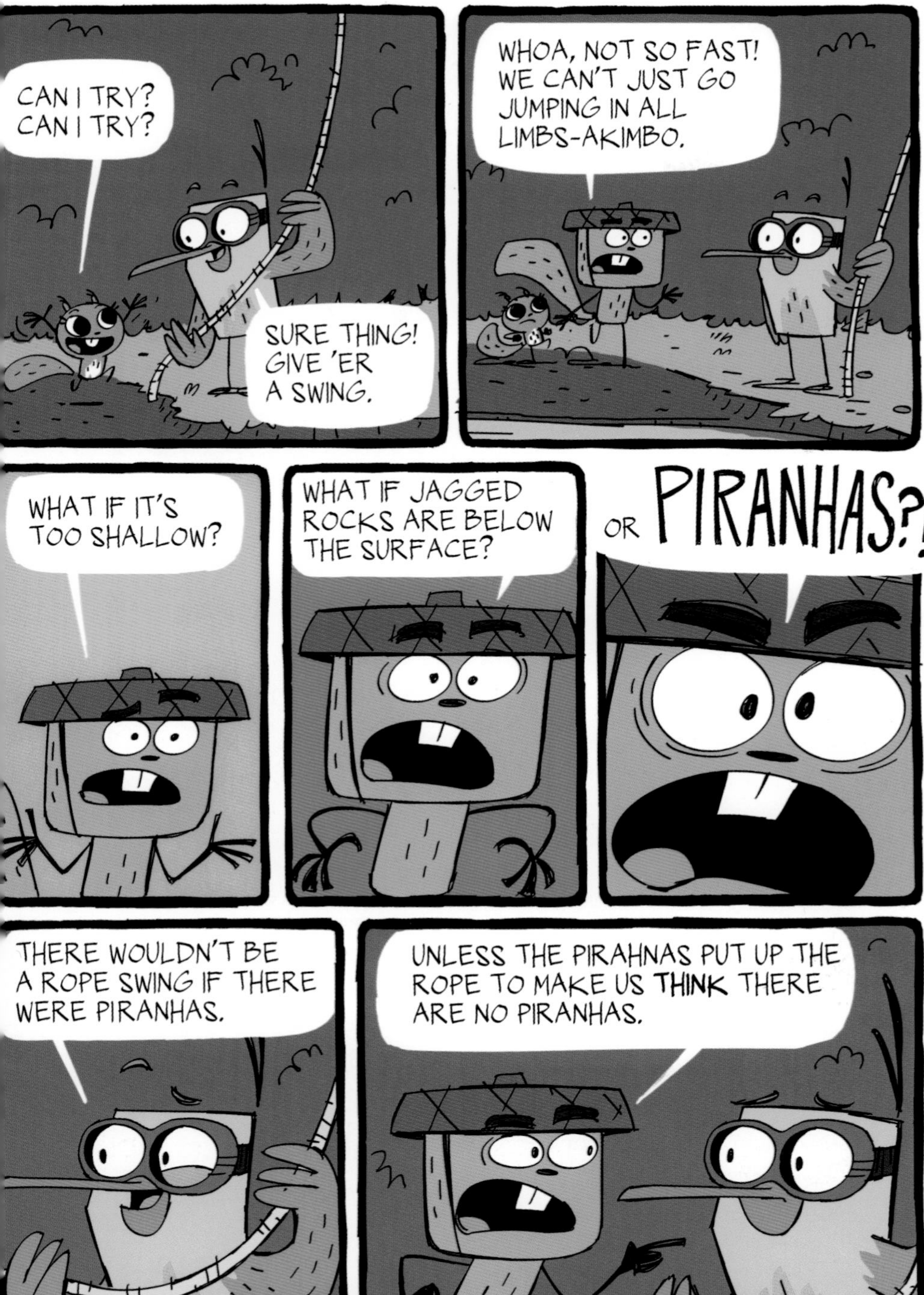
CAN I TRY? CAN I TRY?
SURE THING! GIVE 'ER A SWING.
WHOA, NOT SO FAST! WE CAN'T JUST GO JUMPING IN ALL LIMBS-AKIMBO.
WHAT IF IT'S TOO SHALLOW?
WHAT IF JAGGED ROCKS ARE BELOW THE SURFACE?
OR PIRANHAS?!
THERE WOULDN'T BE A ROPE SWING IF THERE WERE PIRANHAS.
UNLESS THE PIRAHNAS PUT UP THE ROPE TO MAKE US THINK THERE ARE NO PIRANHAS.

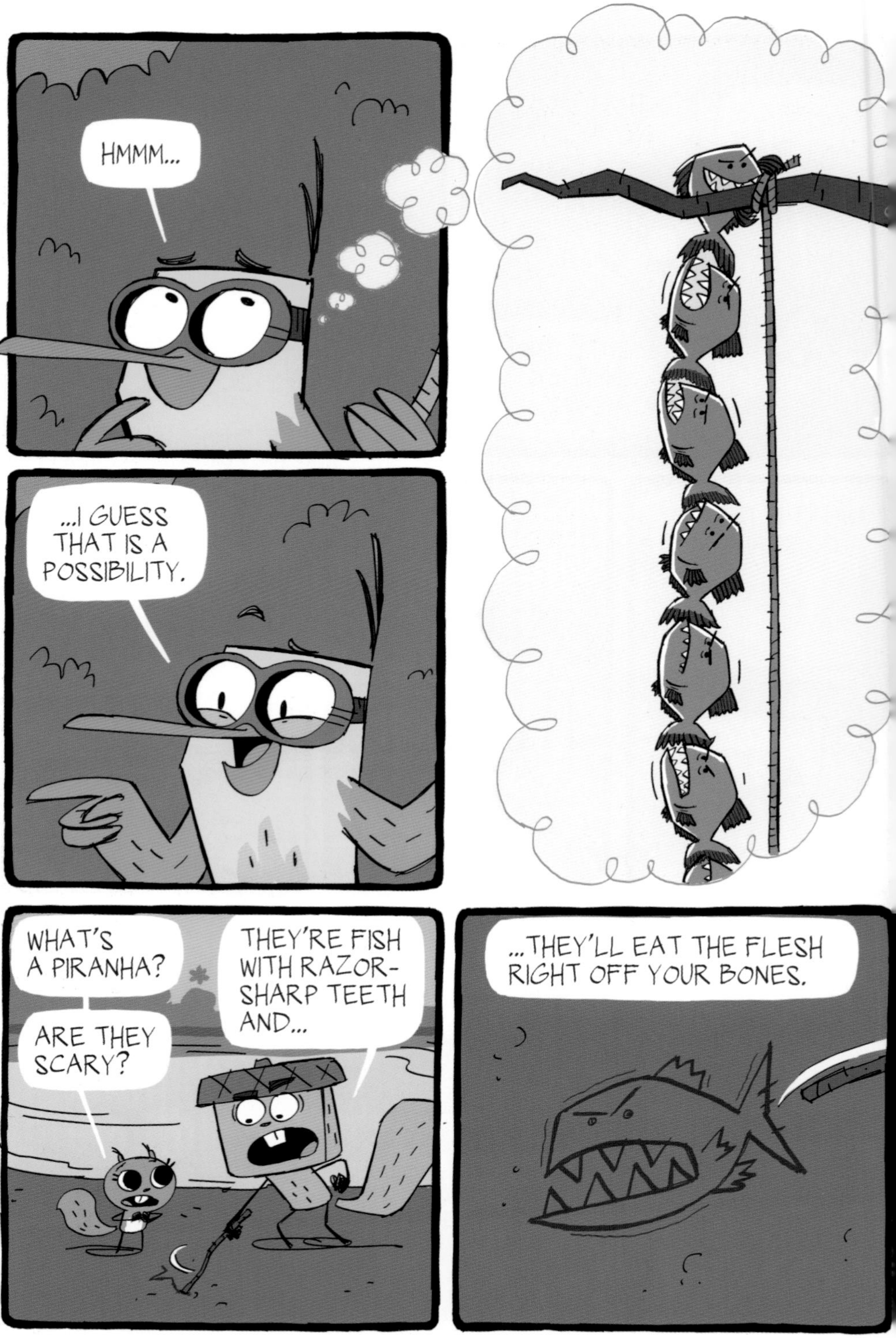
HMMM...
...I GUESS THAT IS A POSSIBILITY.
WHAT'S A PIRANHA?
ARE THEY SCARY?
THEY'RE FISH WITH RAZOR-SHARP TEETH AND...
...THEY'LL EAT THE FLESH RIGHT OFF YOUR BONES.

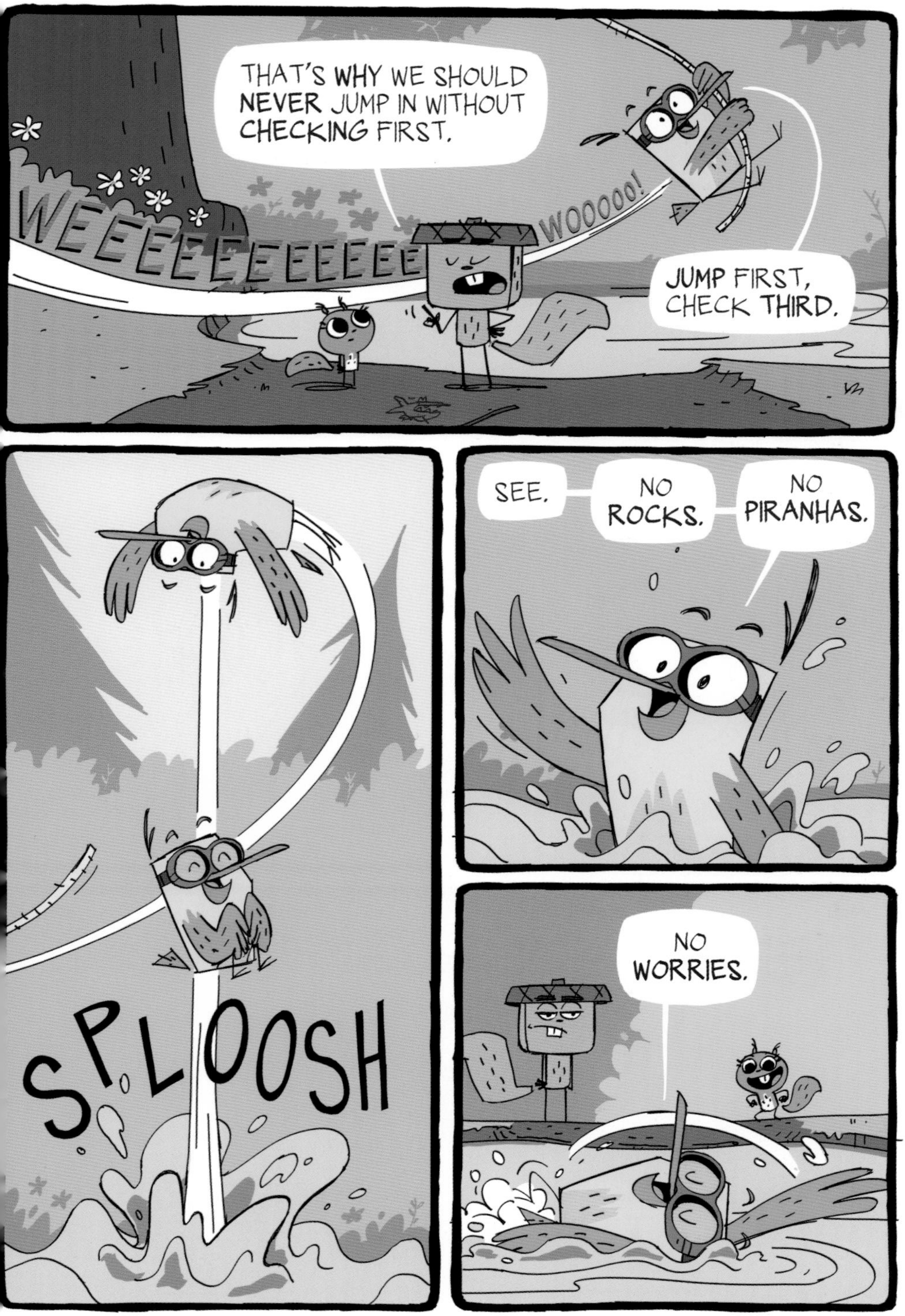
THAT'S WHY WE SHOULD NEVER JUMP IN WITHOUT CHECKING FIRST.
WEEEEEEEEEEEEE
WOOOOO!
JUMP FIRST, CHECK THIRD.
SPLOOSH
SEE.
NO ROCKS.
NO PIRANHAS.
NO WORRIES.

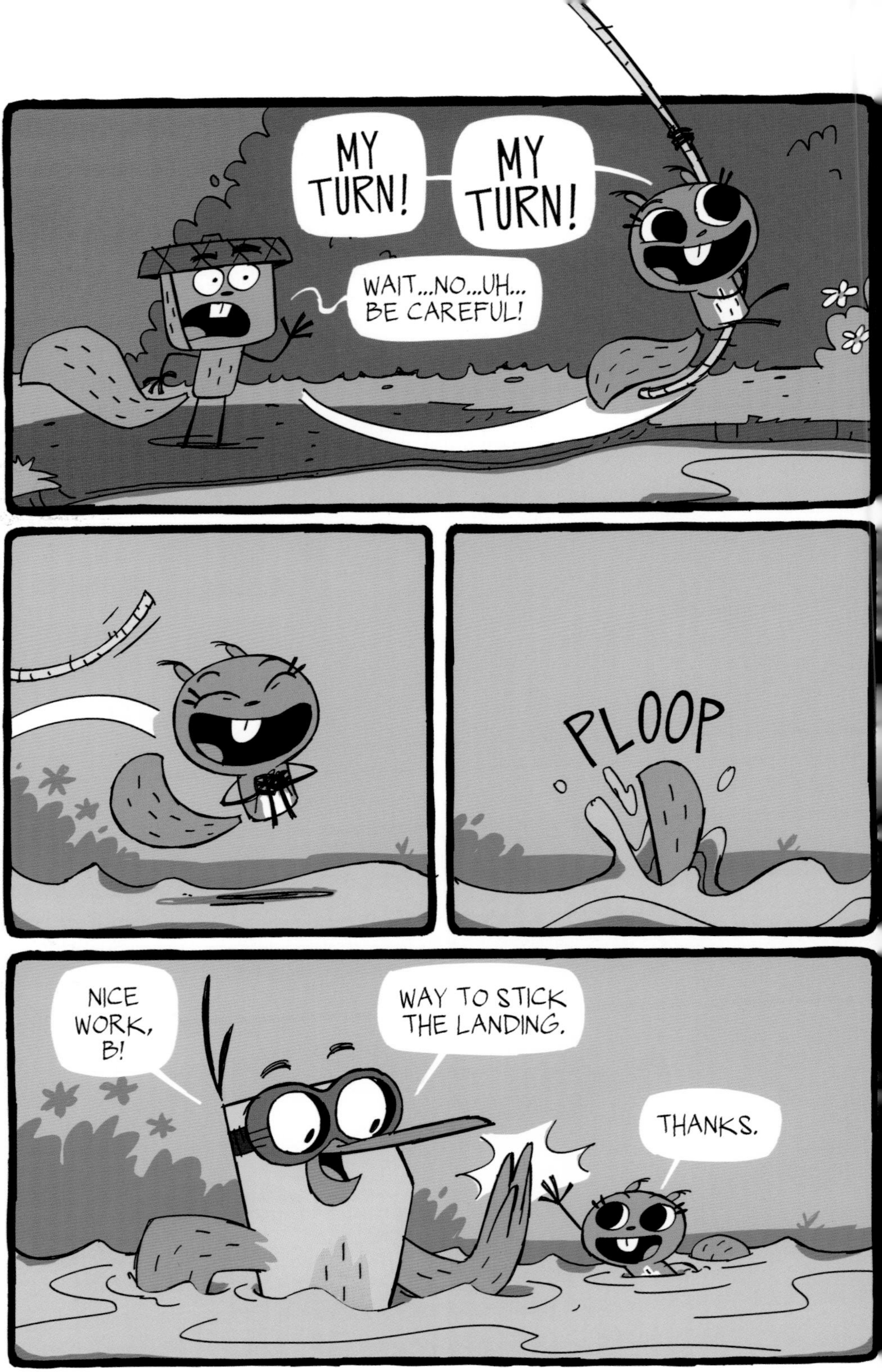
MY TURN!
MY TURN!
WAIT...NO...UH... BE CAREFUL!
PLOOP
NICE WORK, B!
WAY TO STICK THE LANDING.
THANKS.

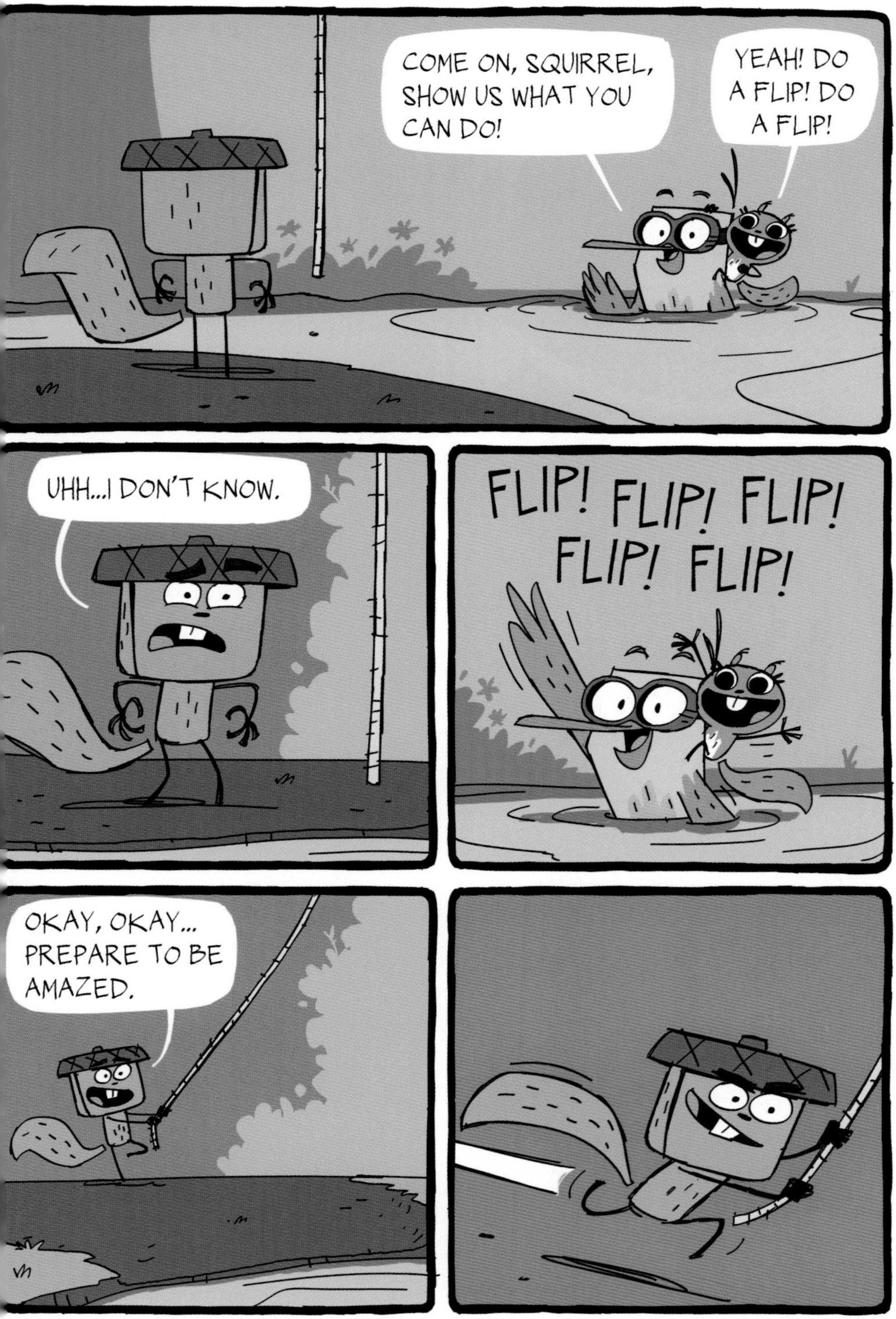
COME ON, SQUIRREL, SHOW US WHAT YOU CAN DO!
YEAH! DO A FLIP! DO A FLIP!
UHH...I DON'T KNOW.
FLIP! FLIP! FLIP! FLIP! FLIP!
OKAY, OKAY... PREPARE TO BE AMAZED.

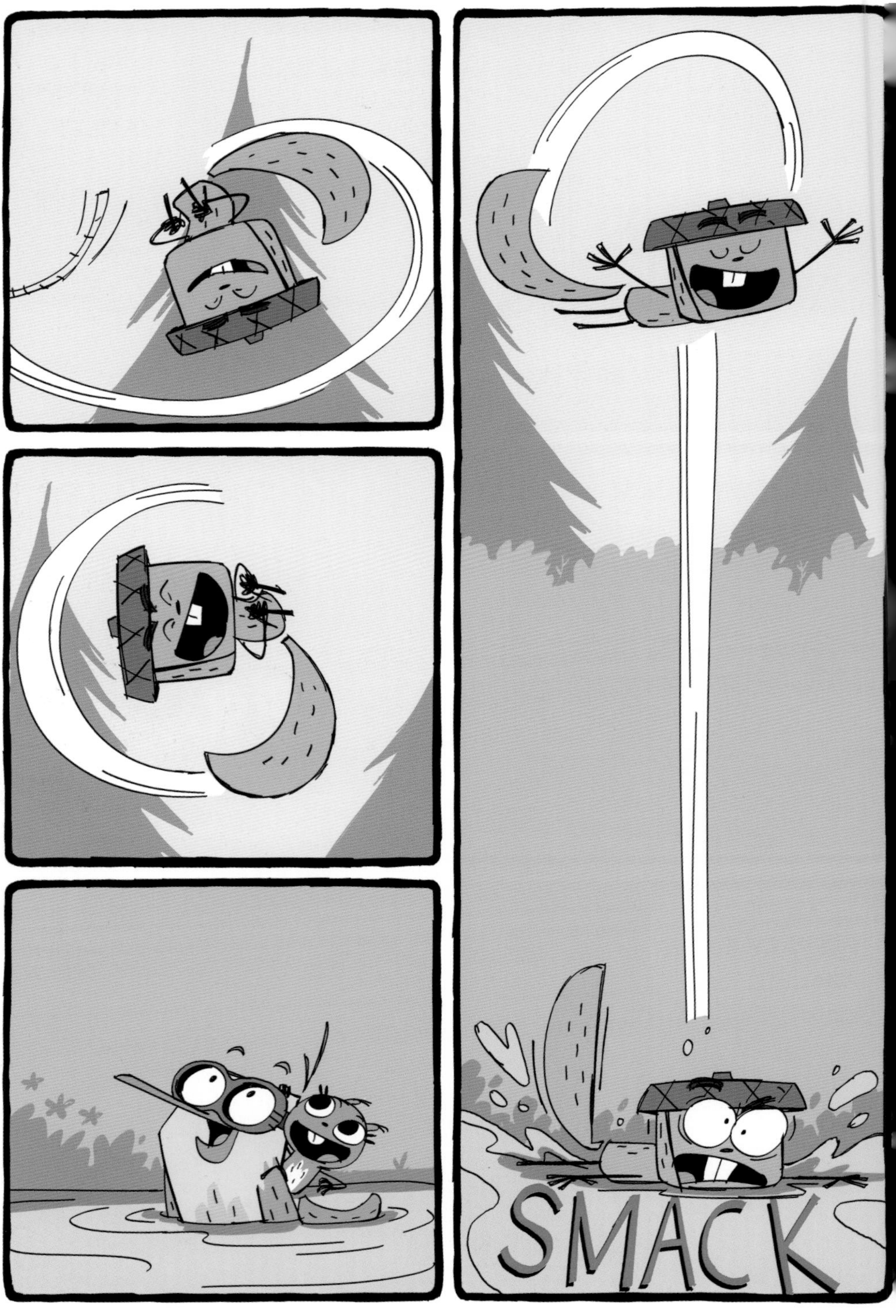
SMACK

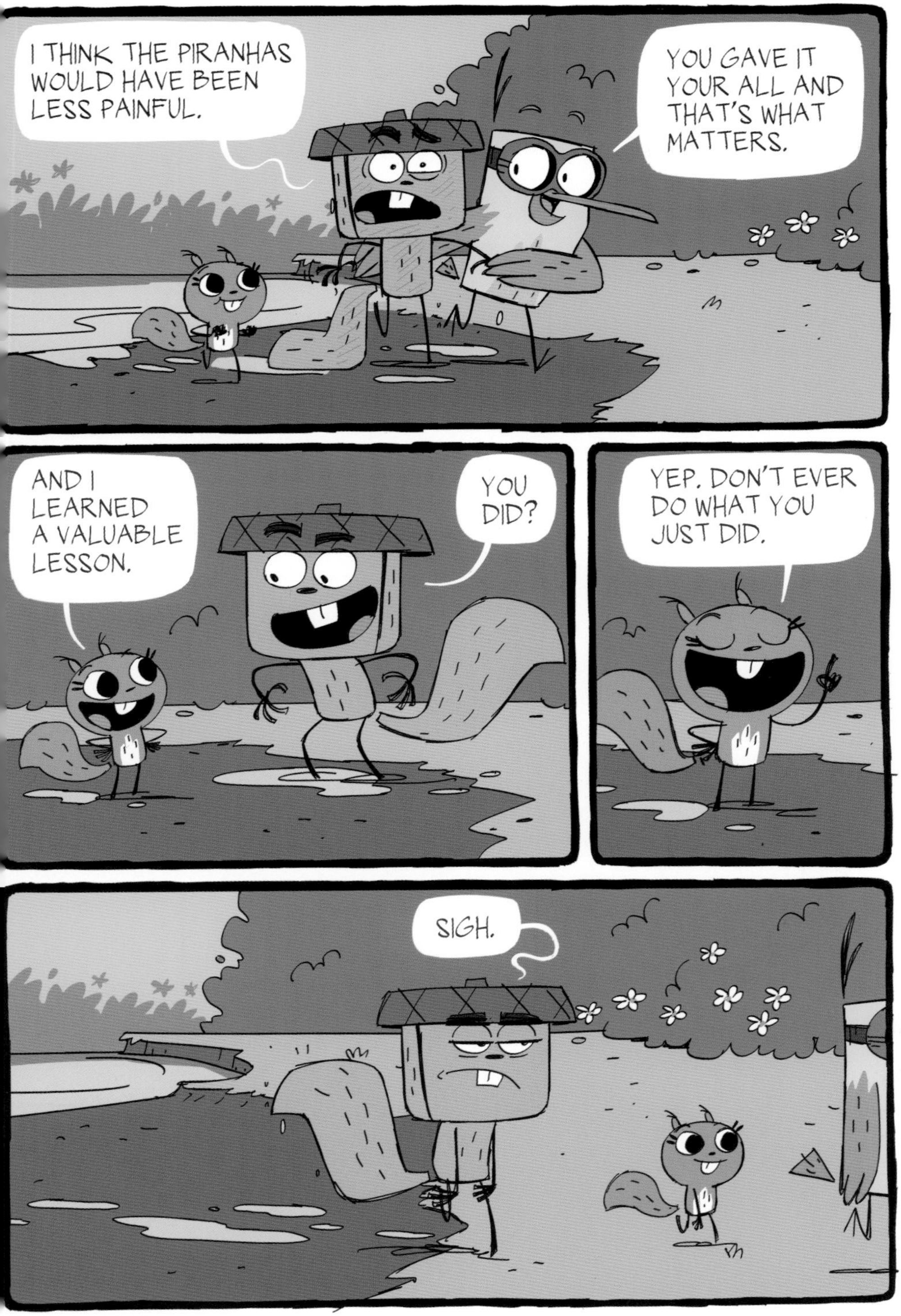
I THINK THE PIRANHAS WOULD HAVE BEEN LESS PAINFUL.
YOU GAVE IT YOUR ALL AND THAT'S WHAT MATTERS.
AND I LEARNED A VALUABLE LESSON.
YOU DID?
YEP. DON'T EVER DO WHAT YOU JUST DID.
SIGH.

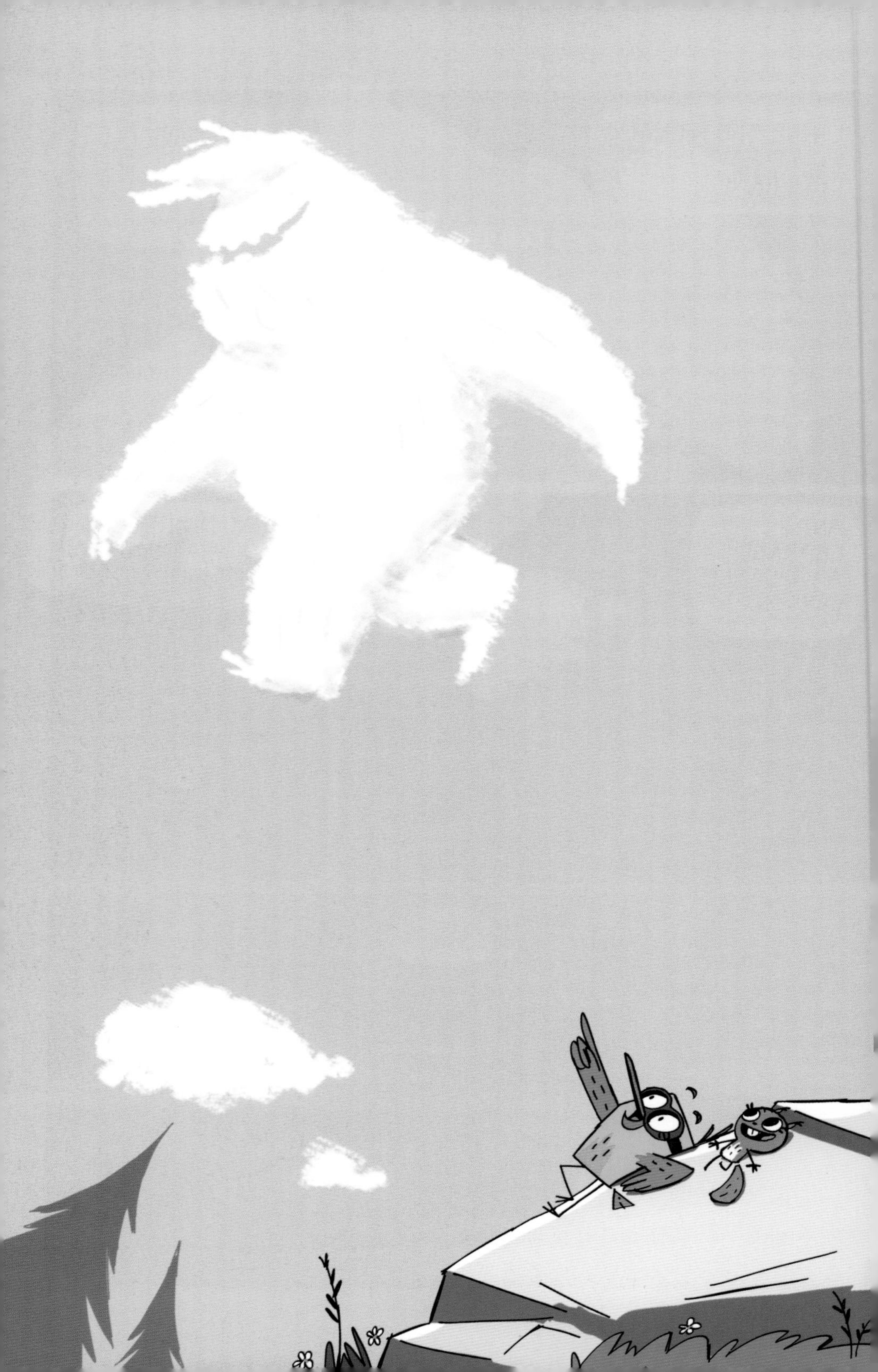

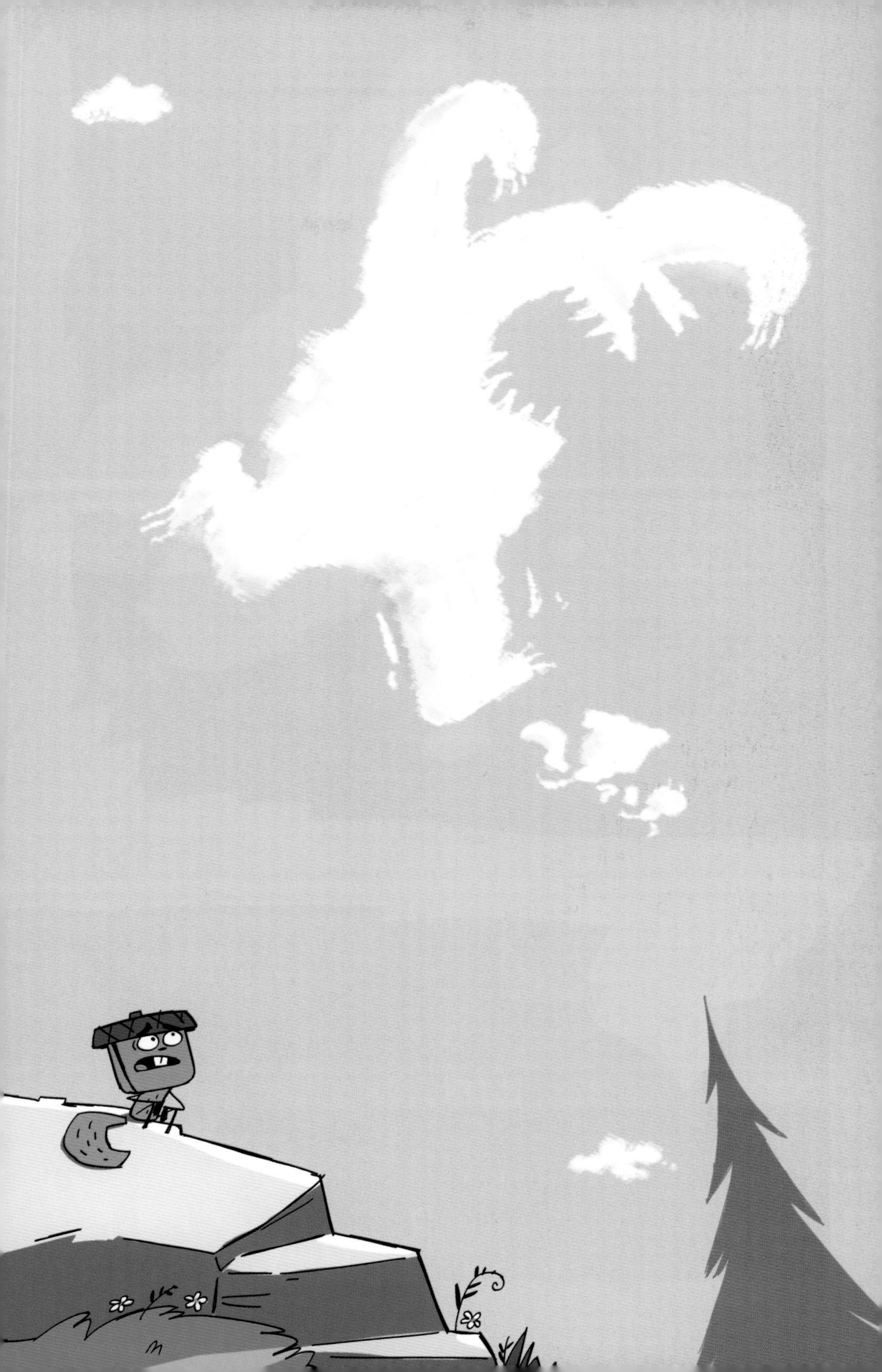

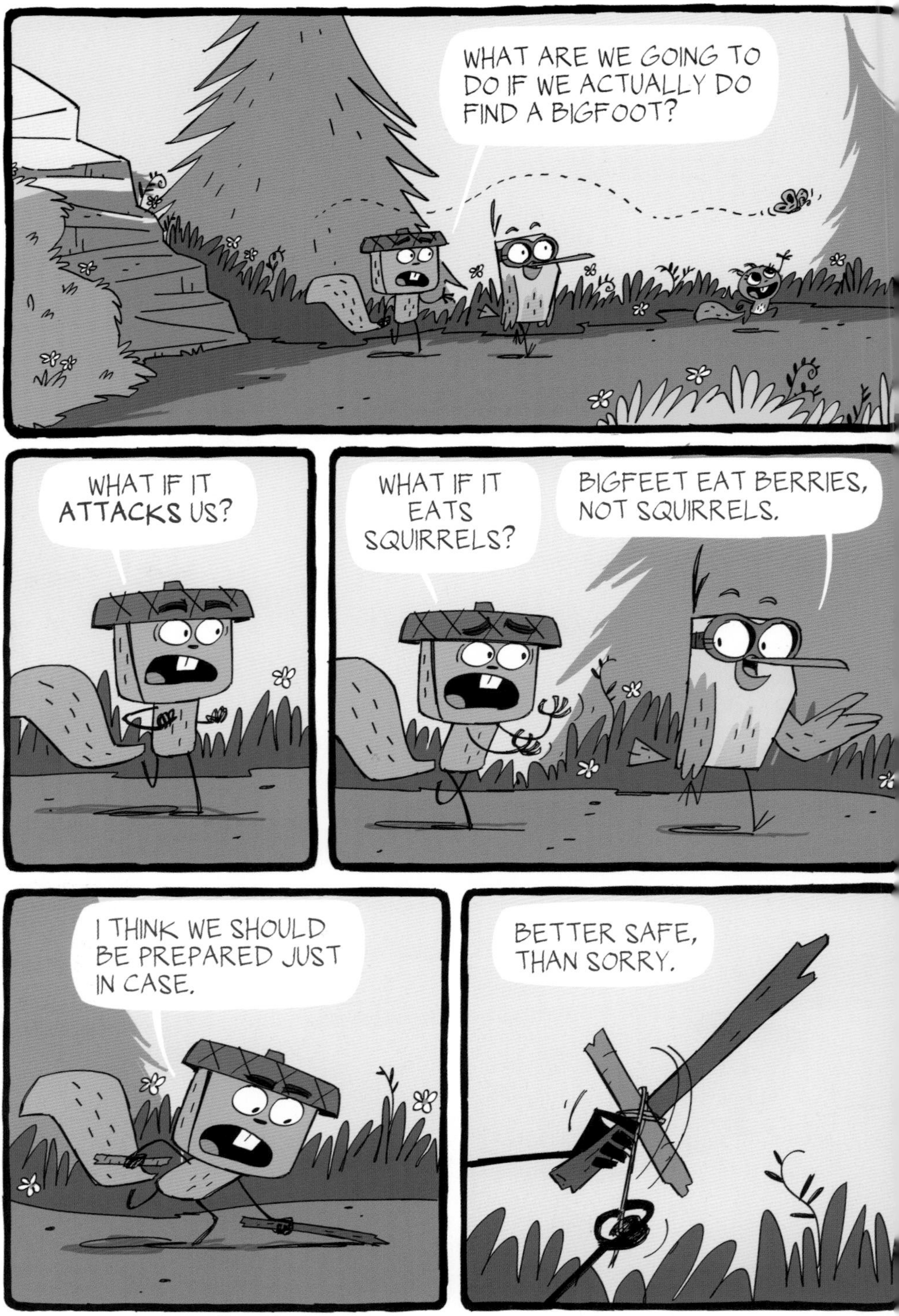
WHAT ARE WE GOING TO DO IF WE ACTUALLY DO FIND A BIGFOOT?
WHAT IF IT ATTACKS US?
WHAT IF IT EATS SQUIRRELS?
BIGFEET EAT BERRIES, NOT SQUIRRELS.
I THINK WE SHOULD BE PREPARED JUST IN CASE.
BETTER SAFE, THAN SORRY.

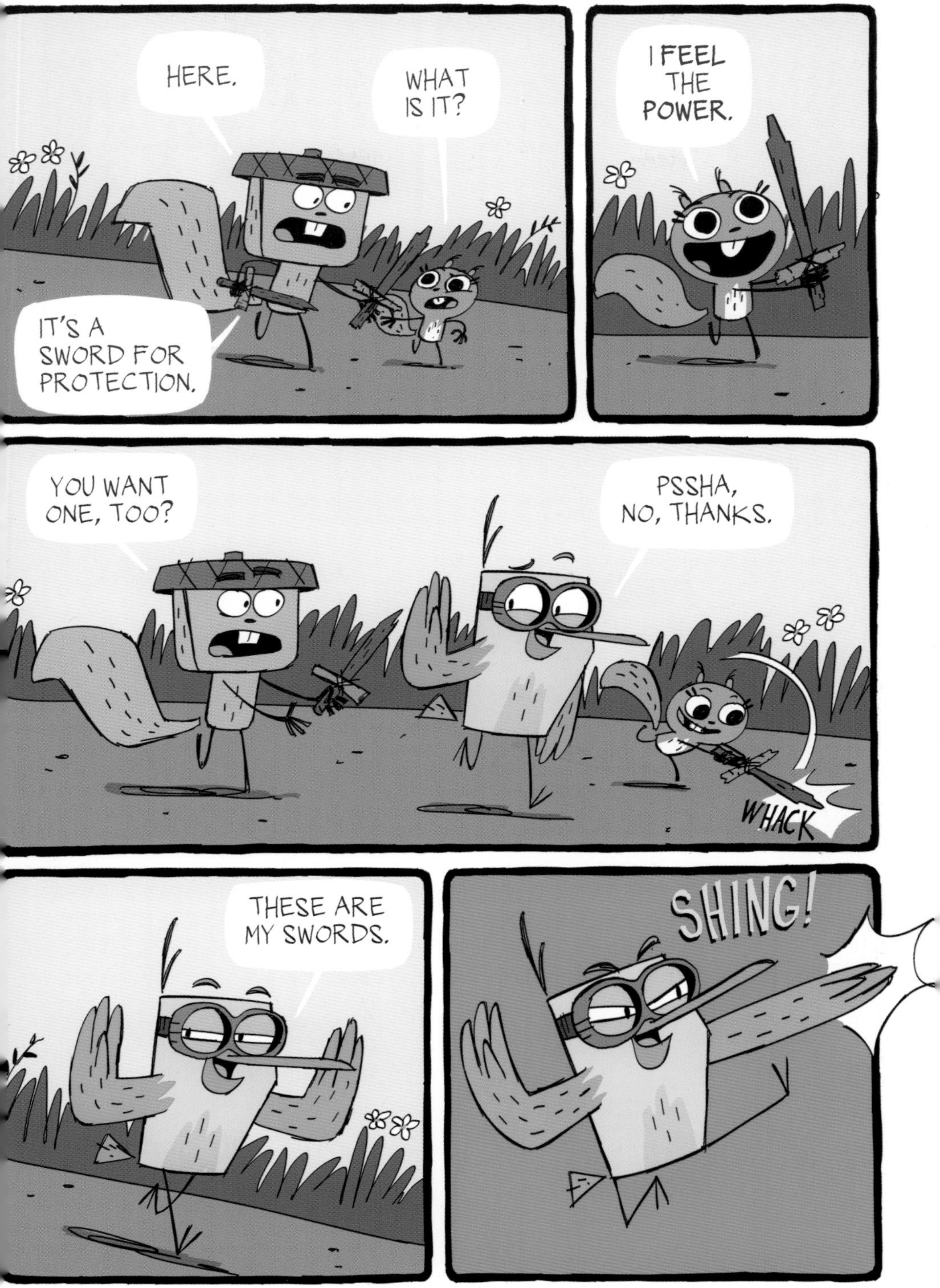
HERE.
WHAT IS IT?
IT'S A SWORD FOR PROTECTION.
I FEEL THE POWER.
YOU WANT ONE, TOO?
PSSHA, NO, THANKS.
WHACK
THESE ARE MY SWORDS.
SHING!

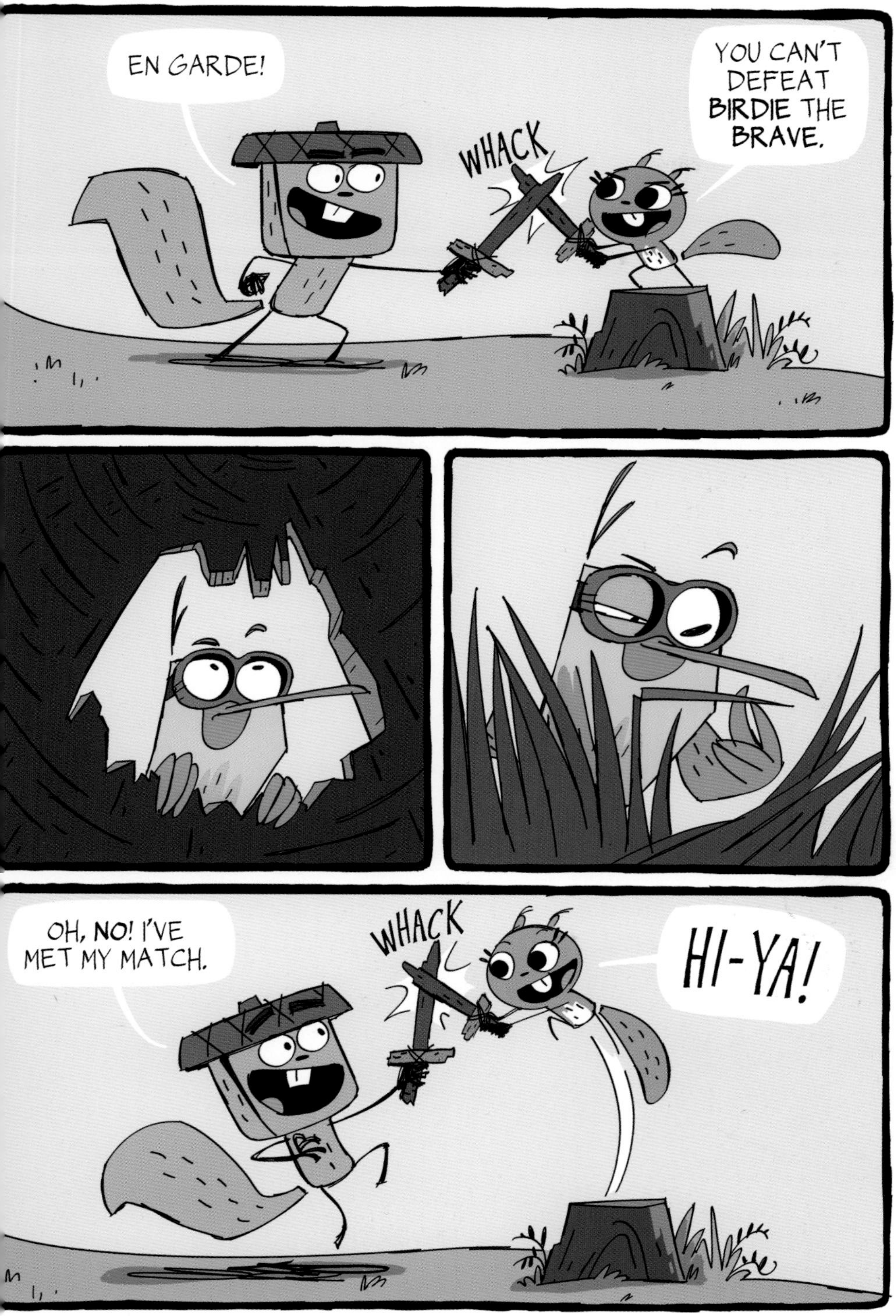
EN GARDE!
WHACK
YOU CAN'T DEFEAT BIRDIE THE BRAVE.
OH, NO! I'VE MET MY MATCH.
WHACK
HI-YA!

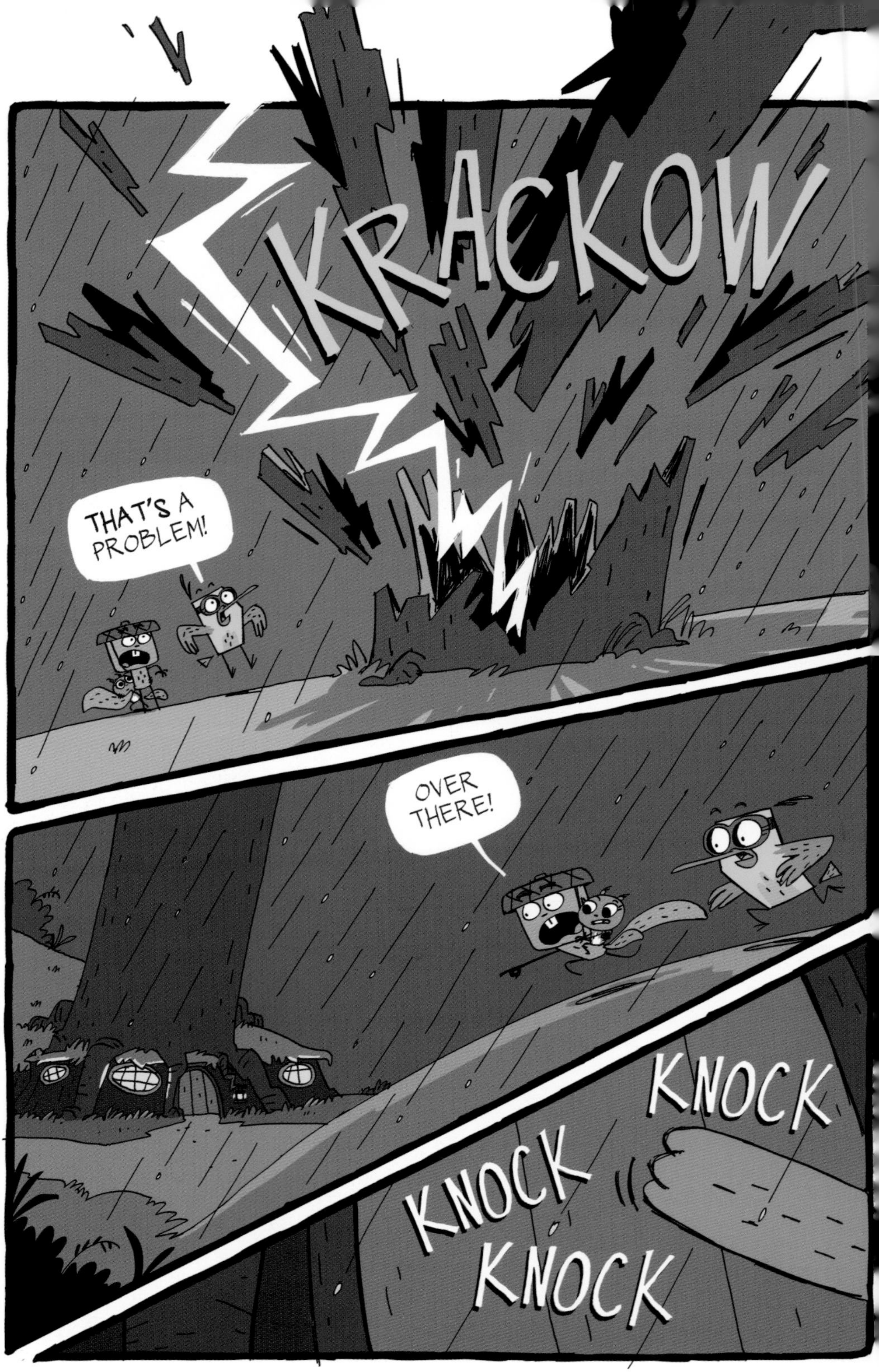
KRACKOW
THAT'S A PROBLEM!
OVER THERE!
KNOCK
KNOCK
KNOCK

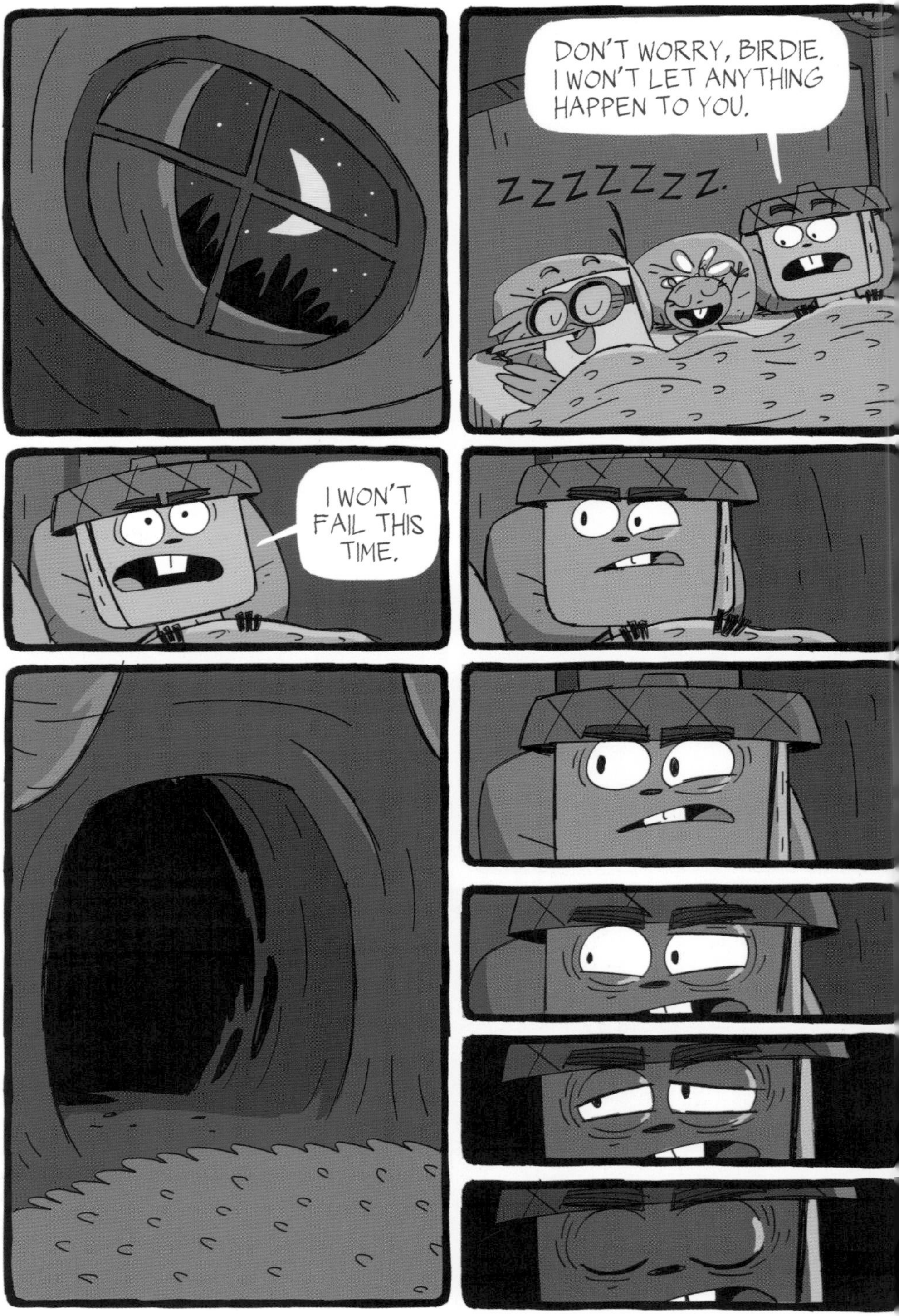
DON'T WORRY, BIRDIE. I WON'T LET ANYTHING HAPPEN TO YOU.
ZZZZZZZZ.
I WON'T FAIL THIS TIME.

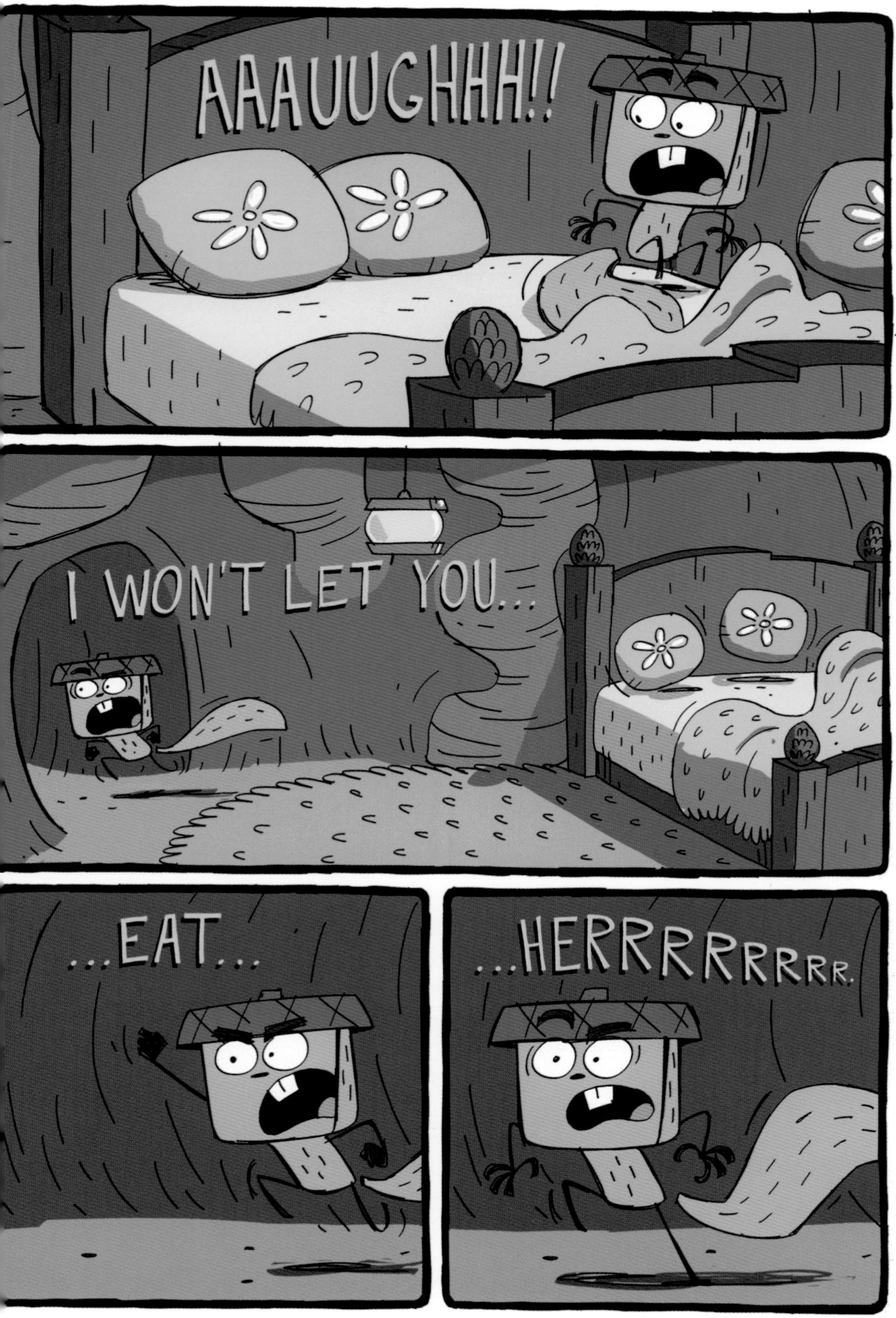
AAAUUGHHH!!
I WON'T LET YOU...
...EAT...
...HERRRRRRRR.

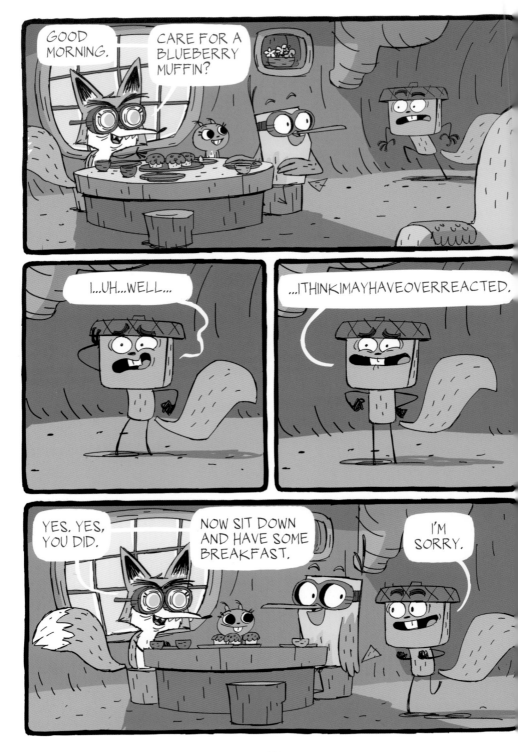

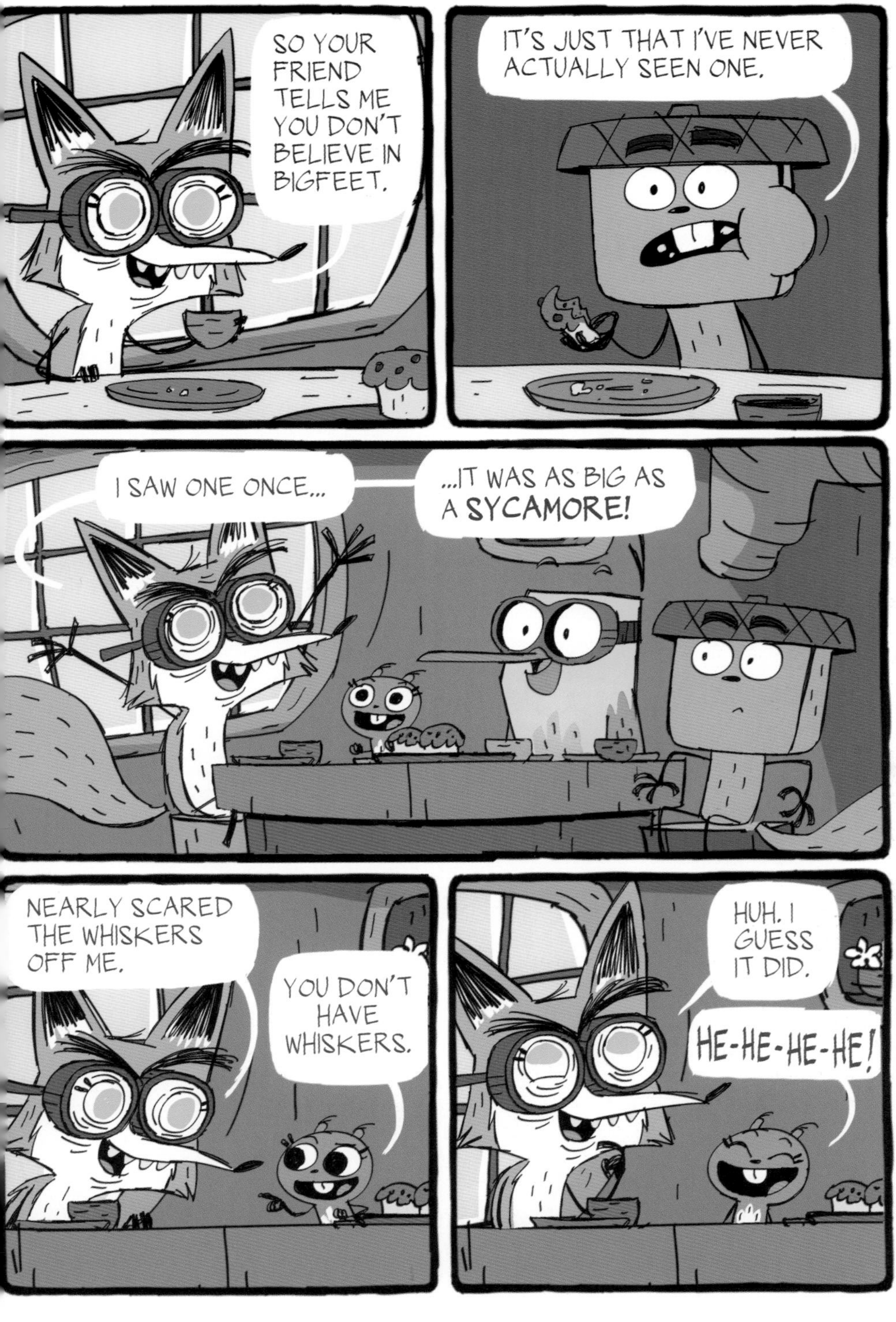
SO YOUR FRIEND TELLS ME YOU DON'T BELIEVE IN BIGFEET.
IT'S JUST THAT I'VE NEVER ACTUALLY SEEN ONE.
I SAW ONE ONCE...
...IT WAS AS BIG AS A SYCAMORE!
NEARLY SCARED THE WHISKERS OFF ME.
YOU DON'T HAVE WHISKERS.
HUH. I GUESS IT DID.
HE-HE-HE-HE!

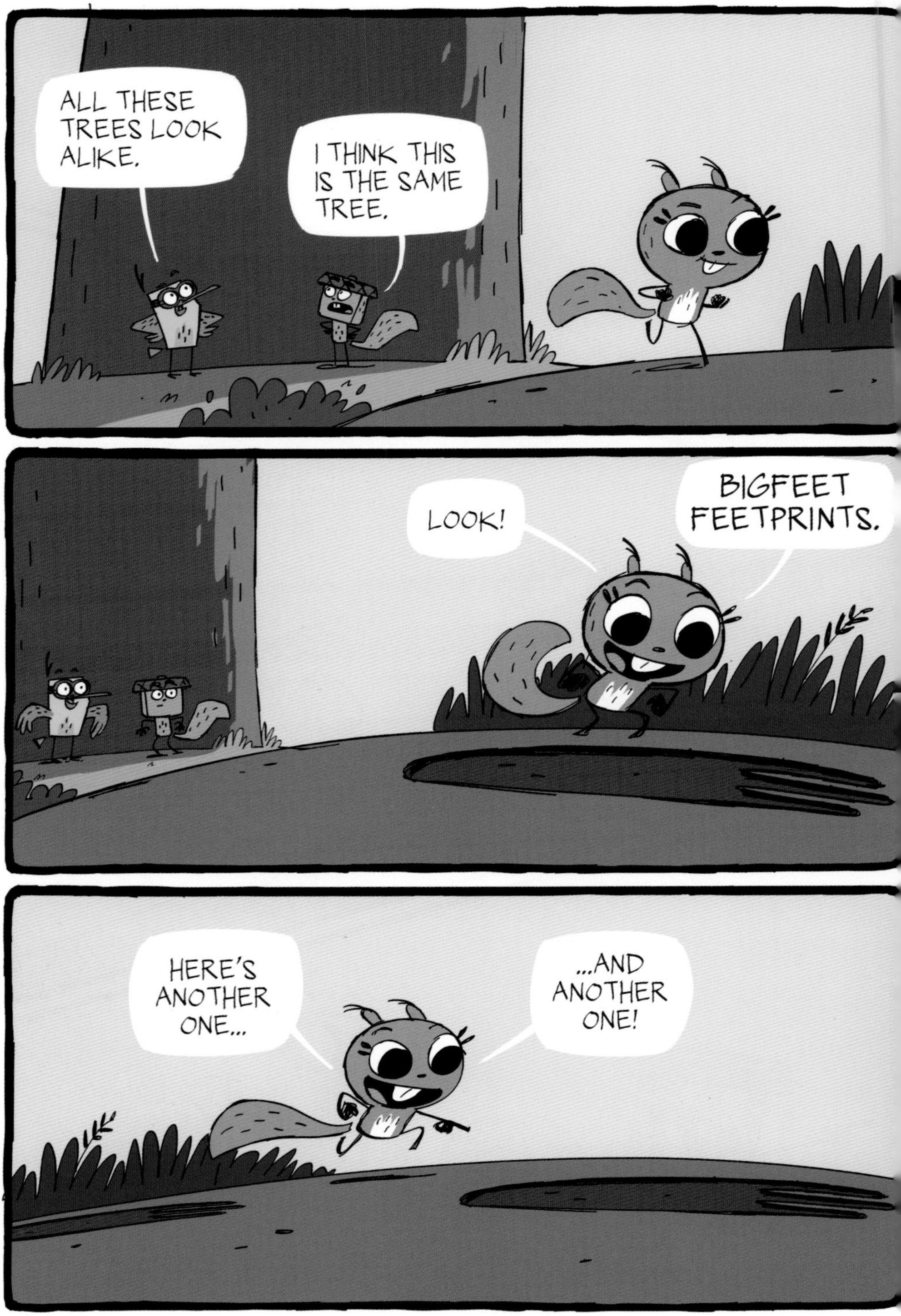
ALL THESE TREES LOOK ALIKE.
I THINK THIS IS THE SAME TREE.
LOOK!
BIGFEET FEETPRINTS.
HERE'S ANOTHER ONE...
...AND ANOTHER ONE!

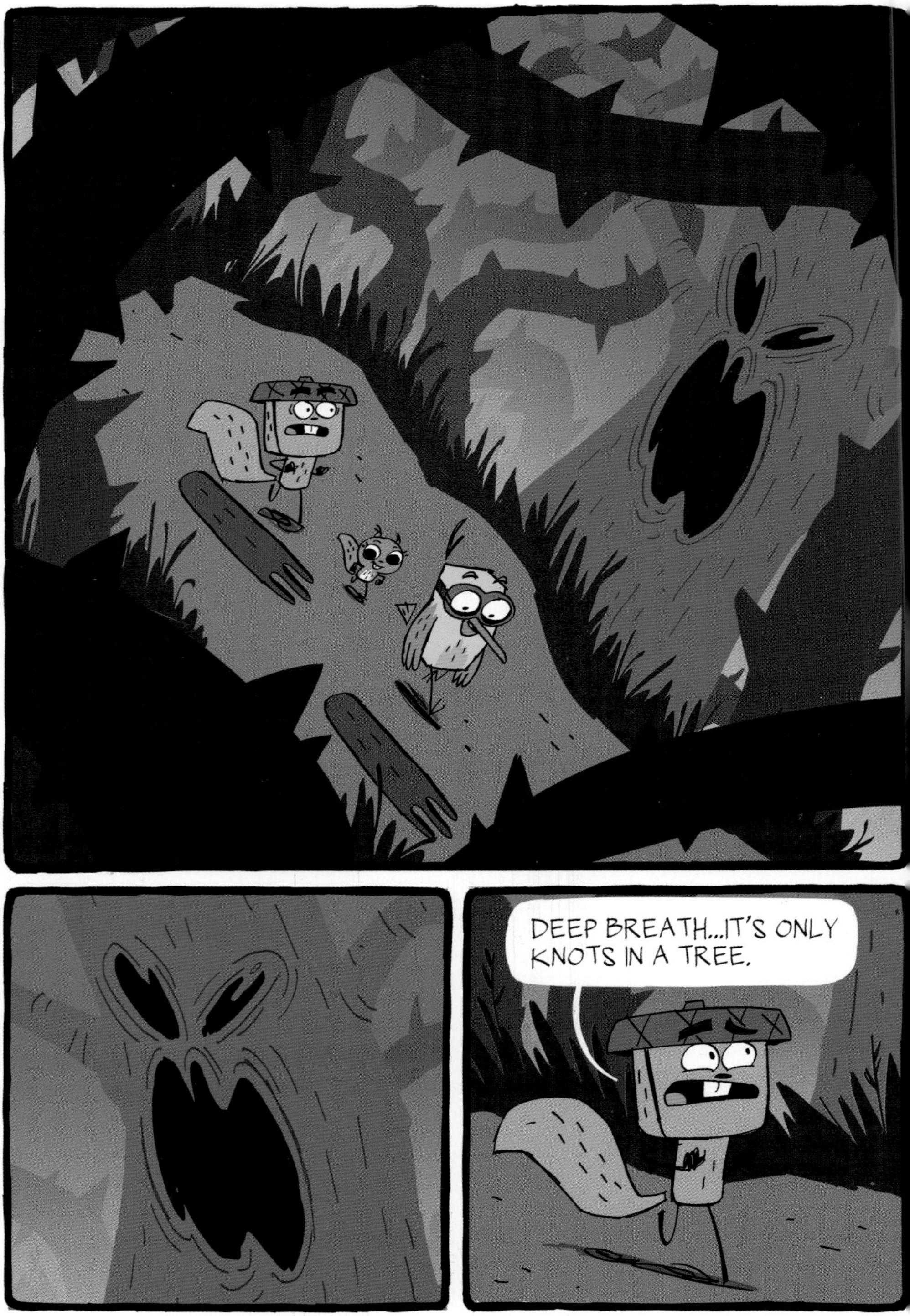
DEEP BREATH...IT'S ONLY KNOTS IN A TREE.

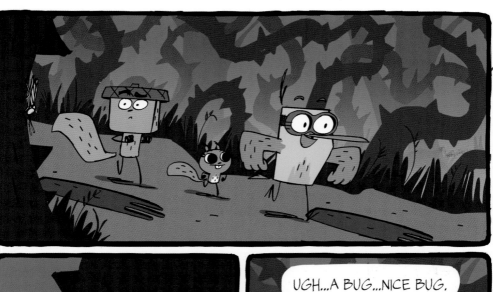

BZZT

UGH...A BUG...NICE BUG.

SWAP

CRUNCH SLURP CRUNCH

SNAP

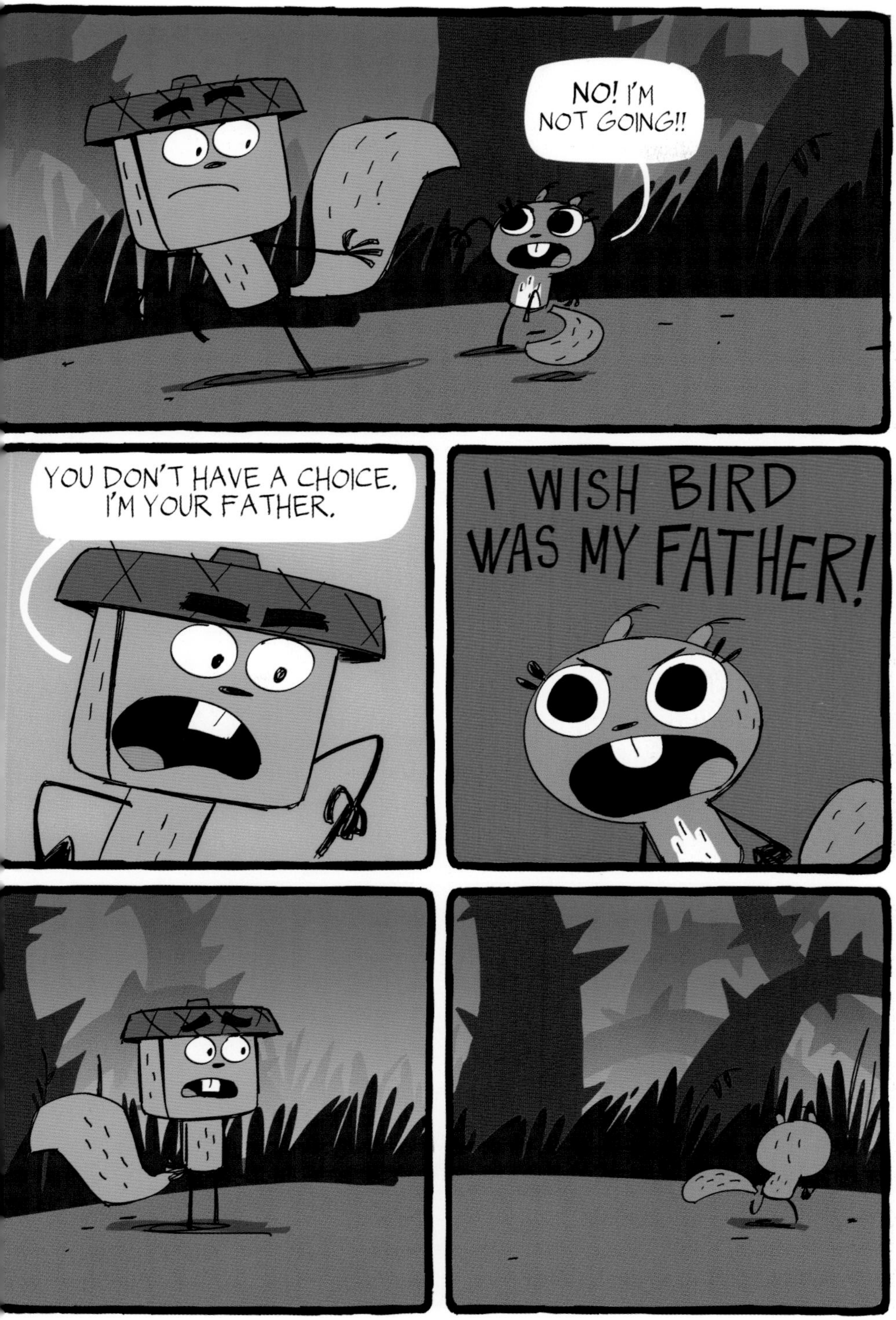
NO! I'M NOT GOING!!
YOU DON'T HAVE A CHOICE. I'M YOUR FATHER.
I WISH BIRD WAS MY FATHER!

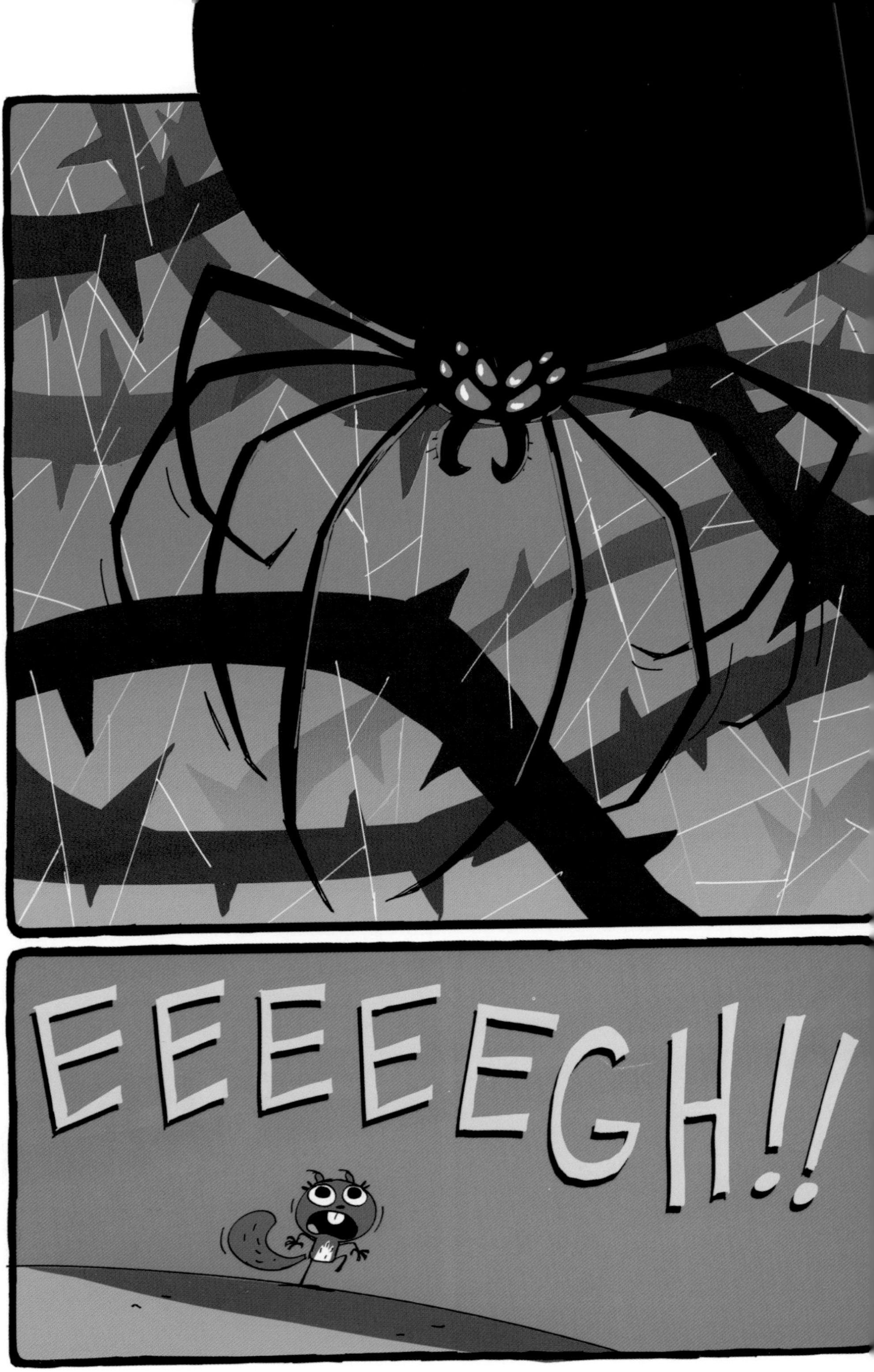
EEEEEGH!!

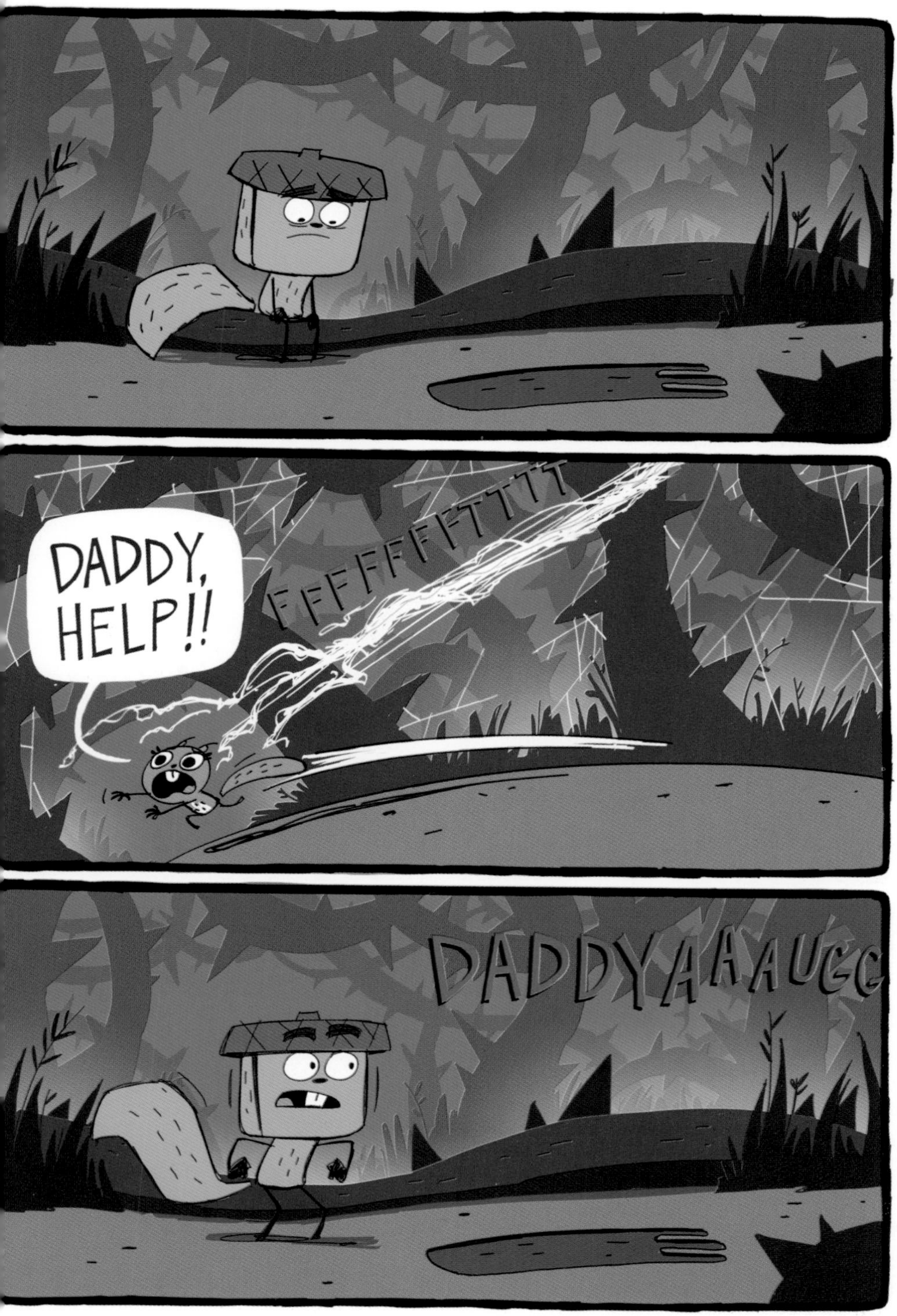
DADDY, HELP!!
FFFFFFFTTTTT
DADDYAAAUGG

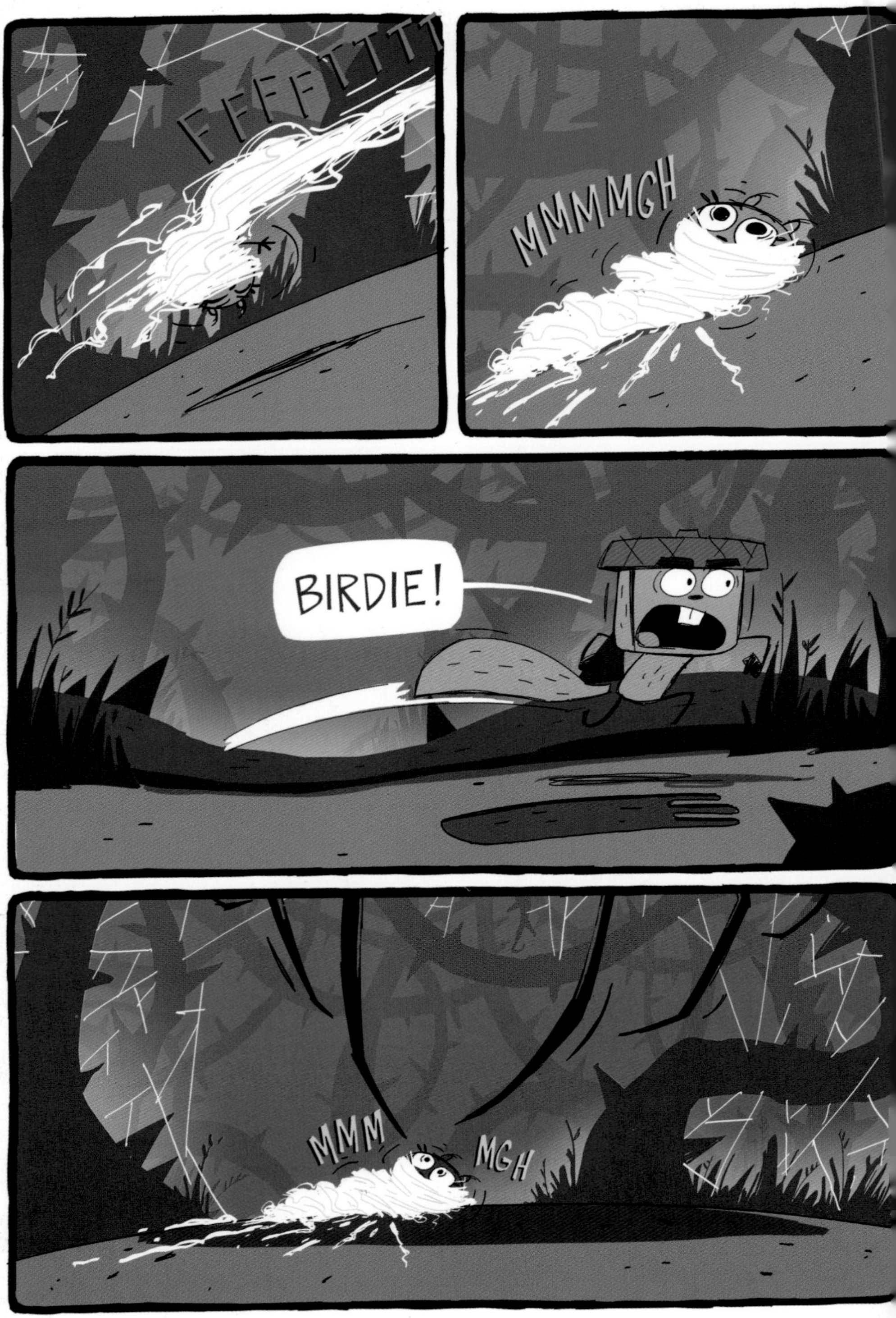
FFFFTTTTT
MMMMGH
BIRDIE!
MMM
MGH

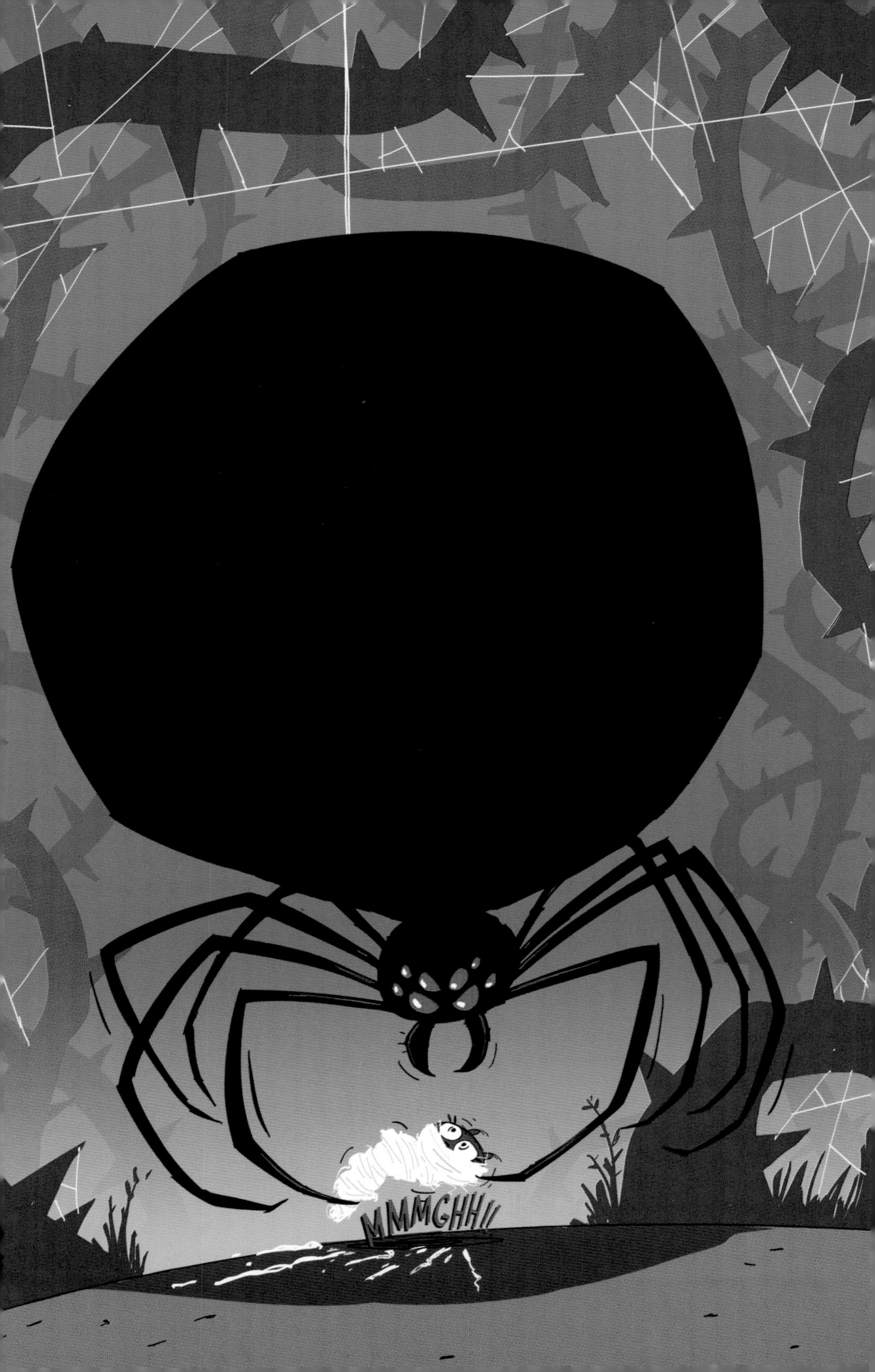
MMMGHH!!

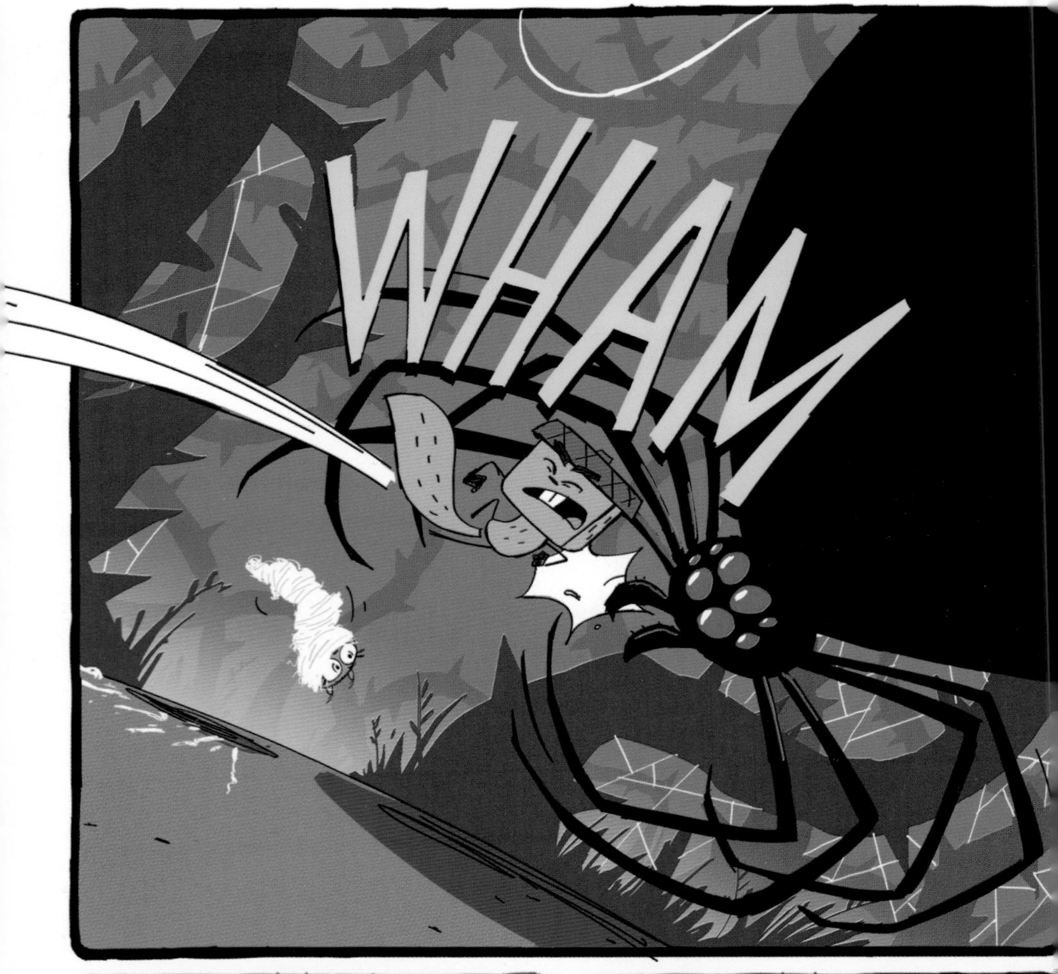
WHAM

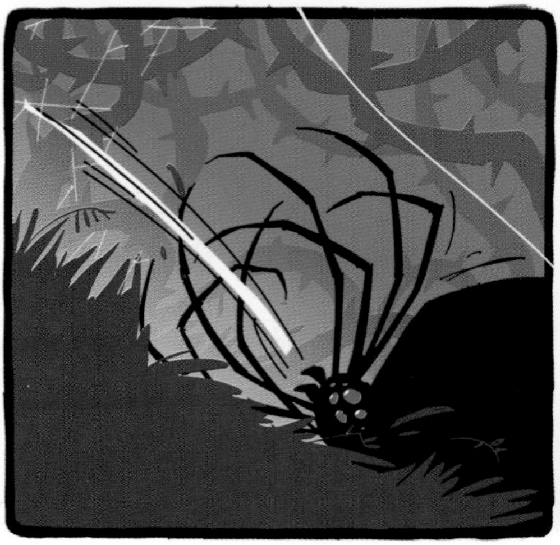

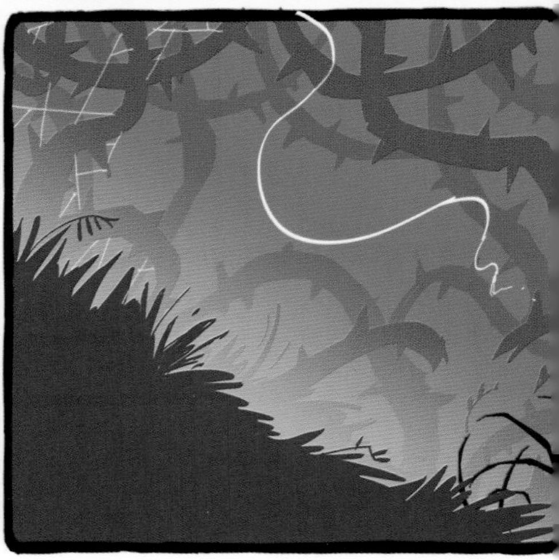

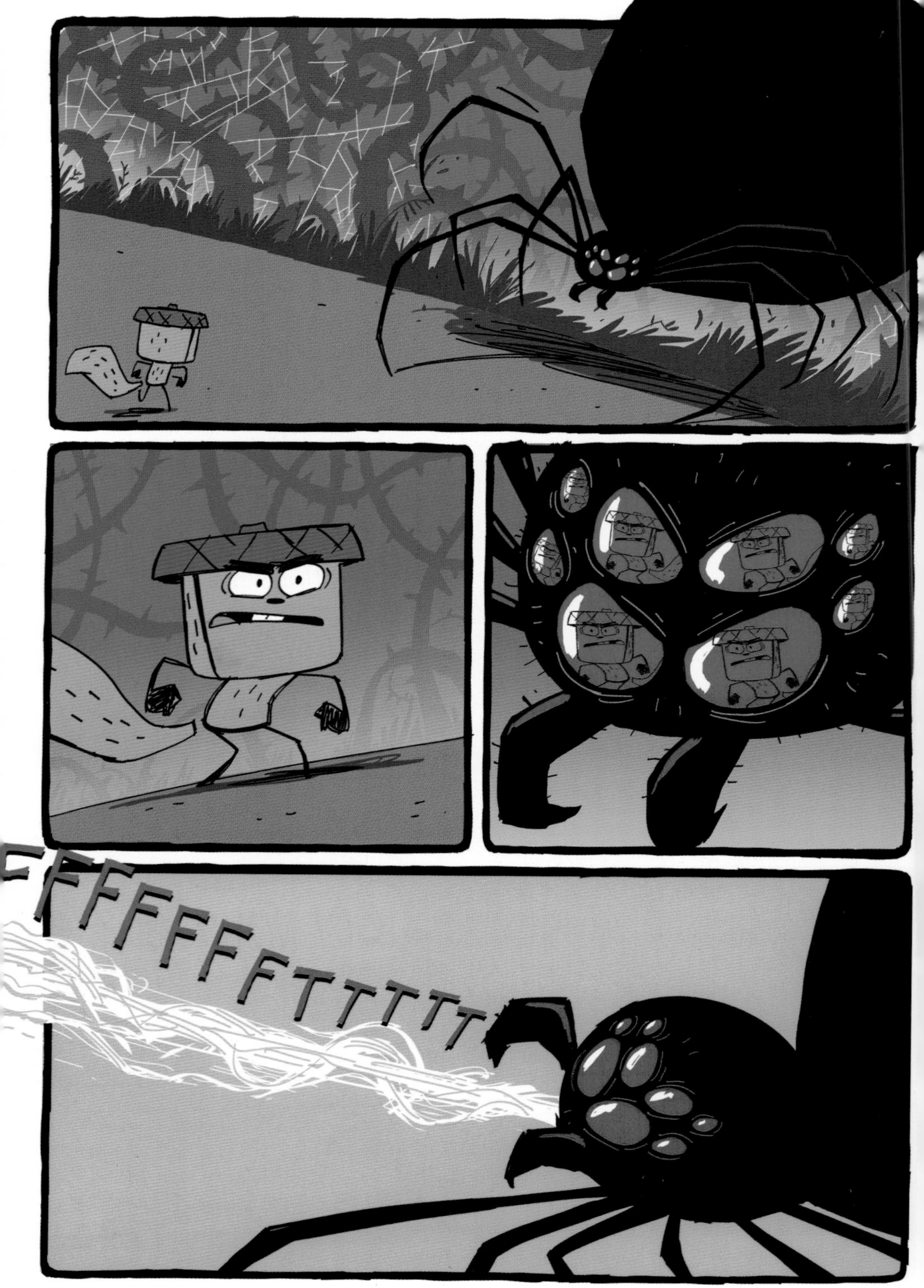
FFFFFFFFFTTTTTTT

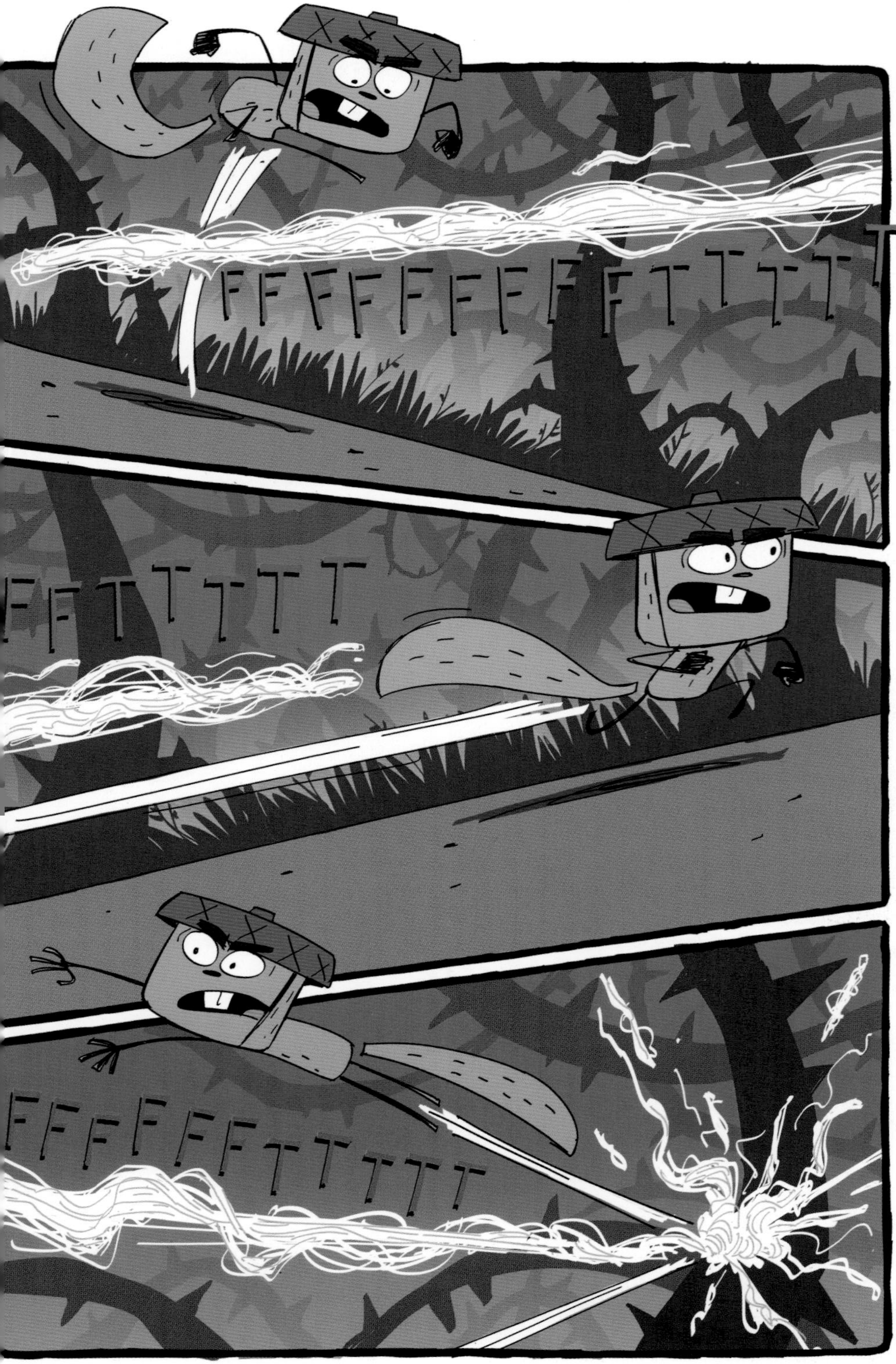
FFFFFFFFFTTTTT
FFTTTTT
FFFFFFTTTTT

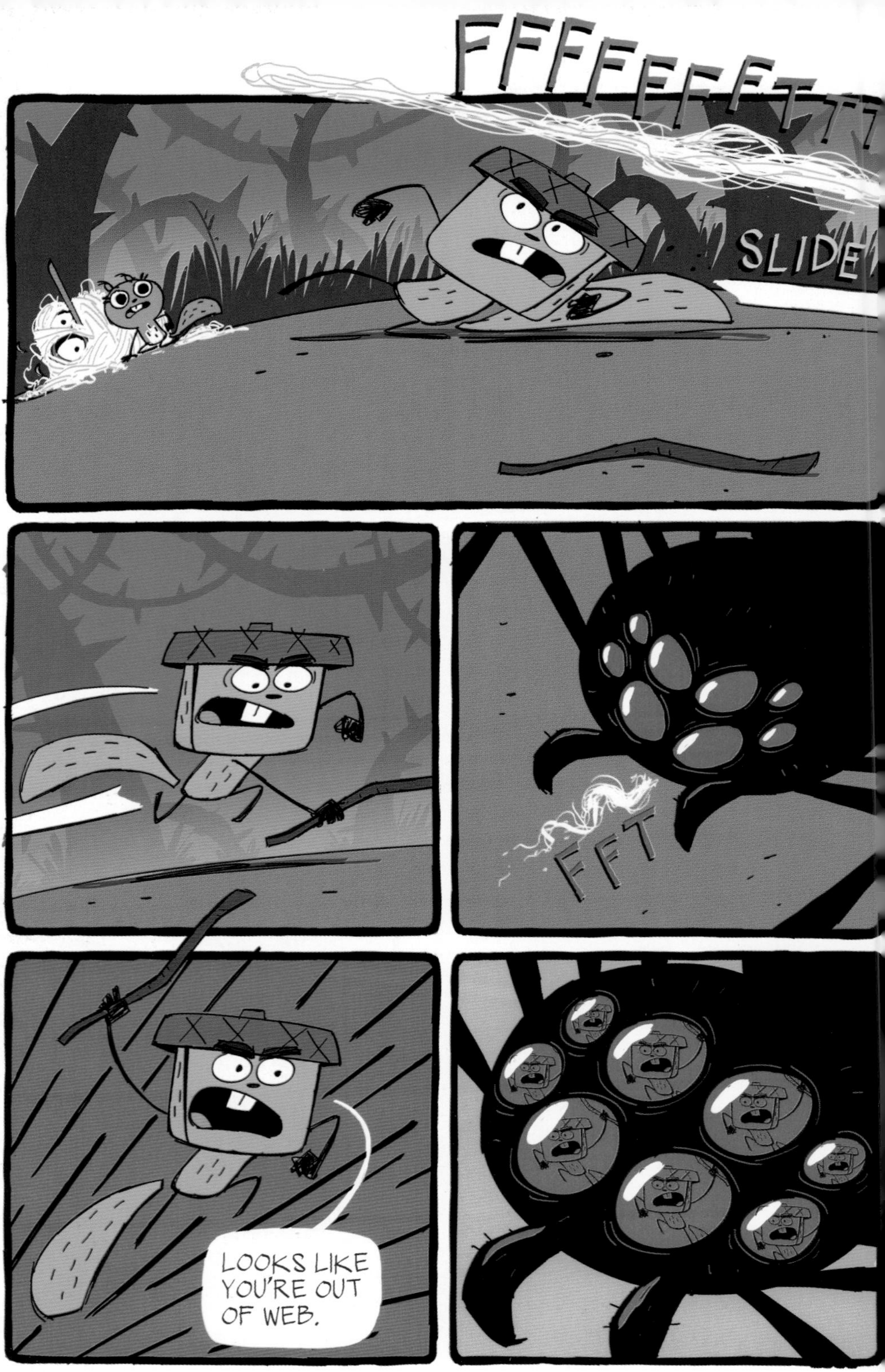
FFFFFFFTTTT
SLIDE
FFT
LOOKS LIKE YOU'RE OUT OF WEB.

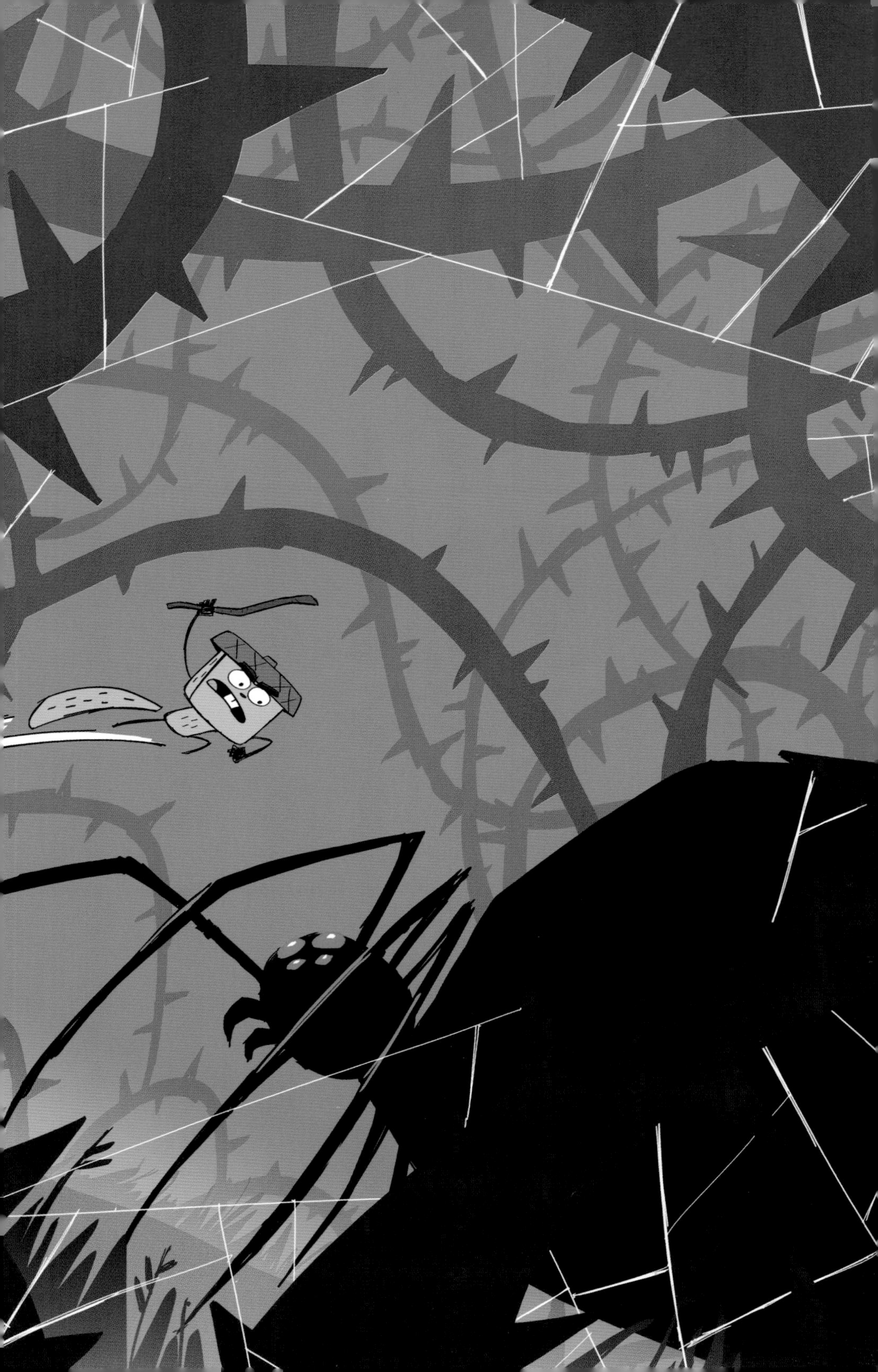

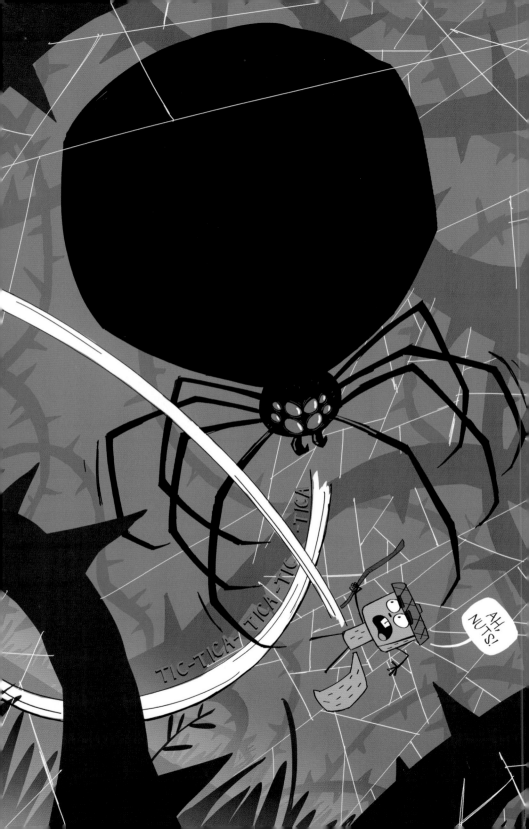

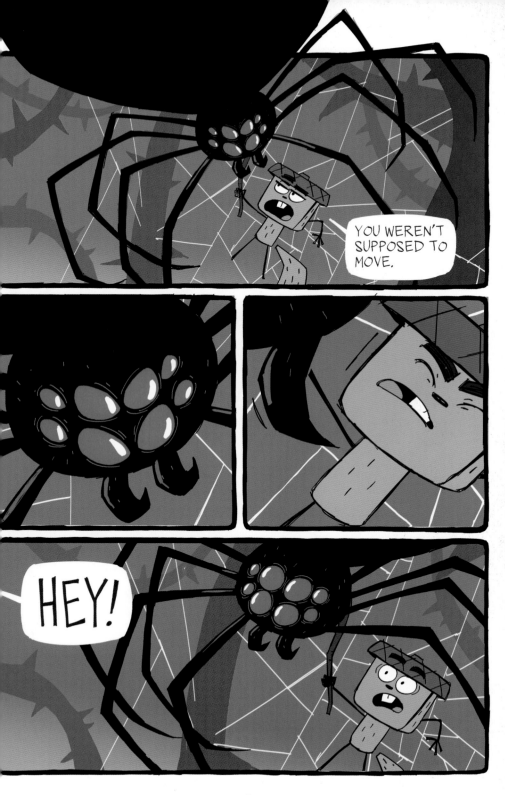

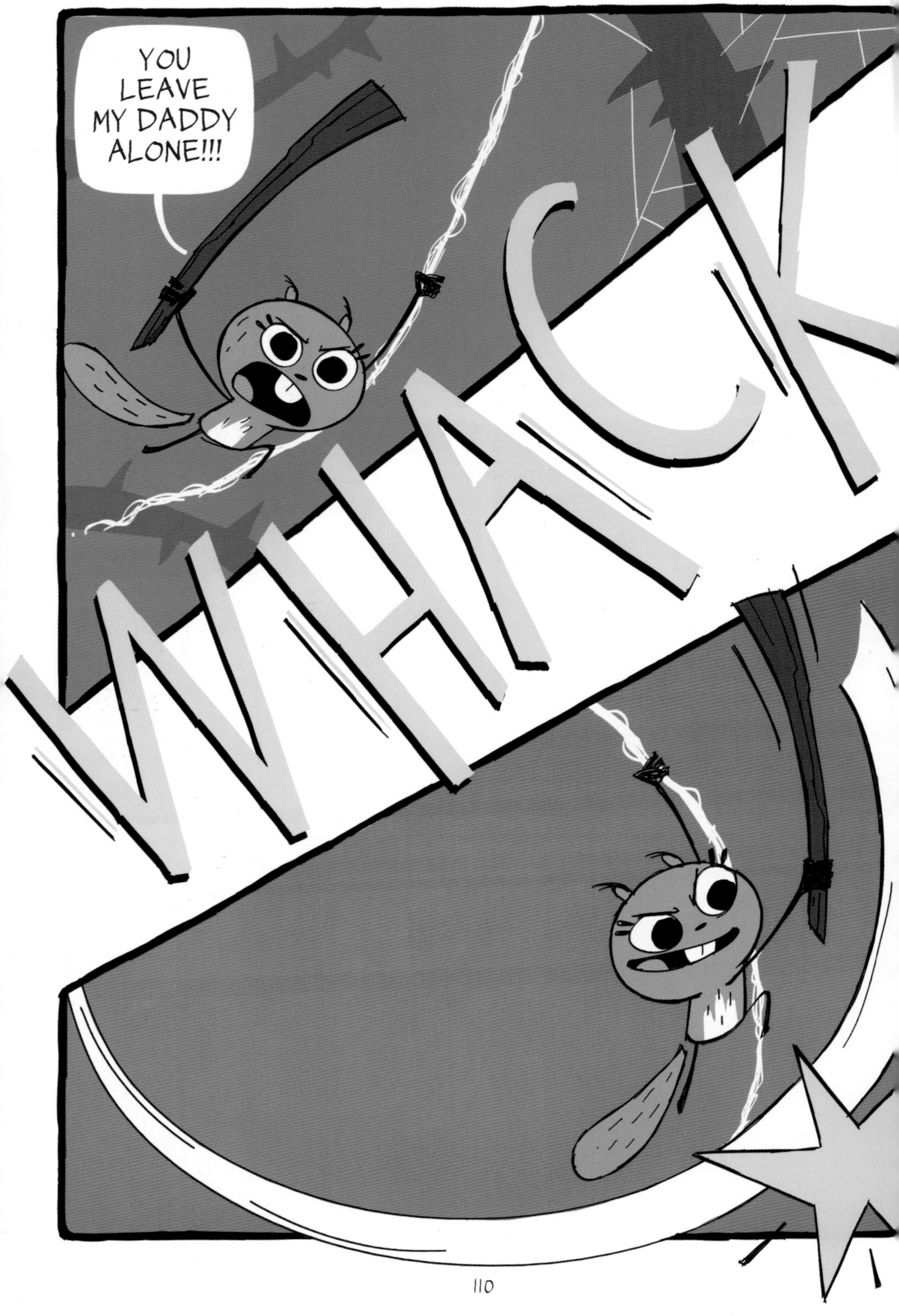
YOU LEAVE MY DADDY ALONE!!!
WHACK

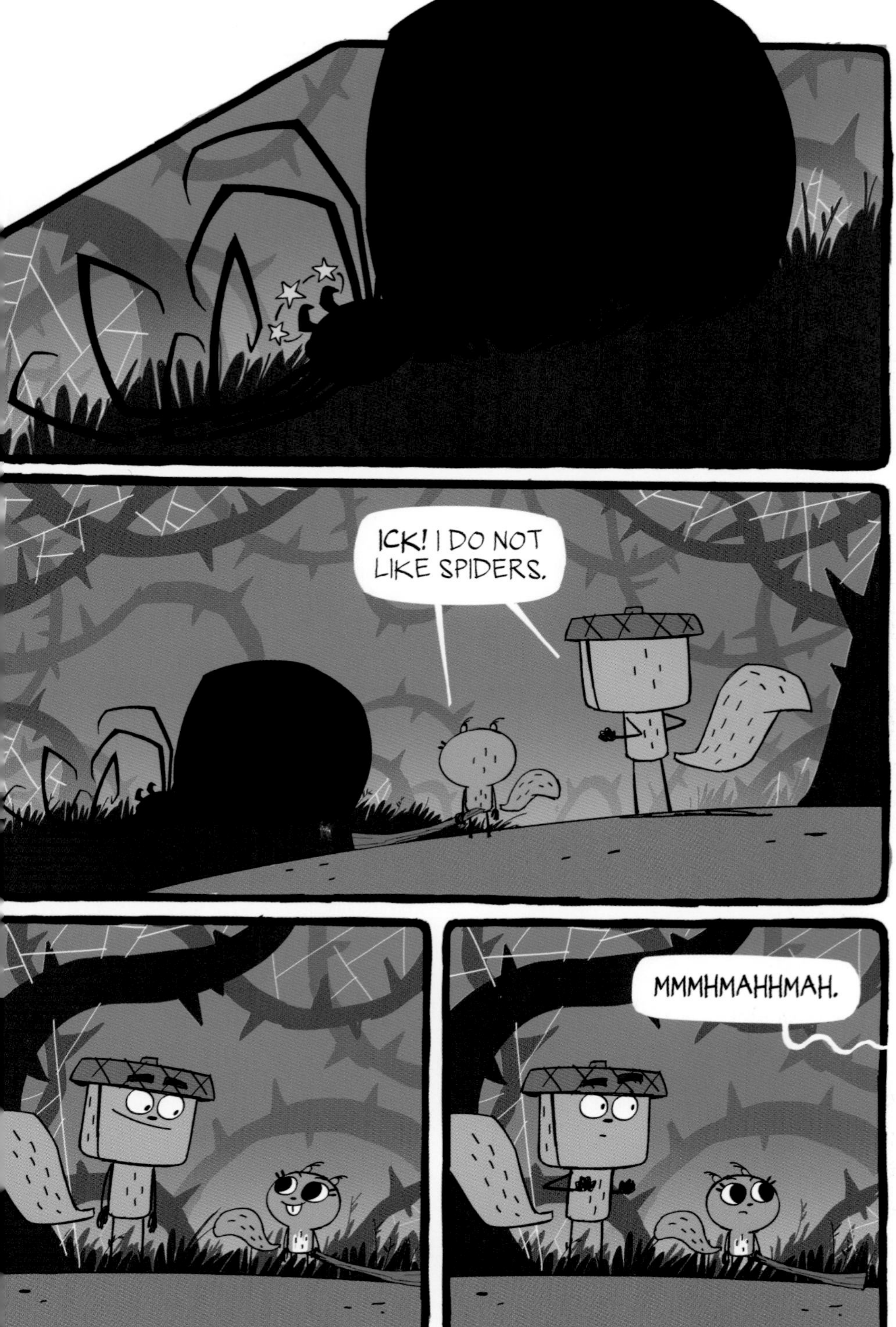
ICK! I DO NOT LIKE SPIDERS.
MMMHMAHHMAH.

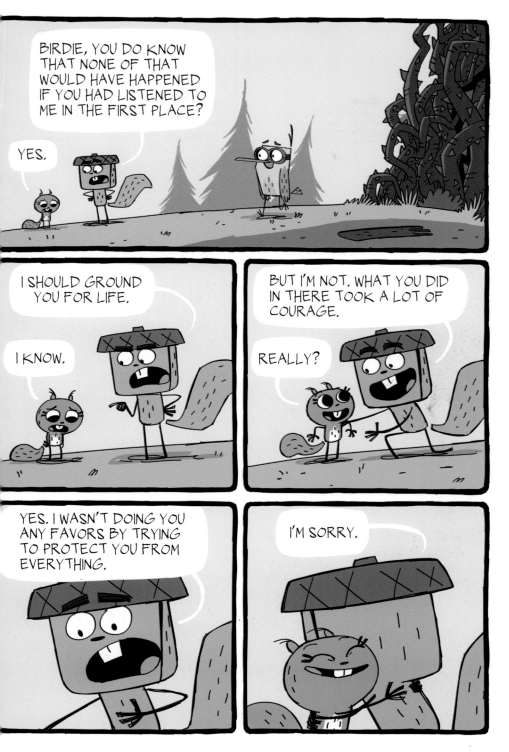

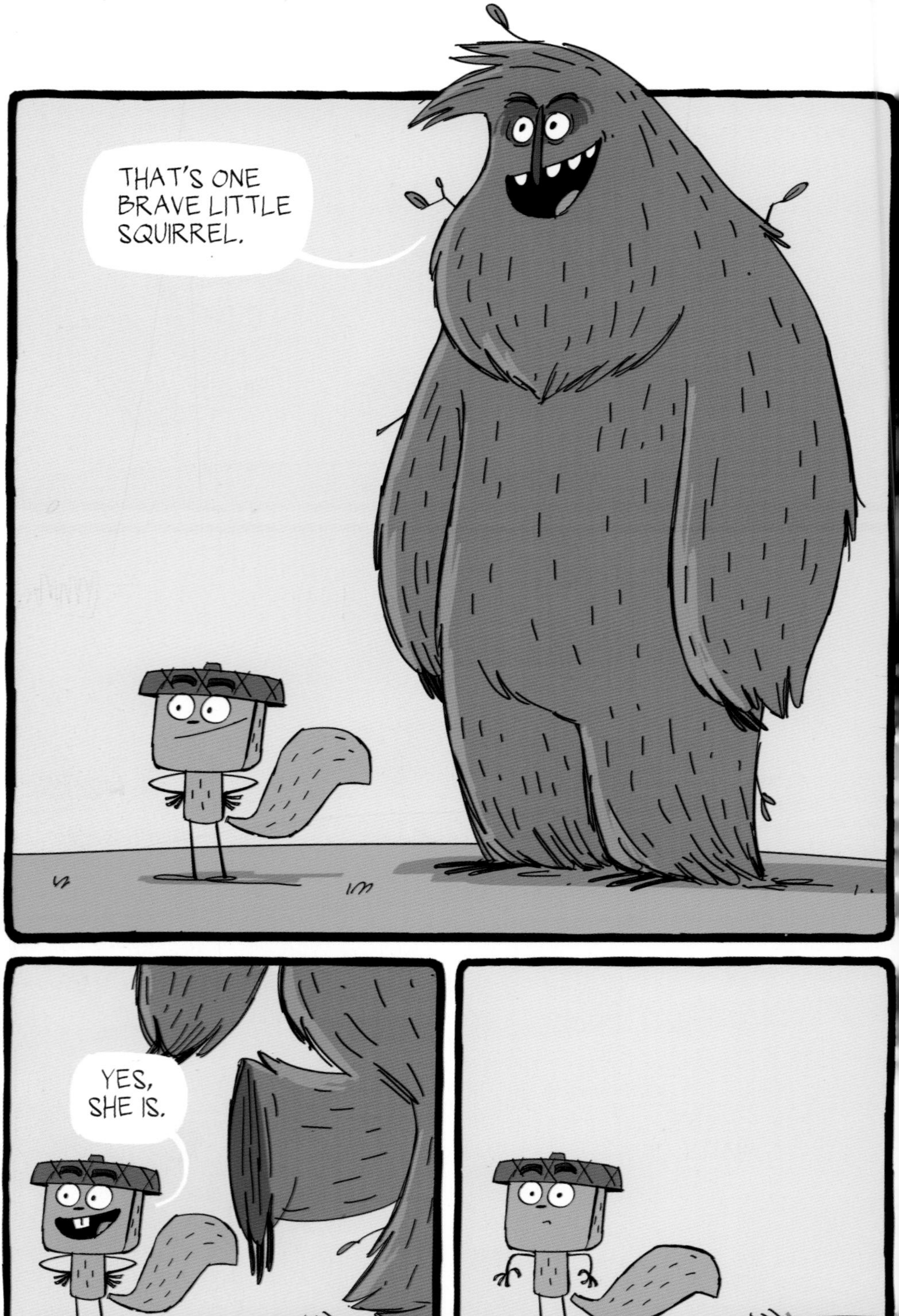
THAT'S ONE BRAVE LITTLE SQUIRREL.
YES, SHE IS.

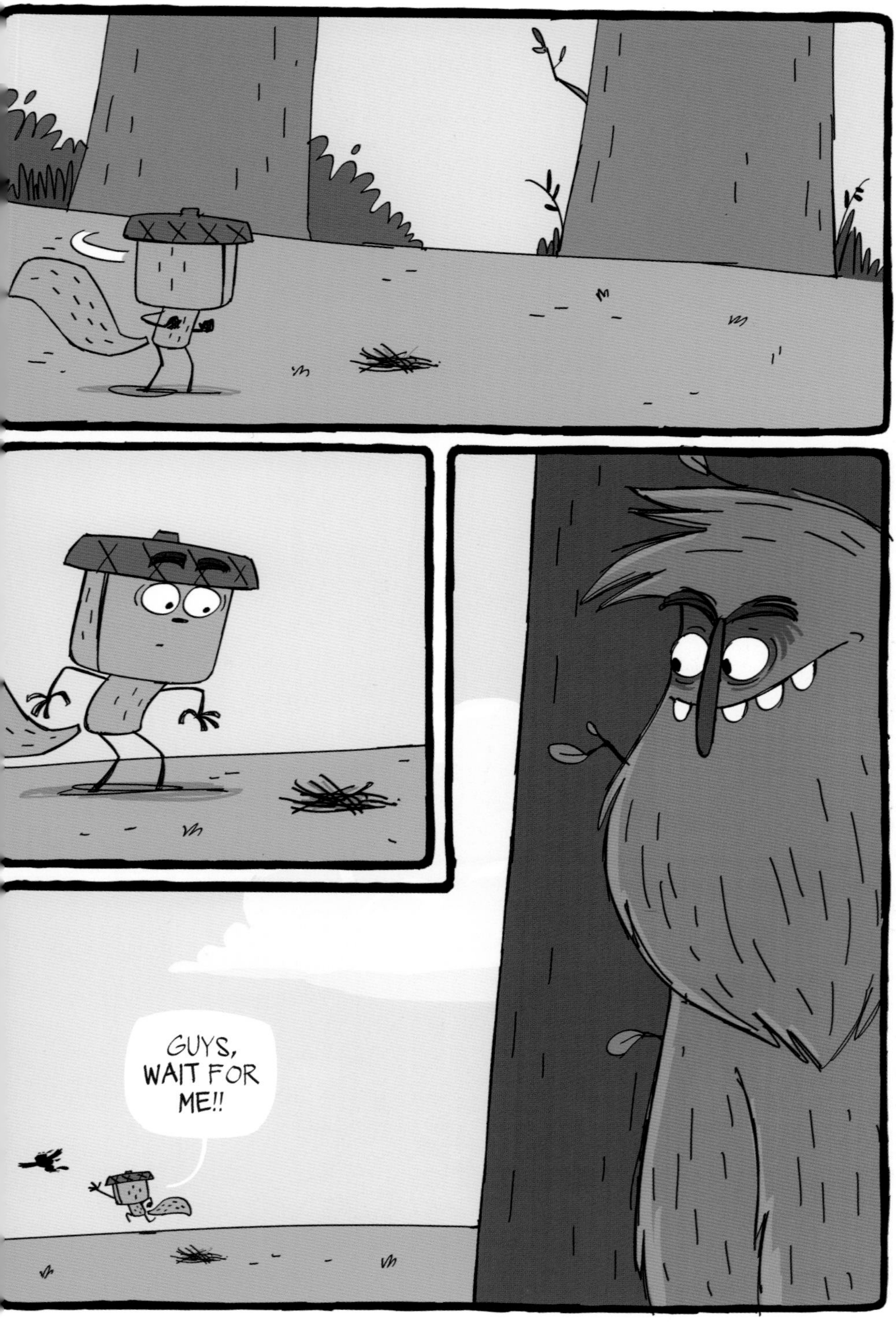
GUYS, WAIT FOR ME!!

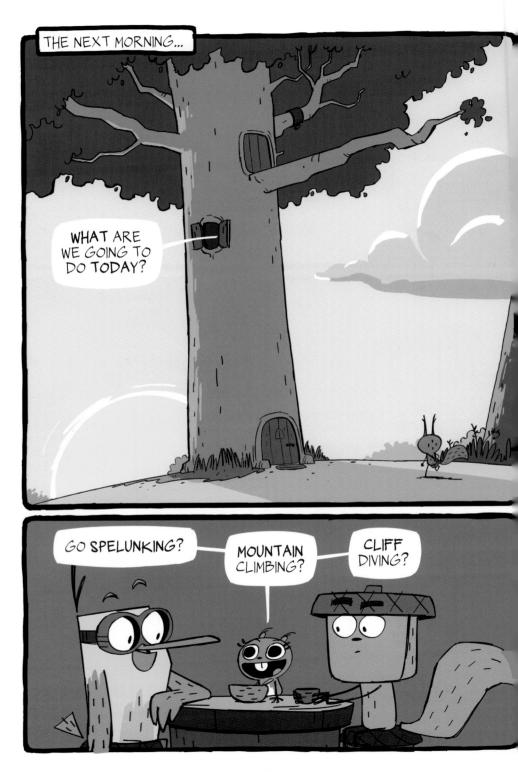

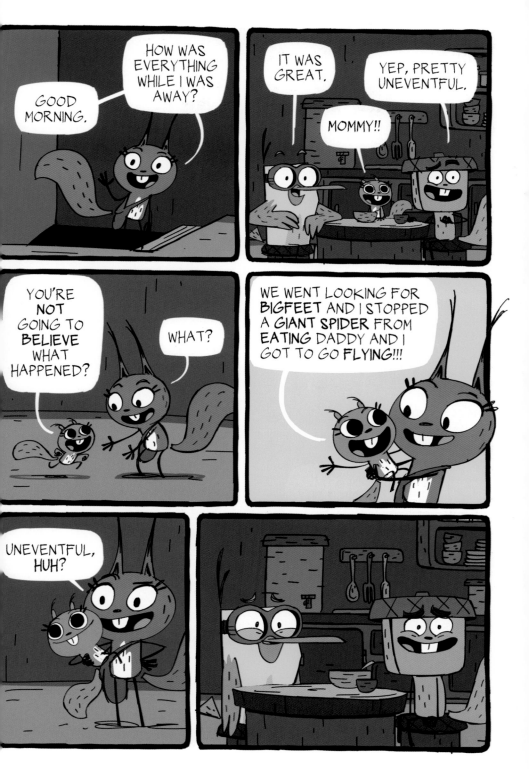

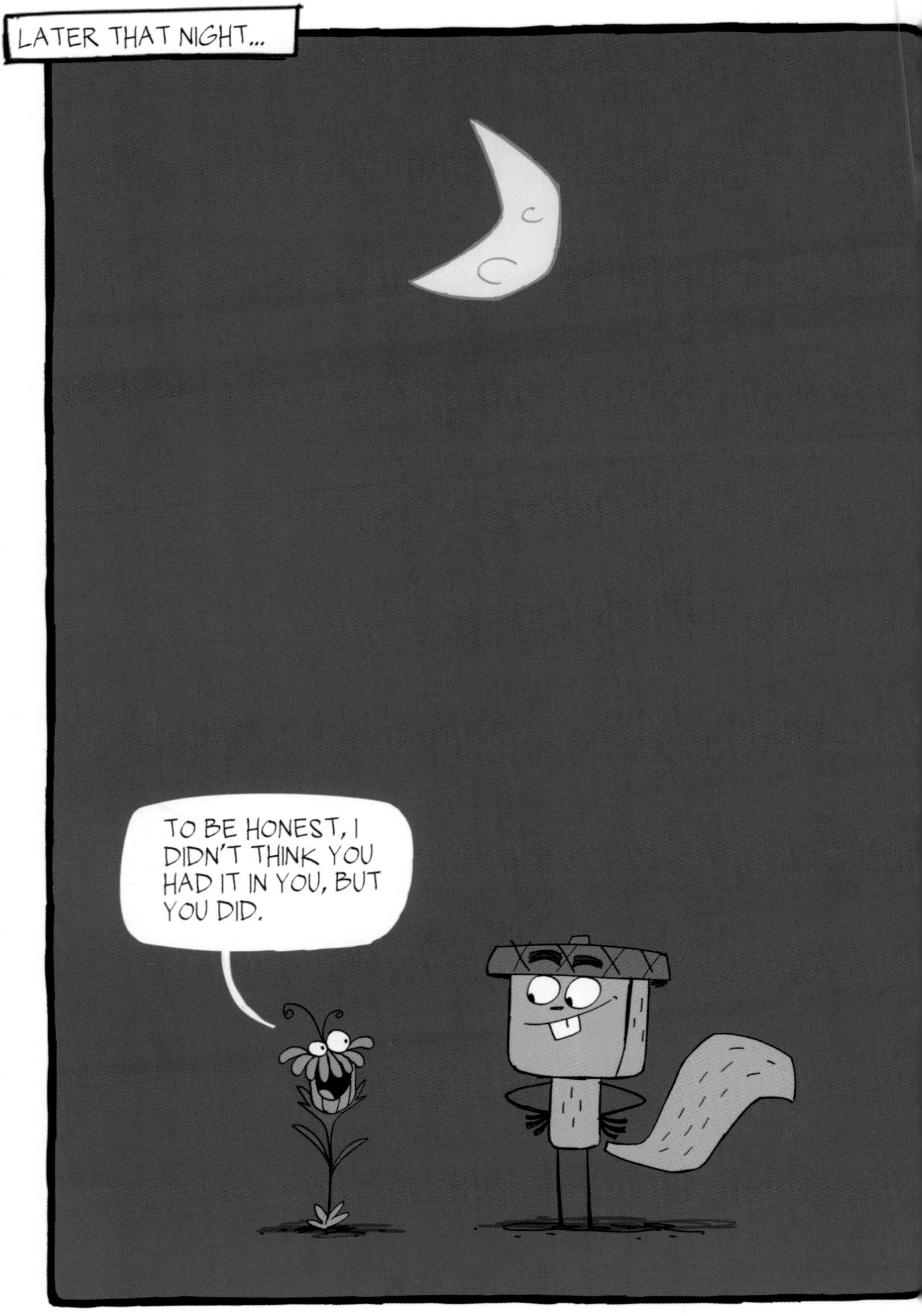
LATER THAT NIGHT...
TO BE HONEST, I DIDN'T THINK YOU HAD IT IN YOU, BUT YOU DID.

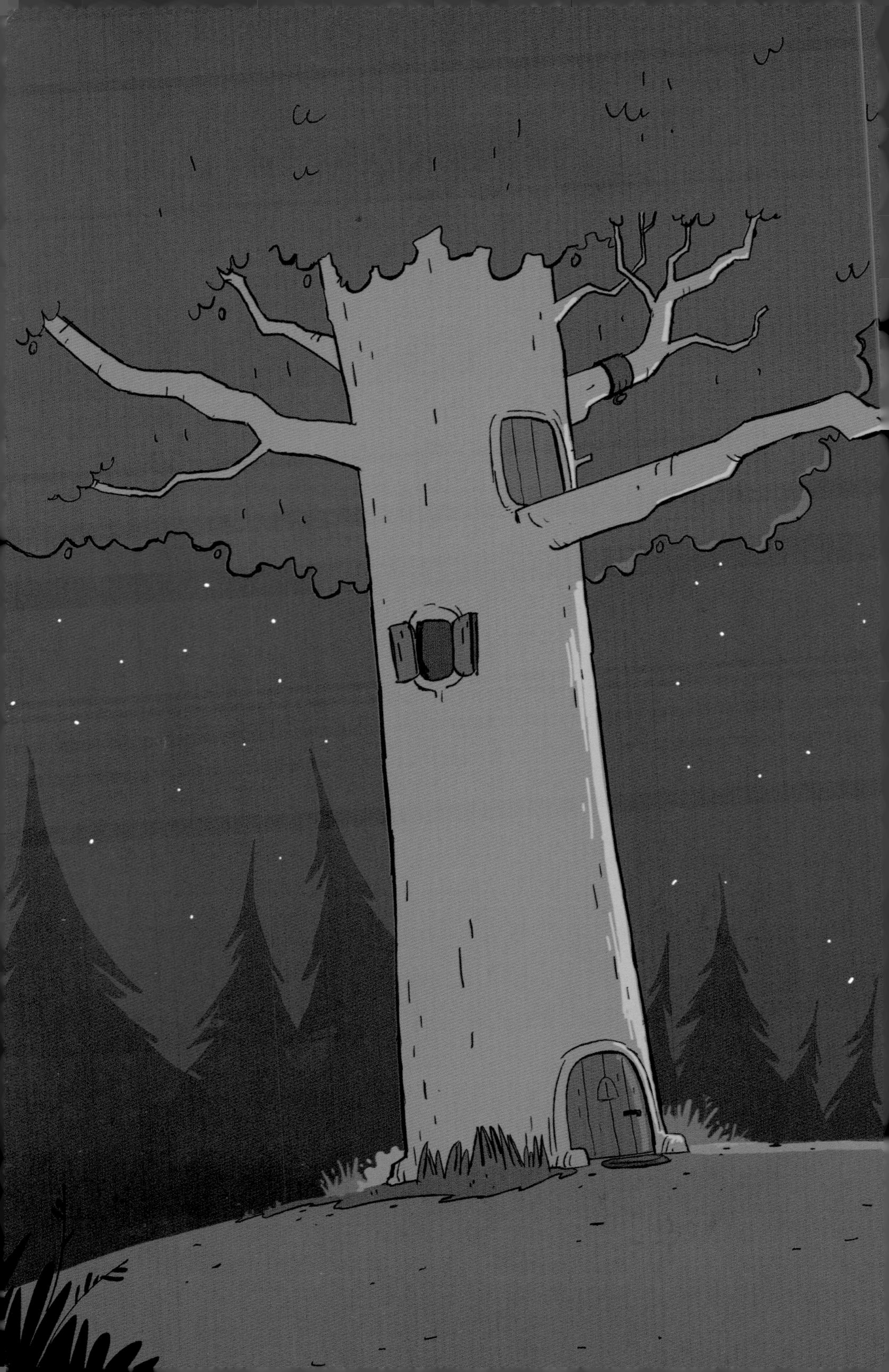

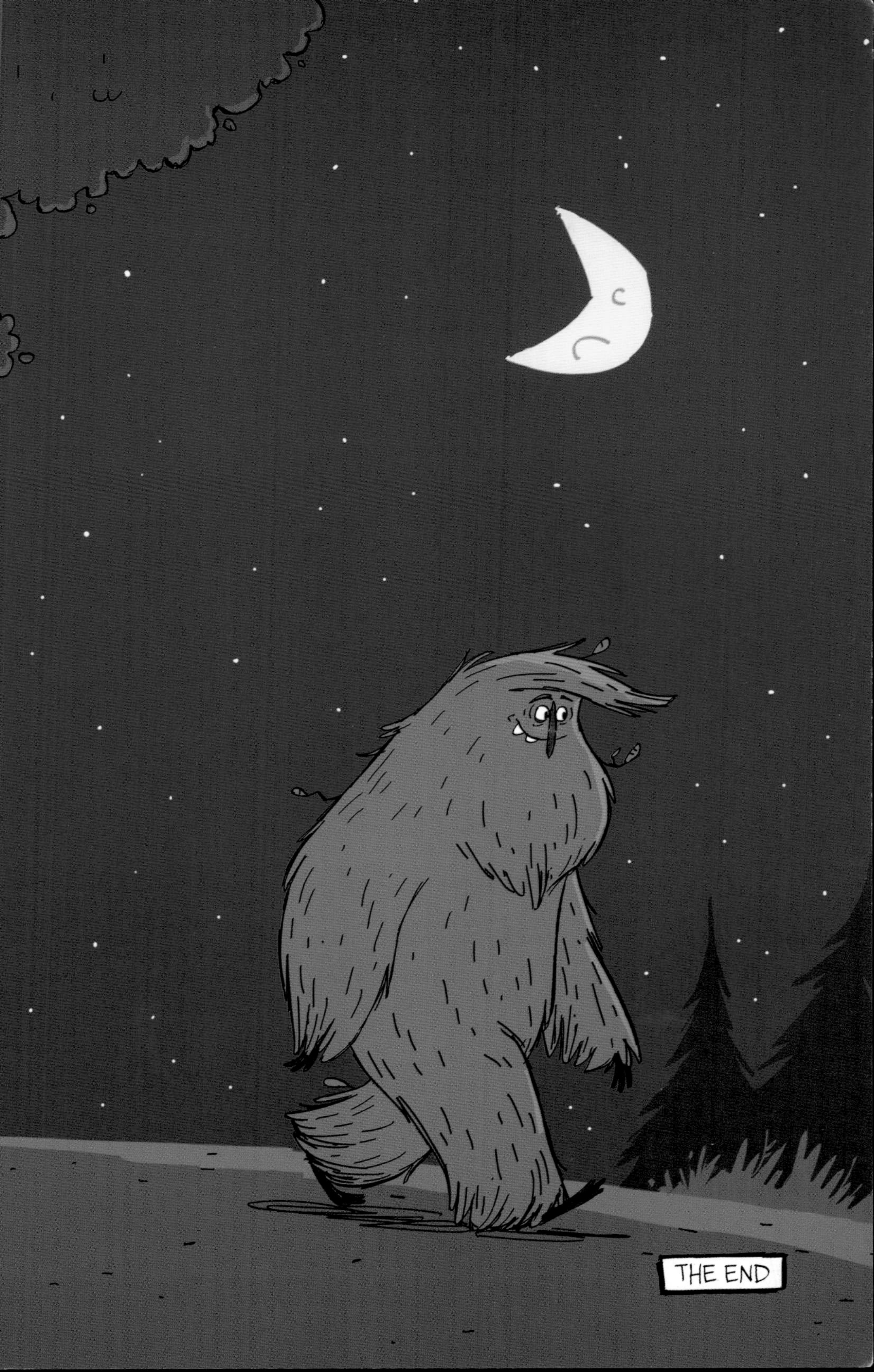
THE END

DON'T STOP HERE!
THERE'S MORE BIRD & SQUIRREL
ADVENTURES TO CATCH UP ON!

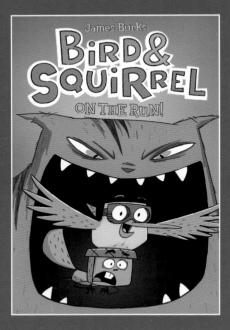